ALSO BY DAVID DAVIDAR

The House of Blue Mangoes

The Solitude of Emperors

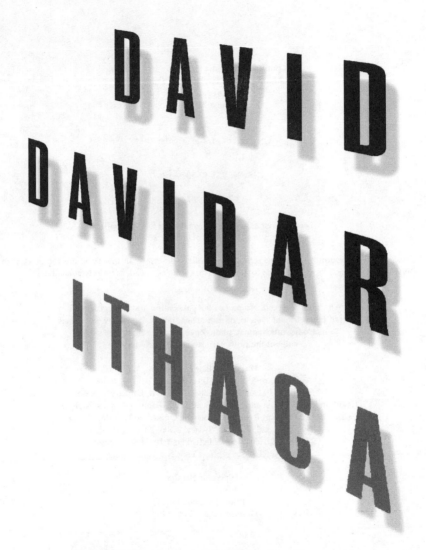

DAVID DAVIDAR

ITHACA

FOURTH ESTATE • *New Delhi*

First published in India in 2011 by Fourth Estate
An imprint of HarperCollins *Publishers*
a joint venture with
The India Today Group

Copyright © David Davidar 2011

ISBN: 978-93-5029-104-7

2 4 6 8 10 9 7 5 3 1

David Davidar asserts the moral right to be identified
as the author of this work.

This is a work of fiction and all characters and incidents described in this book are the product of the author's imagination. Any resemblance to actual persons, living or dead, is entirely coincidental.

HarperCollins *Publishers*
A-53, Sector 57, Noida, Uttar Pradesh 201301, India
77-85 Fulham Palace Road, London W6 8JB, United Kingdom
Hazelton Lanes, 55 Avenue Road, Suite 2900, Toronto, Ontario M5R 3L2
and 1995 Markham Road, Scarborough, Ontario M1B 5M8, Canada
25 Ryde Road, Pymble, Sydney, NSW 2073, Australia
31 View Road, Glenfield, Auckland 10, New Zealand
10 East 53rd Street, New York NY 10022, USA

Typeset in Bembo

Printed and bound at
Thomson Press (India) Ltd.

For Rachna
Always

As you set out on the road to Ithaca
Hope that the road is a long one,
Filled with adventures, filled with discoveries . . .

– from "Ithaca" by C.P. Cavafy

PART ONE

Hope that the road is a long one,
Many may the summer mornings be
When – with what pleasure, what joy –
You first put into harbors new to your eyes . . .

– from "Ithaca" by C.P. Cavafy

THIMPHU

It is the most dramatic flight path in the world. Four tremendous mountains, feet planted in snowfields, peaks ventilating the sky: Everest, imperious and distinctive, a plume of snow jetting from its crown; Makalu, saw-toothed and threatening even when the sun is shining; Lhotse, a thunderclap of a mountain, its bulk dwarfing its neighbours; and finally the ramparts of Kanchenjunga, stretching as far as the eye can see. The great peaks seem to be just inches from the windows of the small plane crawling across the face of the eastern Himalaya.

"Killers," Zachariah Thomas says to his wife, Julia, "every one of them." His eyes are riveted on the mountains below. "Hundreds have died on their slopes and yet the climbers keep coming. Oh, I'm not being macabre, just telling it like it is. Wonder if any of them have scored a planeload of passengers yet? You would think that any self-respecting death zone peak would be pretty pissed if it hadn't knocked an Airbus out of the sky."

Julia does not reply, possibly because she is not on the plane. She has been gone eighteen months and it was then that Zach's troubles started. Hammer blows, one after the other, pounding his life into something resembling a coffin. All that needs to happen now is for the lid to slam shut. Perhaps these mountains will do it for him.

As if in response to that thought, the plane encounters a patch of turbulence, shivers in its skin. The pilot's voice crackles over the speakers, reminding passengers to fasten their seatbelts and stay calm. The man next to him – bearded, overweight, and smelly – starts to pray loudly in French, grasping the crucifix around his neck. Zach glances at him irritably, what better way to go than ramming into a mile-high wall of ice, stone and flying snow at several hundred miles an hour? He puts up with his neighbour's panic for a minute or two, then leans across and whispers into his ear.

"Relax, mon ami, God's mighty host will not let this plane fall, I should know, I am quite knowledgeable about angels." The Frenchman looks at him as if he is mad but he isn't joking – well not entirely, he does know a bit more about angels than his terrified neighbour, although it would be stretching it to say he can predict how they will behave.

The plane sails out of the turbulence, the juddering ceases and the Frenchman smiles vacantly. His teeth are large and yellow.

Zach has always spent a lot of time watching his own thoughts, and has grown even more introspective since his troubles began. He loses interest in his neighbour, begins to brood on the events that have put him on a plane to Bhutan.

[4]

Julia (now an imaginary friend) walking out of their Kensington flat; his mother dying a year later; and then, the last foundation of his seemingly unassailable life beginning to crumble – being told by his boss that the publishing company he has devoted fourteen years of his life to is in deep trouble.

So he is on holiday, ironically the only palliative he can think of, he who has always been indifferent to nonsense like work-life balance and holidays – it's one of the things Julia and he had fought about for the six years they were married. Once the decision had been taken he hadn't known where to begin, his holidays this far having been taken at the behest of others, usually with him cast in the role of reluctant participant. All he knew was that he needed to get as far away as possible from London. He had phoned Julia and told her that he was thinking of going to Bhutan after the London Book Fair – he had quite enjoyed himself the only time he had visited the kingdom. He had refused to be pathetic and say what he had actually wanted to – that the reason he had so enjoyed that vacation (if you discounted weekend getaways and visits home, one of only two proper holidays he had taken with her) was because she had been with him. She had thought the call was another of his ploys to get back together. He had told her quite emphatically that it was not, although he could tell she didn't believe him. It was late at night and she had terminated the conversation quickly after pointing him to a travel website. As he surfed the site he had come across the clincher – Bhutan was the only country in the world that had officially adopted Gross National Happiness over GDP as its chief indicator of progress and prosperity. Just what he needed, he had thought savagely, as he booked flights and hotels, a week among shiny, happy people was bound to annoy him so much it would eject him from the pit of depression, and get him back on his feet again.

The plane banks and touches down abruptly at Bhutan's only airport – a feat of flying so demanding that only eight pilots are licensed to land on the terrifyingly short landing strip that lies hidden behind a mountain until the very last minute. The Frenchman is predictably terror-struck but Zach ignores him. Once out of the plane into the crisp, clear air of the mountains, he walks across to the airport building and clears landing formalities. The terminal seems to have grown bigger since he was last here, although it is still the smallest he has seen. He is met by the driver of the car he has booked, and after a nerve-wracking ride on roads narrow as rubber bands, which he quite enjoys, they get to Thimphu an hour-and-a-half later.

The capital, a small tidy town, spreads like a rash across the lower slopes of a valley, at the bottom of which runs a clear mountain river over a bed of flat white stones. The town is in the throes of expansion and Julia would have been upset by the signs of construction everywhere, and by the modernity that has intruded in the form of garish buildings that stand out amid the traditional houses and shops. But for the most part Thimphu seems to have stood up to the onrush of the twenty-first century reasonably well.

He showers, shaves, takes a couple of aspirins for the headache brought on by the altitude, and goes in search of some decent coffee. From memory he knows that the city is not an epicurean paradise, but the travel sites he has searched online are reassuring on the fact that the food, and especially the coffee, in Thimphu has got better. He finds a restaurant that has received good notices and asks the smiling waitress in her dragon-bright kira for a table overlooking the main thoroughfare. He glances at the menu and orders a brownie and a latte. When the order arrives he pulls out a manuscript that he has chosen at random from among three he has brought with him, and attempts to lose himself in the prose style of a writer whom the agent has described as a cross between early Saul Bellow and Martin Amis – which should have been warning enough. The writing is an unholy clash of prose styles of writers the author has evidently admired. Ten pages and he is done. What is it about most debut novelists? Don't they realize theirs is the best chance any writer could have to make a mark? Don't they understand that every pub-lisher in the world is looking for the flawless debut, the novel of genius that does not have a dispiriting track record to weigh it down? Why on earth don't they throw caution to the winds, give their work a great clawing distinctiveness, an irresistible force that will sweep the reader along from the very first page? A cross between Bellow and Amis indeed! This protagonist is no Augie March or John Self command-ing the reader's attention! He resolves not to look at any more submissions from the misguided agent, whom he hasn't bought anything from in a couple of years anyway, and turns his attention to the dancing policeman outside his window.

He remembers from his previous visit that Thimphu is one of only two cities in the world – the other being Pyongyang,

a city that sounds so dire it might be fun to visit – which lacks
traffic lights; instead it has policemen who, with movements
as smooth and choreographed as those of temple dancers,
direct the sparse traffic on Norzin Lam, the city's main street.
As he watches the gloved hands moving languorously in the
thickening evening light he wonders how the dancing policeman would fare if he had to regulate traffic on Oxford Circus!
Ah, London, how distant it seems. He thinks about his colleagues at Litmus Publishing ("*We are the test of a good book*,"
the company's slogan reads), and then tries to put them from
his mind. He is here to steady himself, to recover, and he is
not going to do that by thinking about Litmus. Through an
effort of will he manages to keep out what is waiting for him
back home for a few moments but it soon forces its way back
in – next year will be the first time in ten years that he will
have to meet his budget targets without a new Seppi. In an
industry that appears to be dying, to be without the one
author who has insulated them from all the ills that the
competition has to deal with, is a terrifying prospect. They
have nothing on their list that will come close to the 2.5 million
copies they sold of his new book in the UK alone two
years ago. No new hardback. No movie tie-in edition. Just an
A format edition of the last novel. Plus a hundred or so
regular books, of which approximately eighty per cent will
barely live up to expectations or fail to recover their advance
no matter how desperately they massage them into shape,
or how vigorously they hawk them to a largely indifferent
media or even more indifferent customers. Stop worrying, he
tells himself, you are on holiday. And who knows, this might

be the place where his luck will turn; maybe he can stick a prayer flag into a mountain top, there to flutter away madly, sending out entreaties to God that will eventually be answered.

After all, it was after his previous visit to Bhutan that he had published a novel by an unknown Sicilian writer called Massimo Seppi. It was the first book he had ever bought, and it was more thrilling than he could have ever imagined – watching, awestruck, as characters that he had worked on for months rose up from the page like latter-day Lazaruses and made their way into the hearts and minds of readers. There were other things that he was excited by, of course. He was still just a glorified assistant when he acquired the book, no matter that his designation was associate editor, and the Seppi acquisition marked his passage to bigger things – an office, and the authority to acquire a few books entirely on his own – but there was nothing that compared with the elation he had felt when the production director personally handed him the newly published novel and said, "It's all downhill from here, mate. Cheers!"

The book, about the rise and abrupt fall of a Palermo crime lord, was not a success. A translation from the Italian that had come to him unagented (Seppi's translator had sent it to Litmus, where it had landed on the slush pile that was his responsibility to oversee), it sold less than five hundred copies, and received only two reviews at a time when reviews still meant something to readers and publishers. But he had believed in Seppi's talent and had somehow managed to persuade his publisher to allow him to publish Seppi's second novel. It hadn't been a hit either, and he knew that was the end so far as the connection between Litmus and Seppi was concerned. It was one thing to persist with homegrown writers who might just come up with a winner, but a foreign author in translation who flatlined at the very beginning of his career – well, there was no way he was going to get his boss, Gabrijela, to sign off on yet another Seppi.

In all this time, he had met the writer only once, at the 2001 London Book Fair, where Seppi had been part of a delegation of writers sponsored by the Italian government. He had taken to him at once, this author whose manner was much like his writing style – spare and unadorned. They spoke about *The Leopard,* a novel they were both passionate fans of, and which he had always longed to read in the original Italian. To his chagrin, Seppi told him Lampedusa's great novel truly shone only in its language of creation, no matter how well made its various translations were. Seppi added that he was lucky with his own translator because her versions of his novels were supple enough to work well in English while remaining true to the style in which he had written them. Seppi, who was a schoolteacher in Palermo, spoke passable English, and told Zach that he might not hear from him for a while as he was moving to Canada, where he hoped to make a better life for himself – a cousin had offered him a position as a manager at his restaurant in Little Italy in Toronto. Zach didn't have the heart to tell him that it really did not matter whether he stayed in touch or not, because he wasn't going to be able to publish Seppi anymore.

A year later, without warning, Seppi's new novel had appeared in his inbox – and its size and content were as surprising as its unexpected arrival. It was 840 pages long, twice the length of both his previous novels combined, and it was an epic fantasy quite unlike his earlier work. *Angels Rising* was the first book in a planned quartet, each featuring one of the great archangels – Michael, Gabriel, Raphael, and Uriel. In his cover letter Seppi explained that several religious traditions put the number of archangels at seven, but that he had decided that he would stick with just the best-known or, more pertinently, the least contentious.

A thin mist softens the lines of Thimphu's buildings; the semaphoring arms of the traffic policeman grow indistinct. Zach remembers ruefully that he was actually glad that Seppi was intending to stop at four; even that many would be a tough sell given the track record of his previous novels. He had the second book in the new series almost finished, Seppi wrote, and the other two closely plotted, and he was willing to give Zach world rights in all four books if he paid enough. His Italian publisher hadn't seen the manuscript, and he was willing to throw in Italian rights for an extra consideration. The restaurant job hadn't worked out, his translator hadn't been paid, and he needed the money urgently.

Even if he had wanted to keep publishing Seppi, *Angels Rising* didn't seem his kind of book. The last time he had read overtly commercial novels with any kind of excitement was when he was a teenager, inhaling westerns and thrillers and sci-fi novels indiscriminately until his passion for literary fiction had swept all that away. But Seppi's circumstances seemed to be genuinely dire, and he thought the least he could do for his very first writer was read and comment on the novel, so he had printed out the manuscript and taken it home with him. He wasn't looking forward to the task he had taken on, angels weren't exactly his thing. Sure, he liked the work of Bernini, Botticelli and Michelangelo and thought the way they had been represented by Brueghel, Blake, and Doré, especially Doré, was extraordinary. He counted the Mitchell translation of Rilke's *Duino Elegies* among his favourite poems, but that was the extent to which the angelic hosts had penetrated his consciousness. Seven hours later, at three in the morning, when he finished the manuscript, he finally understood exactly what Rilke meant when he wrote "Every angel is terrifying." The darkness beyond the small circle of light cast by his bedside lamp seemed to pulse with tremendous unseen presences, not threatening exactly but untamed, awe-inspiring, powerful beyond imagining. When a book could do that, lift you out of yourself into a world that you had not known existed, you knew that you held in your hands the sort of treasure every publisher dreams about.

What Seppi had done was take the fantasy novel out of the restrictions of its genre and invest it with the style, depth, startling insights, and characterization of literary fiction. Most of all, though, *Angels Rising* was storytelling at its very best. It had cracking narrative speed, intricate plotting, and a host of compelling characters – foremost among them the Archangel Michael anchoring the story of the expulsion of Satan and the rebel angels from heaven. Unlike *Paradise Lost*, Zach thought (mentally rehearsing his pitch to his editorial board), Seppi's book did not get bogged down in the theological and religious elements of the story but concentrated on the enormous scope for drama and action that the Fall represented. Later books in the series would cover cataclysmic events that had been set in motion through time by the fallen angels and their monstrous spawn, the Nephilim. In each volume one of the great archangels would be dispatched by God to manage the latest threat to humankind.

The idea behind the series was excellent and, based on the evidence of *Angels Rising,* Seppi was a powerful storyteller, but that didn't mean Gabrijela was going to go for it. She had expressly prohibited the acquisition of any more fiction from Seppi, and even if Zach could somehow get her to read the manuscript and hope she was as blown away by it as he was, they would still have to get retailers and reviewers to take *Angels Rising* seriously. The world had changed irrevocably since retailers had gained access to accurate sales data, and unless they could prove that the author had done something dramatically different with his new work the initial orders of every important retailer were going to be based on Seppi's indifferent sales record. Everyone knew an exceptional fantasy series could set the trade on fire, but Zach wasn't known as an editor of bestselling commercial fiction – why were they going to take his word for it?

A couple of stories that were now firmly part of publishing lore had floated into his mind as he sat up in bed thinking about how he was going to tackle the situation – the ten-year-old son of the founder of Allen & Unwin recommending that Tolkien be published; the enthusiasm of the eight-year-old daughter of the chairman of Bloomsbury getting J.K. Rowling a publishing deal after twelve publishers had turned her down. Unfortunately *Angels Rising* was not for kids, and it was not a debut novel. However, it had supernatural beings and perhaps he could convince his boss that angels were going to be the next big thing after wizards and vampires.

———

Gabrijela Kostic was a true publisher in a profession now awash in suits. At the age of thirty she had thrown up a secure job as the youngest editorial director of one of London's storied publishing houses to take up an offer from a Serbian compatriot to start a firm specializing in the writers of Eastern Europe. Her benefactor was jailed for fraud two years after she set up Litmus, and it looked as though she would have to fold her company, but Gabrijela was as stubborn as she was brilliant. Through the careful management of capital and her personal friendships with some of Europe's finest writers, she kept the firm going. After one of her writers won the Nobel, her finances improved somewhat and she promptly parlayed that slight advantage into raising more funds and giving the company heft with agents and authors. By the time Zach arrived at Litmus it was among the top twelve publishing firms in London, but the trouble the industry found itself in had begun to have an effect; unless they scored a big one the Arts Council grants and occasional hits would not be enough to pull them out of trouble year after year. Litmus did not have the war chest or the backlist that the bigger and older players had, so it had to make at least half of the books it published every year count, and that was a near impossibility, despite Gabrijela's exceptional eye for talent. They weren't giving up, their few recognizable names kept them going, but every Litmus staffer knew that they needed a *Life of Pi*. Soon.

Celebrated editors are superstars at the companies they work for. They are feted for their taste, their ability to make the work of the finest writers even better, and the role they play in launching the careers of authors who go on to become household names. The world is aware of one of the most important skills any editor worth her salt *must* have: the ability to nurture all the writers she publishes, for the editor is the only person with whom the writer works continuously throughout his association with his publishing company. But another equally important skill is almost never spoken about outside the profession: the ability to sell. In an industry that is entirely speculative, where decisions at every stage of the publishing process are subjective, where any mistake can wipe out the company's tiny profit, every great editor needs to be a brilliant persuader. Each time an editor is seeking to acquire a book for her company she needs simultaneously to fall under its spell and remain detached from it, so that she is able cannily and passionately to sell it, to herself, her publisher, her sales colleagues, her marketing colleagues, and everyone in the company with a stake in the success of the book. Flogging an unsuccessful author to your skeptical colleagues is akin to raising the dead. More so, if the publisher you need to convince is someone like Gabrijela Kostic.

When she was eight Gabrijela's parents had fled Yugoslavia, a few years before the Prague Spring had marked the beginning of the end of the fragile peace the region had enjoyed. They came to Leeds, where her mother had family. But although the Serbian community welcomed them to the city, there was not enough to go around. Her father, who had worked for Tito's government, could find only low-paying daily-wage jobs, and spent his time bemoaning his fate with other exiles from his homeland, while her mother, a schoolteacher, cleaned homes, took in washing, scrimped and saved. There was nothing unusual about the Kostics' story – the standard immigrant experience, more or less – but it did invest their daughter with a very low level of tolerance for inefficiency, lack of ambition, indecisiveness, laziness, and dolts.

She ran her editorial meetings like a sergeant major – quick, efficient, with not a lot of room for sloppy thinking or ill-prepared pitches. In a profession where long, rambling discussions are the norm, Gabrijela expected her firm's acquisitions editors to be clear thinking and concise in their pitches. As soon as they started to waffle on pointlessly they would feel her eyes, grey as a submarine's hull, boring into them; if they ignored that warning signal, they could expect to be shut down with very little ceremony. If Zach was going to get Seppi past her he would need a plan.

This was easier said than done. The mystery at the heart of the publishing business, the unsolvable conundrum that every single publishing professional worries about, and the one question to which no one has the answer, is this: no one knows what books are actually going to succeed in the marketplace.

Editors will use taste and skill to acquire and edit authors of quality, marketers will slavishly follow the trends du jour to package them, salesmen will brandish sales data to persuade retailers to stock them, accountants will come up with excruciatingly detailed P&Ls to show how they will turn a profit, but in the end all this masks a simple truth: unless the author has a proven track record, and has written an even better book than the one she published last year, no one in the business really knows how her book will be received. And for unknown authors or those with a less than stellar sales history the mystery deepens, threatens to be practically insoluble.

This means that every action in the publishing sequence has a whiff of desperation about it. Editors frantically sell their colleagues further down the chain on the mythical selling points of the book they are pushing, and these fabrications get ever more elaborate and fantastical as the process unfolds. By the time the salesman is selling the book to the buyer at the retail chain, neither quite knows or believes what is being talked about – partly because the odds are they haven't read the book but more so because they haven't the faintest idea of whether it will work or not. Given this scenario, everyone in a position of authority is cynical about the claims made by those who need them to buy into their arguments. This is what Zach was struggling with.

In the end, he decided to keep it simple. He would let the book speak for itself; there was nothing that could better support his conviction that Litmus should publish *Angels Rising*. Although Gabrijela did not like editors to read from manuscripts at editorial meetings – to her it simply meant

that they hadn't marshalled enough selling points to persuade her to approve the acquisition – this was precisely
what he intended to do. He deliberately did not put the
novel on the list of titles to be discussed at that week's editorial meeting. After they had gone through the titles on the
agenda, he said there was a submission that had come in at
the last minute that he wanted to table. Gabrijela's eyes had
locked on to him as he nervously started to read the first
paragraph of *Angels Rising*.

You do not want to be touched by an angel . . . he began. There
was no interruption, and he steadied his voice and read the
next six sentences unhurriedly and stopped. Editors know
when they have won a room over, and Zach knew he had
caught and held the interest of every person present. The
only one who knew what he was trying to do was Maggie,
the marketing manager, whom he had shared the manuscript
with. She had loved it, but Gabrijela knew they were friends
and he hadn't been sure how persuasive Maggie's support
would be.

Into the spell cast by Seppi's writing he introduced the
things that could sink his campaign – the name of the author,
his dismal track record, the four books that they would need
to buy. Gabrijela's eyes gave nothing away. Maggie spoke
bravely into the silence, said she had loved the book. Still
nothing from the boss. Then, with her usual lack of ceremony, Gabrijela approved the acquisition. The sales director,
Gareth, raised a dissenting voice, said Seppi would be a tough
sell, but he wasn't telling her anything she didn't already
know, and the decision stood. She set one condition: Zach

couldn't pay more than twenty thousand pounds for world rights to all four books.

Zach waited for Toronto to wake up, and phoned his author with the news. Seppi's response was as unemotional as ever. Zach was a bit irritated by this – if only the author knew about the hoops Zach had had to jump through to be able to make an offer. But he tamped down his annoyance and asked why Seppi had decided suddenly to write about angels. "I'm Italian," Seppi had said, "and Catholic. Why wouldn't I want to write books featuring angels?" He then told Zach about the catalyst that had got him started, and the devotion and commitment that had kept him working away at the project. All through the many years that he had spent writing and conceptualizing the quartet, he had kept quiet about its existence because he had wanted to finish the first book in its entirety before getting in touch with publishers. Meanwhile a friend of his had read and wanted to publish the literary novel he had written in homage to Lampedusa (he liked to work on more than one novel at a time, Seppi said, although from now on he intended to devote himself exclusively to the quartet) and that was why things had worked out as they had. Zach told him what he was prepared to pay as an advance at the very end of the conversation. There was no immediate response from Seppi and Zach's elation began to drain away – was he going to be denied the opportunity to publish a masterpiece? Then Seppi had asked if there was anything he could do to raise the advance, he really needed the money. Unusually, for someone as stoic as he was, he had expanded on his circumstances – the vermin-infested, suburban one-room apartment on which he hadn't paid the rent for three months and from which he was in imminent danger of being evicted; the days when he didn't have enough money even for one proper meal and subsisted on whatever he could get from food banks and marked-down items from grocery stores; the inability to send money to his ailing mother in Palermo. Embarrassed, he cut short his litany of woe. Zach felt for his author but explained how hard he'd had to fight to be able to make even this offer; the best he could do was throw in a couple of sales bonuses. Seppi had hesitated, and then agreed.

Angels Rising was published eight months later to modest acclaim. It won a minor award at the World Fantasy Convention and sold seven times more copies in hardback than both Seppi's previous works combined – a grand total of 7,230 copies, although they had given away an equal number at sci-fi conventions, to various reading groups and, two weeks before publication, to random members of the public (each member of staff was given a bag of books to distribute at strategic locations – Tube stations, on buses, Costa Coffee bars, in night clubs). A major Hollywood studio bought movie rights to the first book for a tiny sum by its standards, and Zach recovered the advance from that deal alone.

By the time the second novel, *Angel Dust,* featuring the Archangel Gabriel fighting the Beast and his cohorts against the background of the fall of the Roman Empire, was published (the opening battle scene against Alaric's invading army of Visigoths still gives him goosebumps when he thinks about it), they had got better at publishing a series that was aimed outside their core market. The cover was more commercial, the author's name and title were foil-stamped, and they had their first brush with the joys and sorrows of pushing substantial numbers of a book into the supermarkets. Half the company's marketing budget for the year was devoted to *Angel Dust* – posters on the Tube, window displays, advertising in the broadsheets – Maggie was exhilarated by all the new toys she got to play with, and even Gabrijela, who rarely attended marketing meetings, got into the spirit of things. Litmus printed ten thousand copies in hardcover and to everyone's delight the book sold double the number of copies of its predecessor. The best was yet to come. In the annual Christmas round-ups, one of the world's most famous fantasy authors picked the *Angels* books as her books of the year, and said she couldn't wait to read the third volume in the series. A fourth reprint of ten thousand copies was rushed through, and from that point onwards Litmus and Seppi were in uncharted waters.

The title of the book was propitious in more ways than one, for angel dust was sprinkled over all the events, big and small, that took place in Zach's life that year. The most important, trumping even the rush of publishing a writer who was on the verge of superstardom, was that he had finally begun to feel his life had settled down on the personal front. After the frantic, usually unsuccessful attempts at romance during his undergraduate days in Delhi, his love life had begun to improve, in part, he supposed, because he had stopped trying so hard. He didn't think of the women he courted successfully as conquests – he genuinely liked most of them and thought they enriched his life in some way. Moreover, he treated whomever he was with as though she were the first woman in his life. The freight of past loves, the knowledge that her glory would rapidly dim, none of this mattered; when he was with her, everything about her was beguiling. The problem was that six weeks or six months later, despite being enormously fond of his lover of the moment, he couldn't think of a single reason to continue to be with her. In his moments of introspection about his love life, which happened naturally enough when yet another relationship was about to end, he could see how selfish he was being, how much hurt he was causing. It was to their credit that few of his lovers brained him with their stilettos when he suggested that they move their relationship to a rather less intense plane, possibly because they had regarded him all along as an "idiot boy trapped within an adult frame" (as a cellist with impossibly long eyelashes had declared as she sped out of the tail end of their relationship). It helped that he was unfailingly contrite and blamed himself for everything that had gone wrong with the union that until just a short time ago had passed all earthly understanding. On the couple of occasions that things had got ugly, his sense of guilt and mortification had risen exponentially, and he had resolved never to fall for a woman again – until some enchantress came along and placed him under her spell and the entire cycle started up again. And then he had met Julia, who took him over completely.

By the time *Angel Dust* had started climbing the charts, they had been married for a little over three years and their lives together had taken on the sort of happy domesticity he had never imagined for himself. The initial white heat of their romance had given way to a deep attachment, and although he sometimes missed the electric charge that had accompanied each new romance in his life, this was way better, and something he had never had before – a union with another person with whom he felt he could always share everything in his life. As their relationship deepened and broadened, and his professional career seemed poised to skyrocket upwards, Zach couldn't have felt better about himself.

When it came to publishing the third book in the series, *The War of Angels,* all Litmus's forty-nine employees were stretched to the limit. The company was planning to publish a quarter of a million copies in hardcover, along with half a million copies of the movie tie-in edition of *Angels Rising* to coincide with the release of the Hollywood blockbuster (Seven Star Studios had purchased movie rights to the rest of the quartet after the success of *Angel Dust*) directed by one of Peter Jackson's protégés. Taking their cue from *The Lord of The Rings,* the studio and the director had shot the movies of all three books simultaneously in Iceland, and planned to release them at the rate of one every autumn, which was exactly what Litmus needed, because it would be the perfect platform for the release of their new hardcovers and movie tie-in editions.

Unfortunately, things were not as good on the personal front. The blissful domesticity of less than a year ago had disintegrated to the point where Julia and he were fighting almost constantly. He hadn't seen this coming and, worse, he didn't know how to make things better. In the past he would have shrugged and walked away, every romance had its sell-by date. But he knew he wanted to be with Julia no matter how difficult things had become; the strain on their relationship was compounded when Zach's father passed away from a sudden heart attack. In the end, confused and heartsick, he retreated as far as he could into his work. He immersed himself in all the details required to get the epic story of the Archangel Raphael fighting on the side of the Crusaders during the siege of Jerusalem and the battle of Antioch to as many readers as possible, working long hours, returning home only to bathe and sleep. He wasn't the only one in the company working maniacally hard. Every person in every department was doing the same, including their two-person rights department that was inundated with offers from around the world – rights were sold in twenty-nine countries. The success of the first book in the *Twilight* series published that year helped all books featuring vampires, wizards, zombies and, yes, angels and when they launched *The War of Angels*, it charted on bestseller lists on both sides of the Atlantic. Seppi and Litmus were on their way to becoming very wealthy.

Six weeks after publication Gabrijela took Zach out to a celebratory lunch. She had chosen Sheekey's, an expensive fish restaurant in Soho, in itself a surprise, for Gabrijela entertained frugally. But they were toasting Seppi's success, so he thought he understood why she was splurging. She raised her flute of champagne to Seppi and the company, and then sprang her surprise by ending with a toast to Litmus's new publisher, Zachariah Thomas. She explained that she was dividing her job and would stay on as managing director – he would continue to report to her – but that he would now be responsible for all the books the company acquired. He hadn't thought even once that he might rise to such a position so soon; Gabrijela was only fifty at the time, she embodied Litmus's publishing, it was unthinkable that anyone else could take her place. Overwhelmed, he had looked blankly into his boss's grey eyes – usually flinty, they were now friendly and warm in a rare show of emotion. He had just turned forty and nothing seemed impossible. Perhaps he could even find the inspiration to turn his messy personal life around.

———

Four years later things are as bad as they could be. Zach asks for his bill politely and is rewarded with a smile by the waitress whose expression seems to suggest he has done her a great favour. He has learned to be very considerate to wait staff over the past five months or so, which is as long as he has been with Mandy, his girlfriend of the moment. In her thirties, she is still looking for a break as an actress; she spends the rest of her time waitressing, the latest in a series of thankless jobs, and ignoring his attempts to extricate himself from the relationship. He finds it interesting that this is the first time he has thought about Mandy since he got to Bhutan; it gives him proof, if he was indeed looking for proof, as to where she fits in his scheme of things. He had got involved with her soon after his breakup with Julia but the vivacity and attractiveness (and the French maid's uniform that had so beguiled him whenever he lunched at Noreen's, he has to admit) had soon faded, and as Julia began to seep back into his life, he couldn't wait to see the back of Mandy, especially as he is aware this would be a prerequisite for any reconciliation with Julia.

Unfortunately for him, neither woman sees things exactly the way he would like them to. Julia doesn't seem ready to fully trust him yet and Mandy doesn't seem ready to let go. In the past he would have been able to leave Mandy without too much trouble, but this time around he is finding it unusually difficult to break up – possibly because his view of relationships has changed and he has begun to gain a measure of understanding of what it means to be denied the opportunity of being with someone you want to be with. Or it might simply have to do with growing older and being less able to deal with the fallout of a breakup?

How he thinks he can sort out that situation and everything else about his miserable life by hanging out in a restaurant in Thimphu watching a dancing policeman, he does not know. At least back in London he could fill every waking moment with work, prevent himself from thinking too much. He doesn't have that option now: he has hoped for so much from this holiday that he has even left his BlackBerry behind. The waitress brings him the bill, he pays, is rewarded with a smile that seems genuine enough (Mandy says most wait staff fake it), but it only serves to deepen his anxiety and ill humour. He remembers a Finnish editor friend of his, Kaisa, telling him at a drunken Frankfurt dinner several years ago, after he had been moaning on about a particularly bad breakup, to embrace his misfortune because, as they said back in her country, "Celebrate the bad times for they won't remain bad forever, be wary of the good times for they will end." But he is not a fucking Finn, what do they know anyway, don't they all kill themselves regularly, or is that a Danish trait? No matter, a pox on all nuggets of grand-mother's wisdom!

His annoyance with himself grows. *What the hell am I doing here?* I have no desire to see the sights, I know no one who might be able to divert me from my troubles, and I doubt that there is even a decent bar I can drown my sorrows in. He turns decisive, thinks there is no point in making himself more miserable than he deserves to be — he will just take an earlier flight home. He will not tell anyone he has slunk back to London a day after he got to Thimphu, spending more time travelling than he actually spent at his destination! He remembers a self-important academic telling him at a company bash that the truest sign that you had made it was when you spent more time travelling to and from a destina-tion than the amount of time you had actually spent there (he had just returned from a conference in Melbourne). He had thought that the professor was full of shit then, and now that he is about to put his theory into practice he finds no reason to revise his opinion. He asks the waitress for directions to the nearest travel agency and is told that it will be probably be closed for the day. If he is going to be stuck here for another night, the least he can do is get himself some decent food. He enquires where the Swiss Bakery is; TripAdvisor says it makes decent sandwiches and patties — better to get something that he finds edible rather than face the prospect of eating ema datse in the hotel restaurant – he had found the fiery national dish of chilies and cheese too hot to handle the first and only time he had tried it.

At this hour of the evening Norzin Lam is moderately busy – Thimphu's version of rush hour. As he threads his way through the crowd of locals and the occasional tourist he thinks, not for the first time, that the Bhutanese are an exceptionally attractive people – their natural good looks are accentuated by the national costume most wear, the men in wraparound ghos and knee-length stockings, and the women in full length kiras, garments as effective as saris and kaftans in hiding physical infelicities. As he walks along his mood gradually begins to improve, it's hard to keep glowering when almost everyone looks you in the eye with a smile. A Maruti van screeches by, a pack of stray dogs angles across the street unmindful of traffic or pedestrians, and up ahead a shimmer of Buddhist monks lights up the gloom in maroon and crimson robes. Most of the business establishments have shut for the day, but he spots what looks like a bookshop and darts in to see if he can find any books by local talent. To his disappointment, the selection is poor – eccentric is probably a better word for it – with an unusually large quantity of Spenser's *Faerie Queene* sharing space with a clutch of Indian novels and a rather battered paperback of *The War of Angels*.

The novel spent two years on the bestseller lists, and ended up selling six million copies in various Litmus editions. The company made several million pounds more from the sale of foreign rights, and the movie tie-ins brought waves of new

fans to the Seppi brand. The studio was getting impatient for
the fourth book, as was everybody else who had a stake in
the author, but now, unexpectedly, there was a problem.
Seppi, who had so far delivered a book a year, exactly on
schedule, had overshot his deadline for Book 4, *Angels Falling,*
by six months. Despite repeated reminders, Zach had no
word about when he could expect to receive the manuscript.
Gabrijela and he talked daily about the situation. The *Angels
Falling* hardcover was their biggest autumn release, but there
was only so much pressure they could bring to bear on their
most important author. Moreover, they could not ignore the
fact that Seppi had been a model author thus far, especially
when it came to meeting deadlines – he remembers Gabrijela's
telling him about an author at her previous company who
had overshot his deadline by seventeen years. They had finally
decided to make one last concerted effort, before giving up,
to publish the novel on schedule – marketing, publicity, and
sales commitments had been locked in almost nine months
earlier, and if an author as big as Seppi defaulted everyone's
year would be affected. Zach was told by Gabrijela to go to
Toronto to reason with his star author. This was easier said
than done.

Great novelists are seen to best effect on the page, but in
our time they are expected to be equally adept at perform-
ing and enjoying themselves onstage. Most are pretty awful
when it comes to public performances or interacting with
the media or their fans, but in the relentless, marketing- and
publicity-driven business that twenty-first-century publishing has become, no one is spared. Massimo Seppi was no

Dylan Thomas; his was not an inspiring stage or media presence. They had shipped him to a few festivals and bookstore
readings when the first two *Angels* books were published,
but none of them was a success and Seppi was miserable.
When his star began to rise, he told Litmus firmly that his
publicity effort would be limited to one interview apiece for
newspapers, radio, TV, and the company's microsite devoted
to him. In common with some of the biggest authors on the
planet, as his image waxed and grew gigantic, Seppi became
reclusive to the point of near invisibility. As an unknown
literary author his anonymity had been guaranteed; after his
rise to fame he ensured it was.

Zach had met with Seppi fairly frequently during the
publication of the first two books of the quartet, but he had
seen him only twice since *War of Angels* was published. This
was something he regretted; in his years as an editor, one of
the things he had liked the most about the job was the time
he spent with his authors, those brilliant, fragile, unpredictable people, each of them a character in his or her own right.
Some became close friends, he'd had a destructive relationship with one of them, there were others to whom he was
nothing more than a professional associate, and there were
those with whom the connection was even more tenuous,
mainly overseas authors or those he had published but once.
But he missed those days – he edited only a couple of
authors now, and it bothered him that he had so little to do
with Litmus's most famous author and the very first author
he had published. This was partly to do with the fact that
Seppi lived abroad, partly because he published Seppi in

translation and therefore passed on all his editorial suggestions to the translator, who then discussed them with the
author, and partly because since he became publisher the
constraints on his time had grown. For some time now Seppi
and he had communicated mainly by e-mail and over the past
year and a half even that connection was intermittent, with
the translator, a woman named Caryn Bianchi, taking over
much of the correspondence. His relationship with Caryn
had grown strained after she had begun acting as Seppi's agent
and discovered that her author had signed over all rights in
the quartet to Litmus; it had got downright nasty after Litmus
rebuffed her every attempt to pry rights free, or at least
increase royalties. Finally, Seppi himself had had to intervene
to patch things up.

Now she was getting her own back. Zach had spent
weeks trying to get Caryn to arrange a meeting with his
author, and was on the point of giving up when his phone
rang one day and Seppi asked him politely whether he could
fly to Toronto for a meeting next week.

Unlike the last two meetings, which had taken place in
Seppi's house, this time they were to meet in a coffee shop
in Little Italy. When he got there he found that Seppi and his
translator had already arrived. He hurried over to their table,
disbelieving of what he saw. Gone was the neat spare man in
chinos and blue work shirt he had met barely two years ago.
In his place was a bloated figure, bald and pasty-faced, and
very obviously ill.

"My God, what happened to you? I had no idea —"

"It's nothing . . . I've just been a little ill," Seppi said.

"With what —" Zach began.

But Seppi shrugged off his concern, turning to his translator. "You've met Caryn, yes?"

"I haven't actually but we've been corresponding."

Zach had paid no attention to the woman who sat at the table but now he turned his attention to her. Even if he hadn't been feuding with her, he would have been put off by the scowl on her face and the deeply inset eyes, and thin lips that seemed to be set in a permanent expression of disapproval. He turned back to Seppi, and asked again after his health. With obvious reluctance Seppi told him about the pancreatic cancer that was discovered too late to respond effectively to treatment. Neither his translator nor he was willing to say anything more about his illness, and as the effete waiter brought them their cappuccinos the conversation moved to the fourth book. He could not concentrate for more than a few minutes at a time, Seppi said, and it was therefore taking him longer than expected.

"You shouldn't bug him so much, he's a dying man — you publishers are all alike," the translator cut in unexpectedly. Seppi silenced her with a glance and said simply, "You'll get the book by Christmas." Seppi hadn't touched his cappuccino and looked exhausted. Zach felt deeply sorry to be putting pressure on someone who was so obviously ill. The table fell silent until Seppi suddenly said, "Zach, tell me about your favourite meal." This was unexpected; their conversations had never been about anything but professional matters. Seppi wasn't an author he would count as a friend exactly, so he fumbled around for a reply. He remembered a meal at Nobu with an especially high-powered Egyptian publisher with expensive dining habits, and had begun talking about the exquisite unagi he'd eaten there when Seppi had interrupted, looking puzzled: "You're Japanese?"

"Umm, no, sorry – I don't understand."

"I was just wondering what your favourite food was, from your growing years, your childhood?"

"Ah . . ."

The thought rose in his mind of his grandmother in Kanyakumari making puttu, steamed and fragrant, that he would dissolve in coconut milk or meat stew; he hadn't eaten it in three decades but the taste was rich and warm in his mouth.

Before he could reply, Seppi had begun to speak again, almost to himself. "In Palermo," he said, "the bay lies before the shore like a discus hand-painted by the gods, in blues so shimmering and mysterious the eye cannot quite comprehend them. It is so inviting that you have no option but to jump in, though you have to be careful where you swim, there is so much seaweed in the water. It held no terrors for us, though, my friend Luigi and I grew up swimming in that bay.

"Hours and hours of just swimming, and diving and calling out to the beautiful girls in the tourist boats who would smile and wave out to us, two skinny ten-year-olds who were having so much fun. When we'd had enough we would head back to shore and go in search of street vendors serving our favourite food, babbaluci. For just a few lira we would get a big helping of snails marinated in olive oil, parsley, and garlic, fried in a pan that hadn't been cleaned for a few centuries, giving everything a rich flavour. The vendor would tear off a sheet of the previous day's *Giornale di Sicilia,* twist it into a funnel, and pour the smoking hot snack into it and hand it to us, and we would wander off to explore the evening's delights crunching the fat, juicy, perfectly cooked snails between our teeth, letting that glorious taste slide down our throats."

He fell silent, caught up in the sensuousness of his remembering eye, his best memories his last defence against dying.

You might publish a hundred writers, a thousand, but it is the few who complete you as an editor, Zach thinks, as he turns the pages of the worn paperback in the cluttered Thimphu bookshop with affection and sadness.

———

Seppi's final novel arrived, as he had promised, two days before Christmas 2007. *Angels Falling* was shorter than the previous volumes by about 250 pages, but despite the occasional slack or unpolished passages, the story of the Archangel Uriel fighting the forces of darkness represented by Hitler, Mussolini, and their ungodly armies was told as muscularly and clearly as his previous books. When he presented the book to his sales force Zach was unequivocal in his assertion that the book was a masterpiece, and that Seppi belonged in the pantheon of great authors whose insights and prose were uncluttered and deep, and who did not need props like pretty words and unnecessary disquisition to tell their tale. He had wondered how much of the work was the translator's; despite his problems with Caryn, the company and he were indebted to her; to express their gratitude he sent a magnum of champagne and two crystal flutes.

Litmus published within ten weeks of receiving the manuscript, the fastest turnaround of any book they had published. If that was impressive what was perhaps even more astonishing was that nine of the countries that were translating the book from Italian or English published simultaneously with Litmus. Zach took personal charge of every aspect of publication, from the editing and design, all the way through to the moment the first book rolled off the presses. He drove every one of his colleagues to the breaking-point, starting with his creative director, Alice, a short-tempered genius who threw a coffee cup at him one day when he rejected her fifteenth attempt to come up with suitable typography for the inside text. They got it right on the sixteenth attempt when they chose Aetna Roman, a modern font designed by Jack Yan, based on the typeface created by the fifteenth-century punchcutter Francesco Griffo. Zach loved its smooth-flowing ligatures, the wonderfully buoyant serifs, the balance and exactitude of its stroke weight. When he e-mailed a sample page to Seppi, the author's reply was instantaneous: he loved the look of the page, the fact that it was called Aetna was a gift from God.

Things went more or less smoothly from that point onwards. For the cover, Zach told Alice to ignore the advice of the marketing people and the sales force and go with her most inspired creative instincts – he figured he could sell the book with nothing more on it than Seppi's name. What she came up with was stunning. Eschewing commercial considerations, she created a snowy-white background (to represent the decisive turning point of Stalingrad) on which was superimposed a tiny three-dimensional figure in blue; the type was restrained and elegant and balanced the image perfectly. The cover would win Alice a raft of awards from design organizations that year.

On the appointed date of the launch, shops opened at the stroke of midnight to service the long lines of customers; in an attempt to separate genuine fans from speculators who wanted to sell first editions on eBay, each customer was restricted to two copies. As always Seppi was present at none of the launch occasions. He wanted his illness to be hidden from the world. As he hadn't appeared in public for his last two books, this was easy enough to arrange; the customary print interviews were conducted over the phone, as were radio and television interviews. And that was that. Within twenty-four hours of publication, the book had sold two million copies, and a month later that total across thirty-two editions (sixteen more were in the pipeline) was approaching 8.5 million copies – *Angels Falling* had become one of the five fastest-selling books of the twenty-first century. Massimo Seppi was unaware of this when he died at home on March 8, 2008, a week after the book was published. He hadn't wanted to be visited by any of his publishers during his final days; Caryn was the only one at his bedside, besides a nurse from the Home Healthcare Institute.

On an impulse, Zach buys the paperback copy of *The War of Angels* from the proprietor of the bookshop, who has been giving him the look shopkeepers the world over have perfected when customers linger past closing time. He leaves the shop and goes in search of the Swiss Bakery. He finds it easily enough, an unpretentious restaurant with a limited selection of sandwiches and pastries on offer. It is almost deserted, like every other establishment he has been in since he got to Thimphu; it is one of the things he likes about the city. He is trying to make up his mind between a chicken and cheese sandwich and a plain grilled cheese sandwich when he feels a tap on his shoulder. He turns to find himself face to face with a short, balding man dressed unusually for these parts in trousers, shirt, and cardigan. He looks familiar, but Zach can't place him, and then he does, when the man says, "Its Zach isn't it?"

"Das?"

———

Before he left India for London and a master's degree at Goldsmiths College, Zach studied at one of Delhi's great educational institutions, which was much sought after because of the excellence of its faculty and its proximity to a women's college whose students were renowned for their beauty. Much of his time there has blurred away, but one incident emerges as clear as if it had happened a few minutes ago. All freshers had to endure a few weeks of ragging, a stupid and pointless ritual that was eventually banned when a less than robust junior killed himself after being humiliated nightly for over a month by a particularly vicious band of seniors.

In Zach's time, however, ragging had been alive and well; his worst moment came when he was summoned to a senior's room one Sunday afternoon just before lunch. One of the three seniors present asked him whether he was hungry, and he answered that he was.

"Hot or cold snack, junior pisser?"

"Er . . . hot, sir."

A tub of red chilies was produced from behind the senior's back and he was ordered to eat every one, which he did, masticating each bite thoroughly. The agony was unendurable, spikes of pure pain shot to his brain before being channelled to every part of his body. Tears streamed down his cheeks, his mouth and head threatened to explode, the sound of his heart filled his chest like a mercilessly struck gong, his body was on the verge of giving way from the punishment it was absorbing – but he was determined not to beg, to give in, he was too stubborn for that. There must have been close to a hundred chilies in the tub. He had munched his way through about thirty or so of them when one of the trio, alarmed at the symptoms of near collapse Zach was exhibiting, told his friends to ease off.

"Want some water, junior pisser?" the senior who had given him the chilies asked.

Zach managed to nod. The senior reached under his bed, pulled out a large plastic bucket of soapy water in which his dirty laundry had been soaking, and told Zach to go out of the room into the corridor and drink every drop of the water.

He had picked up the bucket, staggered out into the corridor and, beyond caring by now, started to drink the filthy water in great breathless gulps. Within minutes, he had begun to retch.

Das, who was passing, had taken in the situation and gestured to Zach to put the bucket down. He had curtly informed the three seniors that he was "borrowing" the junior, as he needed him to run an errand. He was a year senior to them; they had no choice but to agree. When they reached Das's room, he was set free with a bowl of curd to cool his tortured mouth and palate. The incident was not the beginning of a deep friendship; Das was graduating that year and was too senior to bother with a newcomer like Zach. But they would greet each other in passing at the hostel or on the way to class, and Zach had never forgotten the senior's kindness.

It has been over twenty years since they last met. The long hair he remembers has vanished; Das is almost bald, the fringe is very grey, and he looks older than his years. He tells Zach he has lived in Thimphu for seventeen years, and that he works for a non-profit organization, is married to his childhood sweetheart, and has three children, ranging in age from six to fourteen. Before they part, Das invites him to dinner the following night.

Das lives in Motithang, a quiet suburb built on an elevation above Thimphu. The night is crisp and clear and the lights of the city stream up to the stars. The house the taxi deposits him at is built in the traditional way: three stories tall, with a prayer flag planted squarely in the middle of the roof, upward curving eaves, wooden shutters, an ochre-yellow façade bright with Buddhist paintings of dragons, tigers, and fertility symbols, including a larger-than-life representation of a brownish-pink penis.

No sooner has the taxi's engine cut off, than Das comes out, and ushers Zach into the house. He introduces his wife, Sonam, a woman with a serene face, and their three children. Instinctively, for he hasn't done this in a long time, Zach raises his hands in a namaskaram and bows slightly. The family smile at him, then Sonam disappears to organize dinner, and the children scamper upstairs to their room.

Das pours Zach a glass of Bhutan Mist, a surprisingly good malt, and they make the first stuttering steps towards re-establishing the slender connection they once had. At first the conversation moves through the great events of the day, especially Barack Obama's extraordinary rise to prominence. Even in this Himalayan fastness people were glued to their TV sets, Das tells him, mesmerized by Obama's charisma and compelling story, the momentary brightness of his election shining through the enveloping gloom of a decade racked by war, terrorism, and economic blight. By the time the second whisky is poured, they have begun delving into each other's lives, and here Das is the more forthcoming of the two. He tells of the years spent working in India in the administrative service, the decision to move to Bhutan where Tenzin, the eldest of their children was born, the job with the NGO that has something to do with education, the building of their own house after years of living with Sonam's parents. He shows Zach around the place, explains the architecture and adaptations he has made to the traditional Bhutanese house that everyone is required to build by law. The ground floor that is still used to house livestock in the rural areas has been converted into the living room they are sipping their whisky in, with wooden floors and glass panes in the windows rather than the usual wooden shutters. There is a proper staircase that leads to the first floor instead of the tree trunk with steps cut into it that the older houses still have. Zach, who has never owned a house, would have usually been bored stiff by these details but he finds that he is quite interested. Would he have behaved differently if the conversation had taken place in London, would he perhaps have been condescending towards Das and his small, uneventful life? Undoubtedly. But as the evening carries on it seems that Das is the one to be envied, with his stable existence and calm outlook on the future. What does Zach have, what has his life of frenzied preoccupation with work, years of short-lived romances, evenings spent drinking with unreliable friends, lunches and parties with the publishing set in London, and an absence of rootedness brought him? A broken marriage. Anxiety about work. And the constant need to experience the next adrenalin rush, take the next step on the high wire his life is balanced on because not to move forward would be to fall – and to fall would be to perish, there are no safety nets in his life – it is why he continues to whip himself on. Whereas Das will continue to accumulate slowly his little triumphs, he will watch his children grow to adulthood, dandle his grand-children on his knee (do people even do that anymore?). And then this train of thought comes to an end: no, Zach could not have led this life; he would have died of boredom, better to go out on his own terms.

They dine without the children, who have already eaten. He jokes about his difficulty in learning how to appreciate ema datse on his first visit here, and Das and Sonam laugh together, their eyes meeting, a reflexively intimate moment born of long years of love and friendship. Zach's mood sours momentarily. He thinks: When Julia and I were together, except in the very early days, we did not have this. Within a couple of years we were leading our separate lives and careers, and when we were together we were not fused but distinct. Sonam asks whether he is married and he replies truthfully that he is, but that work has kept Julia back in London. At some point in the evening, when the conversation has moved away from the personal and back to political and social events, Zach says he is not convinced by the Bhutanese concept of governance.

"Surely you cannot legislate happiness," he says. "People are the same everywhere; they don't give a damn about inner happiness until they have satisfied their craving for material things."

"I think you're oversimplifying," Das says quietly. "What we're trying to do as a society, what the king, and his father with whom the concept originated, are trying to direct us towards is to attain a balance between material prosperity and the things that give us inner happiness. We have problems, just as everyone has problems, but I think the point of GNH is to set different objectives for ourselves as individuals and as a country, objectives that redefine notions of prosperity and wealth, objectives that try to steer us away from rampant consumerism. If we get even partway there we will be better off than we were before."

"And you can do this by turning your back on the modern world, becoming a sort of primitive Utopia?"

Das and Sonam laugh together. "No, that is the way the media depicts us," Sonam says. "Today you can go to a disco in Thimphu, we are connected to the Internet, we have forty satellite channels –"

Das carries the thought forward, "The point is we do not want to be swept away by all these things, we need to remain connected to our culture, achieve the right balance. An extraordinarily high percentage of Bhutanese who leave the country return, so we must be doing something right."

Zach is not entirely persuaded, but he doesn't really want to carry the argument further. If this is the way this country and its people want to lead their lives, who is he to disagree – he can't even manage his own life. He compliments Sonam on the food, and her face suffuses with pleasure. Das says, "Sonam makes a great meen moily; she learned how to make South Indian food like a native when we lived there. And when you visit next we'll give you the best ema datse in town."

After dinner Sonam vanishes upstairs, leaving the two men alone. Das pours them another whisky. They make small talk, and then, all at once and in a way that seems perfectly natural, Zach unburdens himself about what has brought him to Thimphu. As he does so, he thinks that it is his years in London that have made him so uptight, so unwilling to talk freely of the things that he really wants to talk about. In this part of the world they do things differently. He is glad, fiercely glad that it is so, as he tells Das about the lonely death of his mother, his troubles with Julia, his fears about his job.

His host does not interrupt once. When he is finished, Das freshens his whisky, and then says there is something he would like to show him.

He takes Zach to the back of the house, and leads him into a sparsely furnished room – a desk, a chair, and a shelf of books. In the corner something glows in the dim light of the overhead bulb. Das walks him over, switches on a spotlight, and a tremendous bird rockets out at them – an outrageously coloured creature, plumed in howling reds, blues, and yellows.

"What is it?" he asks his host.

"A male satyr tragopan, one of our migratory birds. Its plumage is actually even more stunning than this, I don't think I have done it justice."

"It's extraordinary," Zach says. "But why is it painted on the floor?"

Das doesn't reply directly but says that Sonam and he decided to settle in Thimphu after their first-born, a boy, died in an accident when they were living in Trivandrum. But the change of scene did nothing to calm his mind, he found it hard to concentrate on anything, he was short with Sonam, unable to focus on his work. One day, a group of Tibetan monks from Dharamshala visited Bhutan and demonstrated the art of sand-painting, using small metal funnels called chakpur and coloured sands to create beautiful and detailed mandalas. They spent several days creating a luminous work of art, and then, when it was finished, they swept it up, destroyed it, to demonstrate the impermanence of everything, to show graphically the Buddhist concept of non-attachment.

"It made a powerful impression," Das says, "and I was determined to learn the art of sand-painting, it seemed to show me a way to come to terms with the death of my boy."

They look at the flaring beauty of the bird on the floor; in a short time it will be as if it never existed.

"At first I found it difficult to destroy the paintings I created or even to make good paintings for that matter. I was not trained like the monks, my paintings were not based on religious themes or anything like that, and for me sand-painting was simply a way to work out my grief and my frustration. It didn't help that I wasn't a particularly good artist or that the material I was using was difficult to manage. But I kept at it. The first successful painting I made was of Sonam's parents' house; it had taken so much effort that I couldn't bring myself to erase it, I had to have Sonam do it for me. And then slowly I began to get the point."

"How long did this one take you?"

"About three months."

"And when will you destroy it?"

"Tomorrow. I have just a few details of the crest to complete and I'll be done."

"Thank you," Zach says simply, "for sharing this with me."

———

Back in his hotel he thinks for a long time about Das's method of dealing with sorrow and loss. Although he can't see himself spending months creating paintings of coloured sand in his apartment, the principle makes a lot of sense to him. He thinks that, without really planning it, his life has been built on a platform of detachment. It is the only way he could have survived and learned to thrive in places far from home. The years he's had with Julia, the years he has been sheltered by Litmus and by Seppi, these have eroded his watchful and self-reliant nature. It's why he has been feeling so unsettled, he will need to start rebuilding his defences – here and now would be a good place to start.

———

Novelists rarely agree about anything to do with their craft, but the one thing on which the views of a large number, from Gabriel García Márquez to R.K. Narayan to Graham Greene, seem to coincide is that what fills the well of their imagination is their childhood and early youth. As he lies on his bed in his Thimphu hotel room thinking about his life he gets what they mean – within the noise and chaos of the present, it is only the significant events of his childhood that rise up clear and untarnished.

Zach's ability to fend for himself was formed early on. His father worked for a coffee company high in the Shevaroy Hills; their nearest neighbours were three miles away and Zach, an only child, was pretty much left to his own devices with only a succession of ayahs for company. When he was ten he was sent to boarding school. It was a tough school, and he was the outsider; the student body was largely blue-collar and resented his family's wealth and his life of apparent privilege; he had to fight and fight often just to be left alone.

One incident stood out. Home for the holidays, he had just celebrated his thirteenth birthday, which fell on December 15. His father had taught him to shoot the previous year, and his parents had given him an air gun for his birthday. Although he had been prohibited from indiscriminately slaughtering the bird life that abounded in the vicinity of the house, he tried to do just that when he was unsupervised, which was most of the time. The help weren't able to curb his bloodthirsty instincts (formed from reading too many books on shikar) because they were only permitted to caution him, or threaten to tell his parents, they were not allowed to command. Fortunately his aim was wayward and apart from an unfortunate bulbul that he dropped while it perched on a telephone wire, the birds around the house were terrorized but unharmed. But although Zach had delighted in his air gun what he was really looking forward to was the opportunity to use his father's Purdey shotgun, a beautiful weapon with twin barrels of blue steel and a stock as black as night. Ever since he could remember, Zach had gone out with his father on hunting expeditions; Nirmal was a fair shot and had bagged duck, quail, and jungle fowl, and on one memorable occasion a wild boar. He had promised to let Zach use the shotgun when he turned sixteen.

Two days after his birthday his father was called away to a meeting at the company's headquarters in the plains. He expected to be away for four days. On the second day of his trip, his mother received a call from her neighbour saying the police had informed her about a convict who had broken out of prison in a town approximately three hours away and was last seen heading in their general direction. There was nothing to worry about, the police had said, but they would keep in regular touch until the convict, who had been serving a life sentence for chopping his neighbour to death with an aruval over a land dispute, was captured. The police were telling everybody to stay close to their bungalows, the neighbour said, and to get in touch if they spotted anyone who looked suspicious. The police phoned the house soon after with the same message. Zach's mother told him to stop going out with his air gun until the murderer was caught. He dragged himself around the house that day, trying not to get in the way of his mother or the help. By the evening of the next day he was thoroughly bored.

At around five-thirty, after Thangavel, the butler, had cleared away the tea things in the living room, Zach went to his bedroom to listen to music. His bedroom gave on to a verandah, beyond which there was almost half an acre of beautifully maintained lawn bordered by a hibiscus hedge that stood about six feet high. On the lawn was a swing on which Zach had spent many happy hours as a little boy urging his father or his ayah or one of the gardeners to push him higher, higher. As he lay on his bed listening to an old Jefferson Airplane song on the stereo, he thought he saw a silhouette by the hibiscus hedge. In the winter, night came early in the hills, and the gardeners were normally gone by five, but maybe one of them had stayed on late; then he'd remembered that the gardeners had a half-day on Fridays. Today was Friday. His heart beating a little faster, Zach had stealthily slid off the bed, and crawled along the floor to the window; crouching down, he had peered over the sill into the dusk. Was he imagining things or was that something that looked like a human figure wrapped in a lungi? He dropped to the floor, crawled across the room, pushed open the door, crawled out into the passage that separated his room from his parents' room, closed the door to his room, and ran to the cupboard containing his father's shotgun. His mother was having a bath, and the servants were in the kitchen preparing supper, as the neighbours were coming over that night.

Breaking open the shotgun as he had seen his father do, he had loaded it with two cartridges, shoved a couple more into the pocket of his shorts, snapped the barrels back into position, run back into his room, dropped to the floor, and crawled along to the window where he peered over the sill as he had done a few minutes earlier. There was nothing to be seen by the hedge in what little light remained. Not once did it occur to him to call the butler or his assistant.

Although he was terrified he had quietly unlocked the door to the verandah. Then, as smoothly as he could, he had pushed open the door, before rushing out, the gun held chest high, and screaming, "Who is there? Come out at once or I will shoot!" There wasn't a breath of wind. The emptiness of the lawn mocked his terror. There was no one by the hedge. He heard a slight creaking sound. He turned towards it; in the dim light the swing swayed up and down.

Within minutes, the verandah light had come on, and the butler, who had heard him shouting, was there, a poker in his hand. Zach explained what had just happened. His mother joined them and got very angry with him for having taken his father's shotgun, and for having put himself needlessly at risk. She phoned the police and a police jeep arrived half an hour later and stayed the night. When Zach's father returned he had been as cross as his mother had been; he said if Zach ever touched the shotgun again before his sixteenth birthday he would rescind his promise to allow him to use the weapon. When the murderer was caught four days later in the coolie lines a few miles away, where he had been given shelter by a relative, he admitted to the police that during his days of freedom he had spent some time one evening watching Nirmal aiyah's son in his room. Remembering the incident still alarms him, but he thinks that was the day he had truly begun to learn how to fend for himself.

As he grew up he figured out how to temper his impetuosity, developed the strength and flexibility that would see him through difficult situations; from his father, he inherited traits that he often wished were better formed in himself, such as patience and calm; but it was from his mother that he got the qualities that most defined him: the ability to take risks, a deep stoicism that helped him through the hard times, and the resilience that kept him going no matter how many times he was struck down.

Thinking about her now he feels unexpectedly crushed by her death, especially because he hadn't been able to mourn her properly. This was true of his father's passing as well, but at least then Julia and his surviving parent cushioned his sense of loss. Moreover, he was closer to his mother than his father, not that it had mattered very much, he was always the absent son who phoned home from time to time and visited once a

year. Julia and his mother had not got on and that had strained
their relationship for a while. When his father died, his mother
and he had made up and he had tried unsuccessfully to get
her to return to the land of her birth so he could take care of
her. But there was no moving her. She had turned her face
against her parents and England after they had opposed her
marriage to the Indian coffee planter she had fallen in love
with when she was twenty-two, and so far as she was concerned the decision was permanent. She had stayed away
from their funerals, she had signed over everything they had
left her in their respective wills to her sister, and now, nearly
half a century later, she still would not relent. She would stay
on in the old house on the hill that Nirmal and she had
moved to after he had retired – it did not matter to her that
she was seventy-one years old and arthritic and diabetic.

She had once told him about his paternal grandfather
dying a few months after his beloved wife of fifty-two years
had passed on. Apparently, local superstition had it that the
surviving partner of a long-term marriage was most at risk
of dying within a few days of the birthday or death day of
the departed spouse. Sure enough, his grandfather had died
three days after he'd marked his wife's birthday with a night-
long remembrance ceremony of his own devising. That fact
had stuck in his mind, and every year, for the next five years,
he would become extremely anxious about his mother's
health three days before and three days after the birth and
death anniversaries of his father. He set up an elaborate early
warning system comprising neighbours, friends, and servants
who would check in on her regularly and keep him informed

about her state of health. Last year she had negotiated the days that bracketed the critical dates on the calendar without setting off any alarms, but in the winter she was struck down by the flu and he received the phone call he had been dreading, saying he should get to Yercaud immediately.

He found her listless and worn, and unable to move a few steps without becoming breathless. Her GP suggested moving her to the hospital, and she said she didn't mind going but that he shouldn't expect to see her back in the house again. He had brushed aside her fears, but within a day of being admitted to the hospital she took a turn for the worse. Her doctor was blunt with him: his mother was dying and he would have to start making his peace with that fact. He told the doctor that no expense should be spared to make her well again, she was tough and she could make it. He took one of the rooms at the hospital reserved for the family of patients, and spent every waking moment at his mother's bedside; by now her condition had deteriorated further and she was drifting in and out of a coma.

When you are keeping vigil at the bedside of a loved one who is seriously ill, the one thing that no one tells you about in advance is that you will be bored and frustrated by your inability to make yourself useful, and will often be regarded as an irritant because you get in the way of those who are trying to do their jobs. In large city hospitals nobody but hospital staff gets to attend on critically ill patients, but in the country hospital to which his mother had been admitted the rules were more relaxed and he spent hours trying to talk to her, stroking her face, badgering the nurses for updates on her condition.

Finally, they could take it no longer, and the senior nurse ordered him out of the intensive care unit. He went upstairs to his room. The hospital was surrounded by low, humped hills capped with mist, and he looked out at them, his mind blank. He felt no grief; he could fix no thought or image of his mother in his head. For the next couple of days he was allowed into the ICU for an hour every morning and an hour every evening when he was allowed to spoon-feed her a few sips of porridge. One night when he was trying to sleep, his mind began to fill with memories of her and he knew that she was going to die; at three the next morning a nurse came up to his room and said she was very sorry to tell him that his mother had passed away peacefully a few moments ago.

He had stayed dry-eyed when his mother died – he was so preoccupied with all the details he had to attend to that he was unable to grieve. When he returned to London his memories stayed bound tight within him. But now, in this strange city that he has fled to without really thinking, and at the end of an evening that has touched him in a way that he was not prepared for, the cords that he has used to tie the loss of his mother tightly within him come undone, and he weeps uncontrollably.

When the crying subsides, his mind is rinsed clean and he is able to think calmly for the first time in months. He decides not to return home early. He checks out of the hotel in Thimphu, and takes a room in Paro, a small town surrounded by cloud-welted mountains where he takes long, solitary walks, not thinking about much, trying to centre himself, not forcing it, but letting it happen as naturally as possible. By the time he gets on the plane for the return journey home the anxiety he was gripped by has dwindled to almost nothing and his confidence is restored. The troubles that brought him to Bhutan have not gone away but he is now able to place them in the right context, the first and perhaps most important step when it comes to dealing with them. He has started to make his peace with his mother's death; he will work things out with Julia and Mandy no matter how long it takes. Adopting a more relaxed attitude to the threat that looms on the job front is in some ways the most difficult thing; he has fought hard to get to where he is now, but as he reflects upon his career, he comes to the realization that nothing is ever guaranteed in publishing. He has always known that but had forgotten it as his mind had grown unquiet. No, publishing is not a profession for the faint-hearted or those who crave certainty and results that are commensurate with effort. That is why he has always found it thrilling, the knowledge that the unexpected is always just a minute or a month away, and that no matter how dire things seem, something will turn up, something always does.

2 .

LONDON

She had decided to leave Zach after she'd had night-mares for five days in a row, in which she died in gruesome ways – disembowelled, shot through the eye (the left), set on fire, drowned in a lake of turpentine, and smashed flat by a locomotive. She was no great believer in the interpretation of dreams, but these seemed to point to the fact that her marriage was killing her, a view her best friend, Anthea, agreed with, so she walked out and the dreams stopped. It wasn't that her relationship was some-thing she could write a misery memoir about, she wasn't a battered, bruised, electrocuted victim. No, the truth was far more boring, it was simply that the man she had married because he was passionate and exciting and necessary to her own life had grown distant, dull, and wrapped up in his work. But if Julia Spence thought that leaving meant she was rid of Zachariah Thomas, she quickly found out otherwise. As he bounced from crisis to crisis, she found that they were as present in each other's lives as they had been when they were together, perhaps more so because it was difficult to take each other for granted anymore.

Julia did not want to lead a life that was less than fulfilling, and if it was possible she wanted to lead a life that was above average. She had known this from about the age of four when her mother, frustrated by her inability to make anything of her own life, took her older daughter's life into her hands and attempted to make it into something extraordinary. Ballet classes, tennis lessons, hours and hours spent thumping away on the family piano, perched on a pile of cushions so she could reach the keys – she was pushed into everything she showed any sort of aptitude for, as well as a few activities that she was exceptionally bad at (public speaking came to mind). But in the end she didn't become world-class in anything her mother thrust upon her. By the time she got to Balliol and chose English and Modern Languages for her undergraduate degree, her mother had given up on her. Importantly, Julia had not given up on herself and now that she was capable of thinking independently she understood that she could lead a life that was not ordinary *without* being able to serve a tennis ball at close to a hundred miles an hour or coaxing out of her stubbornly indifferent piano a sublime interpretation of Beethoven's Concerto No. 4 in G major. The key, she figured, was in leading a life that was truly fulfilling to *her*, a life that she could look back on and say, yes, this was a life well lived. She knew what she did not want: the desperate search for love or more likely sex that some of her girlfriends indulged in. She was dubious about the illusory promise of marriage and children struck her as being more trouble than they were worth. She liked travel but did not think she was bold enough to wander through lands that were completely alien to her, which seemed the only sort of travel that would be truly exciting. Nor did she want to end up with a job that she could do in her sleep and that would extirpate within a decade any notion of well-being. That was the easy part, more difficult was finding something that would challenge and fulfill her for the rest of her days.

She briefly considered becoming a foreign correspondent like Anthea, who was forever being sent off by the *Gazette* to places like Beijing and Azerbaijan, but you had to be crazy like Anthea in order to be able to deal with that sort of unstructured, unsettled life. For a while she thought she might become a social worker but the six months she spent at an ashram near Tirunelveli, after passing out of university, cured her of that notion; she wasn't unselfish enough to give of herself so completely. Her fallback option was to become a frustrated academic like her mother, although the prospect of teaching waves of supercilious undergraduates and spending the rest of her life in a place like Broad Street, Oxford, filled her with a peculiar sort of horror. Fortunately, before she drove herself completely mad, she found her niche in publishing; a classmate had found a job as an assistant with Random House and spoke rapturously of her new life – interacting with the best writers alive, never doing the same thing day in and day out, working with intelligent, interesting people. Julia interviewed for and landed a job with a medium-sized publishing firm and soon found out that her classmate had exaggerated. An assistant's job was far from glamorous: when she was not photocopying, stuffing envelopes, scheduling lunch appointments, making coffee, or managing anxious authors who wanted to take things up with her boss, she was editing the least interesting authors on the list or panning the execrable nonsense in the slush pile in the hope of finding gold.

Accidentally, as with most things in life, she discovered her calling. Three years after embarking on her career in publishing, at a book launch she got talking with the founder of a small but prestigious literary agency, Fraser Evans Associates, who was looking for someone who could take care of some of his authors; she decided to take him up on his offer and within a few months she knew she had made the right decision. She was working with authors on their manuscripts, rather than attending production meetings; she was interacting closely with some of the best minds of her generation rather than being a small cog in a vast impersonal machine that spat out hundreds of titles, and she knew that in her future lay the prospect of finding and promoting new and exciting talent. She knew heartbreak for the second time in her life (after the obligatory college dalliance) when she had a brief affair with a young writer who had published an intensely felt and rapturously praised collection of stories and then dumped her and the agency in quick succession, but she recovered soon enough and went on.

Three months after her affair fizzled she met Zach. She was in Edinburgh for the literary festival, and was making herself some coffee in the hospitality yurt when he walked in with someone she knew at HarperCollins. They were discussing the bravura performance that day by Caryl Phillips – she had been in the audience, and agreed with them that he was one of those rare writers whose stage presence was as thrilling as his writing. Her publishing acquaintance had wandered off after a while and she and Zach were left alone. She discovered he had grown up in Tamil Nadu, its blazingly colourful landscapes igniting in her mind as they spoke, and the mental and physical attraction between them had escalated from there. She knew she was looking good that day, her long, straight chestnut hair and brown eyes combining well with the stylish Michael Kors skirt that she had worn on a whim, although it wasn't the sort of thing you normally wore to a book festival (he had later confessed that he had found the combination of sunglasses stuck on top of her head and the flash of white he'd glimpsed under her skirt when she crossed her legs unbelievably erotic). They had dinner that day, and two months after they returned to London they were lovers. He was by far the most intense person she had met in her life, his enthusiasm for his authors and for a life in books bordering on the evangelical; she found his vitality and exotic looks an irresistible combination, and before the year was out they were planning to get married. To her relief he got on well with her parents and her younger sister, but the opposite wasn't true – she had liked his father, a refined-looking man with a shock of unruly white hair and a cutting sense of humour who went out of his way to make her feel welcome, but his mother had shown no warmth towards her prospective daughter-in-law. She didn't know why this was so, she would have thought that she and this Englishwoman who had decided to make India her home would have had at least a few things in common, but when it was clear that her friendly overtures were being snubbed she withdrew into herself and waited for the visit to come to an end. She wouldn't accompany Zach on future visits to his parents' home, she decided, and after the wedding she wouldn't have anything more to do with his mother.

Within six months of moving in with him, however, she discovered that the intensity that she had found so attractive when they were dating could get oppressive when she had to deal with it constantly; if she didn't align herself with his obsessions, she ran the risk of being run over or shut out. Fortunately, during the first years of their marriage, physical passion, their shared love of many of the great voices in contemporary fiction, and the stimulating literary circles they moved in kept their relationship alive and fresh. However, by the time the second book in the *Angels* quartet was published she had begun to have misgivings about the marriage and her husband. By now it wasn't so much his rather controlling nature that bothered her – she had figured out how to handle it – but something that she found rather more distressing: his obsession with literature (and, to be honest, with her) had been replaced by a desire to succeed in the most boring sense possible. Just like any other businessman he had begun to worry about getting ahead, about hitting sales and profit targets; he fretted about the competition, yearned for a showier lifestyle. They moved from their tiny Russell Square flat into a larger one overlooking a park in Kensington, long before they could afford it. He got rid of his rumpled English

"Not this time I didn't but fine, I won't discuss her with you again, all right."

"You know I think it was Einstein who said if an experiment ends disastrously it's pure insanity to keep trying it in the hope of getting a different result."

"Well, I married you, didn't I?"

"And we both know how that turned out!"

"Listen, I didn't call you to fight, I just wanted to talk about Bhutan."

"All right then, but let's talk tomorrow, I've got to go now. I have to finish tidying up this submission before I send it out."

"I hope we're seeing it."

"But of course, my love," she says sweetly before hanging up.

God, that Zach, she thinks, how irritating he is. What on earth has he found in Bhutan? Religion? A new love? She remembers their holiday there when everything was great between them. There must have been arguments, sulks, and that sort of thing but she remembers none of that, just the perfection of long walks through mist-shrouded hills, monks blooming like roses from the windows of fat-bellied dzongs, the exquisite detail of the thangka they couldn't afford but bought anyway. It hangs on her bedroom wall, and she walks over to it, examines its delicate blue and gold tracery. She must get back to the manuscript she has been working on, but she can't seem to stop thinking about the man she once loved, and still appears to be involved with. This is ridiculous, she thinks, it's as though she has never left. They talk every

other day, see each other at least once a week, and her desul-
tory efforts at dating have met with no success, because it is
clear that she isn't interested. She goes to the bathroom,
looks at herself in the mirror. At thirty-nine (five years older
than Mandy, she thinks sourly, but better looking, definitely
better looking) she knows she still looks good – the burnished fall of brown hair with just the occasional furtive
strand of grey, the eyes that Zach had once compared to wild
honey, the face unlined except for a faint latticework of
wrinkles at the corners of her eyes – and could find a man
without any trouble, she has no doubt about that. But until
she can excise Zach from her life she knows there is no point
in thinking about that option. She laughs when she remembers she quoted Einstein at him (where did that come from?);
perhaps she should direct the quote at herself. She brushes
and flosses, creeps into bed, switches off the light, and com-
poses herself for sleep.

———

When the money started to pour in with the third *Angels*
book, Gabrijela bought a Georgian townhouse on a leafy
square in Soho for slightly less than four million pounds
and moved the thirty-two people who worked out of the
London office there. Litmus's employees loved their new
offices, all five floors of it; the best space in the whole building was the top floor, with its oak panelling and tall windows
through which the light streamed in to illuminate the gigantic boardroom table made of Canadian maple, which could

getting his hopes up. He hopes his editors' ideas for book
that they can commission or authors they can shake loose
from the competition are truly brilliant, although he fears that
he might be expecting too much of them – they will not be
able to conjure up world-beating books at a moment's notice.
Further souring his mood is the fact that he will have to let
go of Fiona, the managing editor, soon after the meeting.

He still finds firing people the most difficult task he has
to perform as a senior executive. To make things more difficult, he shuns the most efficient way to get rid of employees
in which all he is required to do is make a short, noncommittal speech to the person concerned, following which Naomi,
Litmus's terrific head of HR, takes over and leads the poor
devil through the various stages that Kübler-Ross and other
gurus have identified – shock, denial, anger, panic, bargain-
ing, depression, acceptance and then the fade into oblivion.
He finds this abhorrent and patronizing. Colleagues, especially long-term colleagues, are not units of inventory or
items on the balance sheet to be managed by the impersonal
tricks the human resources department has up its sleeve. He
has always taken the time and the trouble to do the firing
himself – erring on the side of generosity and refusing to
come up with negative reasons, usually exaggerated, to dimin-
ish the employee, and make it easier to let her go. Naomi
certainly, and even Gabrijela, who is renowned for her loyalty
to her employees, have found his method difficult to take on
occasion. He understands their point of view – that he is
needlessly prolonging the process, and there is no evidence
that slow, compassionate strangling is better for the employee

than the swift bite of the guillotine – but he is not going to change. These people did their bit for him and the company; he will not disrespect them, which appears to be the default position of management. He will do everything he can for them, even if it means he is on edge for days beforehand, and filled with despondency for weeks and months afterwards. To make matters worse, Fiona is his best friend in the office; she was the managing editor when he joined the department as an assistant, and she has applauded and stood by him through every twist and turn of his career at Litmus. She is to be the first victim of the planned cost cuts; Gabrijela and he did everything they could to save her but in the end there was no way out. And if they aren't able to come up with projects that generate positive cash flow quickly there will be more jobs lost. Litmus is the last of the significant London publishers to start laying off people, but without a Seppi it is not immune to the recession. He has been back in London for just three days and already the calm and certainty of his Bhutanese holiday have been swept into the far recesses of his mind.

His colleagues know that he likes to start his meetings on time, and just before nine the room fills with a rush. First in is Yanara. He greets her, liking to speak her name out loud, the consonants and vowels rolling off the tongue like castanets. Of Cuban descent she is exquisite – a tall, willowy woman with an exuberant mane of auburn hair. A non-fiction editor of genius, Yanara does repeatedly what none but the best are capable of; she finds books or authors that anticipate a trend or shift in consumer taste, unlike the majority of non-fiction editors who follow trends and are then surprised to find their improbable name of Plasma, turned vegetarian a few weeks ago. He is mystified by her contribution just like everyone else at the meeting, and it temporarily suspends hostilities between Yanara and Rachel.

He has learned that there is an art to running meetings and if he does not intervene decisively at a particular juncture, the discussion can go on and on. Gabrijela is masterful at keeping the tempo of meetings at a perfect pitch but he lets things slip from time to time. He interrupts Maggie's story about Plasma's dietary habits, and the argument over Yanara's book picks up again. It carries on for nearly ten minutes, at the end of which he has no option but to kill the idea, which is beginning to look increasingly ragged. Yanara looks furious, Rachel looks triumphant, and he has to tell Maggie who looks ready to resume her story that they have had quite enough about Plasma. Half an hour later, it is clear that this meeting is not going to produce any stunning surprises. He cuts short a tedious discussion between Gareth and Maggie on whether a new biography of Hitler stands a chance given the definitive tome by Kershaw, and signals to Prudence to talk to her book ideas.

Despite the gravity of the situation his mind has begun to wander, as often happens when meetings lack the vital spark that brings them alive. What would the collective noun for a gathering of publishers be, he wonders. If you could have a crash of rhinos or a leap of leopards or a murder of crows, why not a persistence of publishers or an optimism of publishers – or, if you were trying to be rude, a folly of publishers . . . He forces himself to concentrate, reminds them once again about why they are meeting: "Please remember what I said in my e-mail. I would only like to hear about big books or books that have the potential to make a mark on the bestseller lists. Save the rest for later." ("Later" means never in his book.)

By the time he winds up the meeting he realizes that there is nothing new he can take to his board meeting next week, except a recipe book of food inspired by angels that Prudence of all people proposes at the last minute; maybe they could tie that into their Seppi franchise. He asks his colleagues for their opinion, Yanara and Rachel start squabbling again, Maggie seems on the point of saying something and fortunately for everyone decides not to, and Gareth says he will come up with a potential sales number after talking to his contact at Waterstone's.

He stays on in the boardroom after everyone has gone, looking at the sheet of paper in front of him that he has optimistically titled BIG BOOK IDEAS FOR FALL 2010.

All he has added is *Angels Cookbook*? It is not enough, and although he doesn't know exactly how much revenue he will be expected to bring in next year, he is already beginning to concede defeat.

———

The next day begins badly. Ever since he has returned from Thimphu, everything about his empty flat has appeared to shout out Julia's absence, mock him for losing her. He can't recall it ever being this bad in all the time she has been gone – it's perhaps because this is the first time since her departure that he has gone anywhere for any length of time. When they lived together, one of the things he had looked forward to whenever he returned from a trip was the big goofy smile she would give him at the door, the long lingering kiss, and the other big and small rituals of return. During his days as a bachelor, his house was his refuge, no woman was allowed to spend the night; now it seems a strange and alien place without Julia, and this sensation was multiplied a hundredfold the day he returned from his vacation. That first day, he had wandered through the rooms noticing, as if for the first time, everything that underlined the fact that she no linger lived there, such as the absence of the murmur of the radio that she had on all the time. They had often scuffled about this, because he loved silence and would only listen to the radio or his iPod when he was exercising or when they were driving. On the rare occasions when he listened to music at home it was quite a production; he would don the Sennheiser HD 800 headphones that he had bought after much online research, get into a comfortable position on his leather sofa, turn on the music, and close his eyes. He would do all this very deliberately, paying no attention to Julia's good-natured mocking. He had noted the missing sofa that left the seating arrangement in the living room incomplete; the two paintings that she had taken with her, marked by the deeper shade of paint on the walls and the nails that he hadn't bothered to extract; the ornamental pot-holder in one corner of the living room (without a pot or indoor plant, the latter having expired less than a week after her departure);

and other less obvious details that would have never registered when she was around.

She had taken very little with her when she walked out – her clothes, her toiletries, her jewellery, some stuff from the kitchen, a piece or two of furniture and art. On good days he would take this as a positive sign, an indication that she intended to return; on bad days he would feel crushed, thinking she had left with almost nothing the better to be able to forget him. In the first hour or so after returning he had felt so desolate that it had taken a tremendous effort of will to keep from bolting out of the house and checking into a hotel or, even worse (because he had known it would upset her greatly), turning up at Julia's doorstep. Things had got slightly better since then but not by much, and any gains that he made were wiped out on days when he was feeling low for other reasons.

This morning's despondency was mainly on account of Fiona. He had spent the night tossing and turning, unable to dislodge from his mind her calm acceptance of the news that she was being laid off. The entire office seemed to think he was solely responsible for her departure, that he had somehow betrayed her and them. There was nothing he could do – he was her boss so of course he was responsible, and he could not whine to them about how difficult it was for him personally and how he and Gabrijela had tried everything possible to stave off the inevitable. In a situation like this people saw only what they wanted to see. They would fear him and mistrust him and any affection or loyalty they had for him would be on hold for a while or might never return.

As for Fi – he would probably never see her again, and this had made him very sad.

He switches on the television. The morning news leads with the death of Michael Jackson and the grief and curiosity it was arousing in a billion people – death as public spectacle. He has never been a fan of the King of Pop, even though he acknowledges the genius of his compositional skills and showmanship, but the star's passing somehow (for he couldn't imagine two more dissimilar people) reawakens memories of his mother's death, deepens the grey mood he is in.

He gets to the office late. He is tired and moody and wants to be left alone but a few minutes after he has walked in, Yanara rushes into his office and says she has a brilliant idea for a book: they should publish a quickie pictorial biography of Michael Jackson.

"We're not Michael O'Mara Books, Yanara, this is not what we publish."

"But I thought we were desperate for a big book or two that we could drop into this year."

"We are, but for the sort of books we know how to publish well. And even if we were to go with your idea there will probably be half a dozen books published in the States before we even get started."

She accepts his decision reluctantly but does not leave. They have a disaster on their hands, she says, the new biography of the Thames they had commissioned from Sir Reginald Zogoiby, the distinguished geographer and writer, is unpublishable. The book, which has been delivered two years late, was to have been their high-priced gift offering for Christmas; Zach has nothing to fill the hole should it drop out.

Yanara is succinct. "What the fuck do we do?"

"Any chance of the old boy doing a quick rewrite?"

"He is eighty-eight and practically senile, everyone knows that. God knows why we ever commissioned the book."

"Isn't it yours?"

"I inherited it."

"Well, his last book on the Tower of London made the bestseller lists."

"So what do we do?"

"Let's get someone in to tidy it up, and pad it out with a lot more pictures."

"Christ, Zach, think of the permission fees!"

"We'll just have to increase the cover price by a pound or two."

"I bet the book will have the shortest shelf life of any book in Litmus's history and will be in remainder bins from Paris to Istanbul before the end of the year."

Paris. Istanbul. What the fuck is Yanara talking about? His head hurts. He wishes she would go away. He asks her to do so, but no sooner has she departed than Lea, his assistant, says that Maggie would like a quick word with him. He beckons Maggie to come in. She almost pushes Lea out of the way, shuts the door to his office, and says dramatically, "We've got a problem."

He looks at her wearily. "What is it?"

"It's Ron."

Ronald Carruthers has just scored a hit with a multigenerational novel set in the Cotswolds. It will be one of their nominations for the Booker and a host of other awards this year. He is on tour at the moment.

"What's he done?"

"His publicist, Pam, phoned to say he got pissed just before his event yesterday and couldn't go on. Fortunately the organizers had two other authors reading that night so it wasn't too bad, but apparently he doesn't want to continue with the tour."

"Damn!"

"And this is the first time Pam has escorted an author on tour so she is freaking out."

"Do you think she can handle him?"

"I don't think so."

"Would it help if I talked to Ron, asked him to get his act together?"

"Perhaps."

"Is the tour over?"

"No, he has two more days on the road."

"OK, let me call him, tell him to calm down. I'll stress how important it is for him to continue with the tour."

"I don't think it's that simple, Zach. Apparently Pam screamed at him and they got into a big fight and now he is really cross with her."

He is proud of Litmus's publicists. Hard-working and conscientious for the most part, they valiantly put up with an enormous workload, a punishing schedule, a largely indifferent media, ungrateful authors, and demanding editors, with grace and good humour. Because they spend a lot of time with authors, they are often at the receiving end of atrocious behaviour.

"This is crazy. Who do we have who could replace her?"

"Mark should be good with Ron."

"So why didn't we use him in the first place?"

"Come on, Zach, you know that he and all the other publicists are run off their feet!"

"OK, OK, get Pam back to London immediately and send Mark up there to relieve her. I'll talk to Ron meanwhile, pacify him."

"That should do it."

"OK, I'll ask Lea to get Ron on the phone."

No sooner has Maggie left than Yanara is back.

"It has to go!"

"What?"

"That creature pretending to be Janice is actually a vile zombie pretending to be a human being."

"For heaven's sake, Yanara, I have a busy day ahead."

"You're not the one being asphyxiated, so obviously you don't care."

"Yanara!"

"It's my new temp, she has the most godawful BO and I can't bear it, I simply can't."

"Why don't you go to Naomi?"

"You're my boss."

"Well, OK, why don't you just talk to her about it without being offensive?"

"And be fired for personal discrimination or something like that? I think we should have an official policy about it, I hear in some New York offices they have a perfume policy, your perfume can't offend the person sitting next to you."

"Yanara!"

"Oh, all right."

Then Rachel is at the door just as his phone rings. He picks up the phone and holds up his other hand to tell Rachel to wait. Lea tells him that Albert Wallace wants to talk to him urgently. He groans – Albert is quite possibly the worst agent in London, but in accordance with the law that says idiots will every now and again snag first-rate authors he represents Boris Gaponenko, one of the hottest young writers in London, and the other writer on their list they intend to nominate for the Booker. He mouths "Albert Wallace" to Rachel and is about to take the call when his fiction editor waves her arms about, gesturing to him to put the phone down. He tells Lea he will speak to Albert later and turns to face Rachel.

"He'll want to talk to you about the talking chicken."

"What?"

"Boris has a talking chicken in his novel and I've asked him to take it out."

"Kafka did OK with a cockroach."

"This is not *Metamorphosis*. Halfway through the novel a chicken on the protagonist's farm abruptly starts talking in Latin – it's supposed to be a narrative device to take the character back into the past, or a metaphor for the dumbness of the twenty-first century, I'm not sure what, but it's ludicrous, completely implausible. The reviewers will rip the book to shreds, but Boris refuses to listen to reason."

Rachel is a thoughtful, skilled editor who doesn't tamper with manuscripts unnecessarily; if she wants to chicken out it must be with good reason, but Boris is a star and if he wants the chicken in everyone has a problem.

"Let me take a look at the manuscript," he says irritably.

———

By the time he gets to Orso, where he is meeting Julia for lunch, his spirits have sunk to his toes. He would have taken the rest of the day off except he feels that a meeting with Julia might be the only thing that can salvage his day. In the taxi over he remembers with gratitude how, when he returned to London from his mother's funeral, she would arrive every evening after work to eat dinner with him, talk, just be around for him. She had done this for a month – essentially putting her life on hold until he could get going again. Why did he ever let her go?

The low-ceilinged restaurant is full of publishing types doing a last bit of business before they take off for the summer. He spots a top agent from Curtis Brown in a corner with a glamorous South Asian woman. An executive from Faber deep in discussion with an author who is expected to win the Nobel within the next five years. A table of Hachette editors. He greets a couple of people he knows as he makes his way to where Julia is waiting.

"Hey, have you seen the wall-to-wall coverage of MJ's death?" she asks as he sits down.

"Yeah, apparently more people tuned in for news about it than for any other event since Princess Di's funeral. The massive interest almost single-handedly crashed the Internet, isn't that something?" he says grumpily.

"Is everything OK?"

He could talk about his need to get back with her, but this is not the time to do it; when he gets into one of his moods, he is too aggressive, too selfish about his own needs, it scares people off. With an effort he pushes the darkness aside, musters a smile, tries to interest himself in what she is saying. One of her closest friends, Laura, who works for one of the Big Seven companies is afraid she is going to be laid off in the autumn, there are rumours that all the big companies are planning another round of job cuts. He wants to tell her about Fiona, how awful he felt letting her go, but he doesn't, because he knows she will see it differently from him. He can hear the exact words: *It's not always about you, Zach! So you think it was tough for you, have you thought about what it might have been like for Fiona?*

Their conversation veers to happier things. She brings him up to date with the latest gossip; she is incredibly well connected with the younger editors in London and nothing escapes them. For some years now a group of about fifty editors under forty (this is not a formal organization like the Society of Young Publishers) from across the publishing spectrum have voted annually on the worst-behaved author to be published that year, and this year the prize has gone to a much loved YA author who has a pristine image in public but is apparently a grade A bitch with her editors, assistants, and publicists. The award does not make the trade papers or the mainstream media – if it did heads would roll – but at Christmas the mystified and enraged author will receive an appropriate gift from an anonymous fan that all the editors

have contributed to (the current thinking is that Miss V—
should receive a life-size marzipan capuchin monkey making
a rude gesture – the publicist the suggestion came from is an
enthusiastic and accomplished baker). She then tells him her
UEA star has sold for a healthy sum to a Big Seven imprint
and that she is preparing the ground for a big push at the
Frankfurt Book Fair. Her enthusiasm for her author is
palpable. Being an agent suits her, he thinks. She isn't yet
one of the superstar agents like David Godwin with his
stable of prize-winning talent, jetting off to Delhi or
Durban to snap up the next big international attraction, and
she may never be, but her ability to spot talent, and more
importantly nurture it, will ensure she makes her mark on
the publishing scene.

"So why didn't you sell us the book? I know Rachel was
really keen."

"You know why, you guys didn't offer enough. Besides you
wouldn't budge on your ebook royalties, they were willing to
offer more than twenty-five per cent of net receipts."

"Come on, Julia, it's the industry standard."

"According to whom? Just because five or six of the big
publishers get together and decide on something doesn't
make it fair or right. You have a tiny production cost attached,
no distribution costs."

"But we still have all the other costs, the cost of acquisition, selling, marketing, and editorial costs. And, of course, the
cost of making printed books, which still accounts for the
majority of an author's revenue. So you can't just treat ebooks
in isolation."

"So what will you do when ebooks constitute fifty per cent of sales within five years, as some people think?"

"We'll think of something."

"I don't get it," she says, "why must you people be dragged kicking and screaming towards a conclusion that everyone can see is inevitable – whether it's this year or two years from now you are going to have to give authors a higher ebook royalty."

"So that people like Laura can keep their jobs for a couple of years more," he snaps, regretting the comment the minute it emerges from his mouth. Julia colours and turns her attention to the halibut on her plate.

Why does everything have to be so difficult? he thinks disconsolately. During his long walks through the pine-scented mountains of Paro, the way ahead seemed so clear, with Julia, with Litmus, with Mandy; now all the issues that he thought he could isolate and deal with neatly have begun to merge with one another and he appears to be rapidly going backwards to where he started. Let me at least salvage this lunch, he resolves, and forces himself to talk lightly and entertainingly about Bhutan, talking chickens, and a collie named Plasma. They part civilly enough, but he knows there is going to be a lot of work ahead if he is ever going to get together again with Julia.

———

On the morning of the board meeting he still has nothing to show for his efforts of the past few days in terms of workable ideas for big books. All the major agents in London that he has talked to tell him that there is nothing big in the UK and the Commonwealth that hasn't already been snapped up. The scouts are reporting the same thing from the States.

The mood in the boardroom is somber. As Gabrijela takes them through every aspect of the crisis they are facing Zach realizes that the situation is graver than he had realized. Ever since he was appointed to the board, he has dutifully attended all the meetings but he has been guilty of not paying attention to anything that does not have to do with the editorial aspects of the business. This time he listens closely to his boss's doom-laden review. During the company's best years from 2005 to 2007 they paid off their debt to the bank, doubled the size of the domestic publishing program, bought the new office building in London, acquired a small company in the US that they hoped would form the nucleus of Litmus's American business, and declared handsome dividends. In 2008, they started a tiny two-person operation in India, and this year they are intending to open an office in Singapore. The hardback of *Angels Falling* and the Seppi backlist and specials were expected to pay for all this; unfortunately it turns out they were too aggressive with their forecast for the company's revenue and profits. Although *Angels Falling* exceeded its initial budget in terms of sales, they were left with too much stock (in hindsight their last reprint should have been 15,000 copies instead of the 85,000 copies they had ended up printing), the illustrated editions of the first three books flopped, and the mass market edition of *Angels Falling* sold less than expected. As part of their effort to restore Litmus to good health, they sold a majority stake in their US company to Globish Inc., but that hadn't generated enough revenue to make up the shortfall in Seppi sales.

They have missed their 2009 budget targets for two quarters in a row, and what they have on their autumn list is not enough to make their year-end number. As Gabrijela lays out the measures she intends to take to deal with the existing state of affairs the gloom in the room grows – there will be no bonus for employees this year, salaries will be frozen, and there will be more job cuts in line with the lowered 2009 numbers. She proposes that the board abstain from declaring a dividend. Also, if they do not have enough confidence in the list over 2010 and beyond, she intends to cut the publishing program, overhead, and other operating costs by half.

There is more. She recommends to the board that they sell the rest of their holdings in the US company to Globish and then she drops a bomb – Globish has made an offer to her and to the chairman for the UK company. God, Zach thinks, so that's who is after them. When she first told him about the trouble the company was in, she had casually spoken about the threat of being taken over, but hadn't given him a clue as to who had made the offer! They have no intention of selling, she says calmly; at this point Sir William Boyce, the majority shareholder in the company, and chairman of the board, takes over. He reminds them about the shareholding pattern of the company (he holds 39 per cent, and two of the investors he brought in, and who vote with him, hold a further 20 per cent; Gabrijela owns 18 per cent;

and the remaining 23 per cent is divided among three others) and says that he and some of the other directors who, between them, own a majority stake in the company are seriously concerned about Litmus's future as an independent publishing company. They have agreed with Gabrijela that they will not sell to Globish but if Litmus does not grow over the next three years it could well mean the end; they cannot afford to have another year like this one. There are further investments to be made in digital; there are pressures on pricing; and in a market that isn't growing, if they don't find another Seppi, it might not be possible to hold out. As Olive, the finance director takes them through a PowerPoint presentation on the financial state of the company, and hands out spreadsheets on their current three-year plan, the tension grows within Zach. It is going to be his turn next and he has nothing that will lighten the mood in the boardroom.

In just a moment all eyes will turn to him. This is the part he hates the most about board meetings, trying to present to hard-core businessmen, in language that they will comprehend, why what they are asking of him is impossible. One part of him would like to say, "Look, I'm just an editor," that it is too much to expect him to worry about profit and loss, spreadsheets, operating costs, cash, capital expenditure, depreciation, returns on investment, net present value and all the other eye-glazing stuff he had to learn about in the Finance for Non-financial Managers course he had had to take when was elevated to the position of publisher and to the board of directors. But he cannot duck his responsibility, he is just as much a part of this as the others present in the room – he could have always turned down the promotion when it was offered to him.

When times were good, he looked forward to board meet-ings, and the praise of his fellow directors as the latest sales figures were announced and the quarterly forecast kept being revised upwards, but now he would much rather be any place but here, looking down at the orange shine of the boardroom table and wondering how he is going to conjure up some-thing magical from the pitiful list of books he has in the bag.

He thinks wistfully of his years as an editor when his entire existence revolved around books and their creators. He misses the joy of being the first reader of an exquisite piece of fiction, the satisfaction that came with adopting the voice of the author and working within it to make some-thing that was first-rate even better, and then the final thrill of propelling that beautiful work of art into the world. He remembers his enormous delight when he saw a scary-looking Goth kid on the Tube reading the first book he had ever worked on as an editorial assistant. It was impossible to reconcile the two, progress in his career and the purity of doing nothing but the precise manipulation of text that had filled his days and nights as an editor – he gets that. Moreover, he knows too that much of what he is hankering after is nothing but a sepia-tinted fantasy that exists only in his head. Little of his time as an editor had actually been spent editing manuscripts – nobody *edited* books anymore, you merely did some cursory tidying up of a text before hurrying it through the production process – and even less of his time had been spent editing masterpieces. Of the millions of new books published every year, how many were genuine masterpieces or, opening the filter a little, books that had made a genuine impact on readers? Two? Ten? A couple of dozen? And of those how many had passed through his hands? Seppi, for sure, Ron Carruthers, Muhammad Khan, Emily Baines, Wu Chen, and Sandy Knowles maybe, and that wonderful series that highlighted just one outstanding feature in London's greatest monuments for the casual visitor (with text and pictures provided by the country's best-known writers and photographers) that had sold and sold to their delight – but that had been it more or less. Like most other London publishers, and publishers everywhere for that matter, he had spent his years as an editor, and then as publisher, chivvying on his troops to turn books that were second-rate into ones that would muster a B+ with a very lenient examiner marking the sheets, until it had become a self-fulfilling way of doing things. He was now exactly like every other publisher he had spent his formative years in the industry decrying – a cynical purveyor of mediocre texts that he and everyone else in the company hoped would sell enough to enable them to do it all over again the next year, and the year after that.

The eyes turn to him. He makes his presentation and it falls flat, as he and Gabrijela, with whom he had shared it beforehand, had known it would.

"Nothing from the Seppi estate?" the chairman booms. He is a chunky man with a jowly face, and he looks troubled.

Zach glares at him. He recognizes the need to be polite, but Sir William gets under his skin. He is not a book man, he is a wealthy investment banker who got out of the profession before bankers became the pariahs of the business community; now he makes a nuisance of himself on the various boards he sits on, and spends the rest of the year relaxing on his country estate in Oxfordshire. Zach doubts he reads more than a book a year.

"The estate is in a mess," he replies. "As his mother, the person he was closest to, died a few months before he did, Seppi left everything to a cousin in Toronto, with a small bequest to his translator. The translator complained about the will, but that went nowhere; the last I heard she was thinking of suing the cousin – unless a settlement is reached, of course."

"And if a settlement is reached, and title to his work is established once and for all, do you think that there might be more unfinished work, unpublished stories from his early writing life that we can lay our hands on?" Gabrijela asks.

"Even if something existed, why would Seppi's people give it to us?" Zach asks. "They are still upset with us for not giving up any of the rights in the quartet to them. They will merely sell it on to the highest bidder."

"Can we help them reach a settlement? Lubricate the works, become the mediator?" Sir William says, looking grave. "If we don't do something soon, we might not be able to hold off Globish."

Zach shudders inwardly; Globish is the least well regarded among the Big Seven publishers and with good reason. The youngest and smallest of the publishing giants, Globish is also the fastest growing thanks to the ambitions of Greg Holmes, the Californian software billionaire who owns it, and Mortimer Weaver, the latest in a series of CEOs who have been charged with making it the largest and most profitable English language trade publishing company in the world. There's nothing wrong with the goals the Globish bosses have set for themselves, except that their strategy to achieve them has little to do with the quality and brilliance of the company's publishing. Their method of growing the business is primarily through acquisition and cost cutting, with scant regard for editors and authors; if Litmus was swallowed by them Zach has no doubt he will be one of the first casualties of the takeover. He looks around the boardroom table at the chairman, at Gabrijela, at Olive, and at the two external directors present, and realizes they are not the enemy, they are as concerned about the future as he is and not just because of the looming threat of a takeover by Globish. It is because as the world of publishing spins on its axis, once, twice, three times, a hundred, they have no idea of what it will take to survive and thrive in a world that they do not recognize and do not have the skills to manage. Apple. Amazon. Google. Digital content. DRM. Ereaders. Pricing models. Royalty rates. Marketing to consumers. Readers who would like content for free. Writers who must produce a strange hybrid that is part text, part music, part moving pictures with multiple endings and enough carny tricks to satisfy the semi-literate reader . . . These are just some of the things they will need to take in their stride, see as opportunities rather than death blows, and given the publishing traditions that have shaped them it would be astonishing if they didn't feel threatened. As they dance, dance on the knife-edge of survival, they know everything they do will only be pushing the day of reckoning a little further into the future. Is it any wonder that the majority want to cut and run? For how long will Gabrijela be able to persuade them to remain on board?

————

He has managed to avoid Mandy for eight days now, but he has finally run out of excuses and agreed to meet her at Ronnie Scott's on the weekend. On the appointed day, he turns up a little earlier than he had intended and heads to the upstairs bar.

Half an hour later, he sees her enter the room dressed all in black – black sleeveless top, black skirt, black boots – and festooned with about seven hundred chains around her neck. Her hair, which she dyes a different shade every three months, is now strawberry blonde with black highlights. He takes in her tattoos, an eagle on the left bicep and a vaguely Manichean figure on the right, and thinks it's funny how everything you thrill to when you are in the first throes of an infatuation turns muddy when the fire is banked. As he gets up to kiss her he wonders whether this relationship would have stood a chance even if his need to get back with Julia had not been so compelling. He admires some things about her, especially the way she in which she has supported her two younger sisters after her father died and her mother remarried, but they have little in common, and he doubts that he would have gotten together with her if he hadn't been so emotionally broken. He hopes their parting, whenever it happens, will not go badly. But that seems to be wishful thinking; in his experience relationships end badly if they aren't snapped off cleanly, or if they aren't allowed to dribble naturally away into nothingness. Neither of these scenarios applies in this case. He remembers the worst breakup of his life in the days before he was married – an investment banker with smoky eyes and a fondness for literature he had been mad keen on had smeared Gentleman's Relish on the crotches of the two suits he had owned at the time, and systematically smashed all the mirrors (she was obviously not superstitious) and crockery in his flat when he had suggested they go their separate ways. But Veronique had been spiky and vengeful, and although Mandy had her moments she was nothing like her. He is suddenly overcome by a wave of contrition – what if their positions were reversed, what if she had been the one trying to get out of the relationship and he the one left behind? Would he feel the same way? Of course not. Why did relationships have to be so damned difficult? – maybe he should have become a priest as his mother had once suggested to him!

He's hoping to hear the up-and-coming trumpeter who is billed to play at Ronnie Scott's, he is supposed to be a real talent, but Mandy has other ideas and they take off to a lingerie store that has advertised an opening day sale with extended hours. The store is packed with women of all ages and shapes and sizes. Any forlorn hope that he may have had that he will be mildly stimulated by the spectacle of his girlfriend shopping for lingerie along with scores of hot women is extinguished immediately by the sight of unattractive, wild-eyed shoppers pushing and shoving to get at frilly underwear. Three other male partners lurk sheepishly in the least populated parts of the store, hoping they will not be mistaken for pervs. None of them makes eye contact. After a couple of hours, Mandy emerges triumphant with a set of lacy pink underwear and three boxes of tights. "Got them from under the nose of that rude bitch," she says, holding up the pink undergarments, and pointing to a large woman in a yellow skirt that's too tight for her. "Bet she doesn't find anything tonight."

"But you're five sizes smaller than her, and you don't like pink."

"Oh, I don't want the stuff. I'll just return it at the cash; I just didn't want her to have it."

She makes sure she passes the woman on their way out of the store, and says loudly, "See you next time!"

Startled, the woman gives them an uncertain smile. Mandy looks triumphant and he is mystified by the comment until he twigs to the insult.

They walk along the cobbled streets of Soho to the Tube station, the evening's shopping festooning his arms, and Mandy prattling away about some customer who wrote his phone number on his bill that afternoon – he wonders if she is trying to make him jealous. They stop at a Pret A Manger, buy wraps for dinner, and go to his place where they make arid, joyless love. If this is the best they can do after being apart for over a fortnight clearly this relationship is not going anywhere, surely Mandy can see that!

He manages to bundle her out of his flat at around eleven, and then calls Julia. She is not home, and he wonders unhappily where she might be. He leaves a message, asking her to call him back, then phones a few minutes later, asking her to dinner

next week. Pitiful, he thinks. Abruptly his thoughts about his
less than satisfactory romantic life are displaced by thoughts of
the disaster that threatens at work. Gabrijela has asked for a
meeting in five days, and has told him to do everything he can
to make a better showing than he did at the board meeting.

———

He goes to lunches and drinks and suppers with agents and
publishing colleagues he has worked with for over a decade,
men and women he likes and respects for the most part, all
joined shoulder to shoulder in an endeavour that they have
worked hard to perfect throughout their adult lives – the task
of finding, valuing, and selling worthwhile writing, which
despite all the algorithms and business models that attempt to
convert it into something that can be weighed and measured
like any other product is ultimately elusive and therefore all the
more precious. All its disadvantages notwithstanding, to be part
of this world is a privilege and he is proud to belong to this
company of men and women, who for centuries have nurtured
the mother of all creative arts, storytelling, with dedication and
skill. But as he makes his rounds he finds out that they have
nothing for him this time and he goes into his meeting with his
boss insecure, with his excuses ready, knowing that will not be
enough, because whether he likes it or not a solution will have
to be found to the crisis that is already upon them.

Gabrijela is on the phone and he takes a seat in front of her
kidney-shaped desk. Next to her computer is a little plaque
that says, "Be humble because you are made of the earth, be

noble because you are made of the stars." It describes her exactly, he thinks, this Serbian proverb that she keeps to remember her mother by. She is self-effacing to a fault, and fierce in her determination to live up to a higher standard than is the norm both in the way she conducts herself personally and in the way she leads her company. This sometimes makes her difficult to work for, but for all her prickliness he knows she will always be straight with him and will not let him down, traits that are worth much more than an insincere smile and assurances that mean nothing.

Gabrijela is on the phone for a long time. She doesn't contribute much to the conversation. When she finally puts the phone down, she says, "That was William, he is off to New York tomorrow. Mortimer has asked for a meeting, he thinks Globish is going to sweeten their offer."

"That's not great, is it?"

"No it isn't. I think we can continue to hold them off for a while but to be honest the mood among our shareholders at the moment is to take the money and run, unless we can come up with something really substantial. So, what do you have for me?"

"Not a lot I'm afraid," he says. "Nothing that's going to advance even 20K in hardcover."

She says nothing, so he continues. He has decided to keep the incident involving Pam and Ron from her until Maggie and he can sort it out, so he only mentions the books they are having trouble with at the moment.

"There's some bad news," he says, "the Thames book is not up to scratch."

"Fixable?"

"Probably. If we pad it with illustrations and call in a book doctor, we might squeak by."

"We're positioning it as a gift book, right?"

"Uh-huh."

"Do what you have to do, and let's hope the reviewers won't notice it's a dog."

"And Boris is being difficult."

"What about?"

"A talking chicken – and I had a really tough meeting with his agent, who said if we didn't play ball he would take the book elsewhere."

"Christ! Sometimes I feel that I was happiest in the early days of Litmus when I did nothing but publish dead authors!" She says this without any heat and then adds, "Want to go out and get a coffee?"

"Sure."

This is unusual and therefore alarming; Gabrijela is not known to rise from behind her desk except when there is a real emergency.

When they are seated with their coffees at the Costa Coffee outlet near the office, a latte for him and an espresso for her, she says nothing for a while, just looks pensively at the ebb and flow of people and traffic on the street outside. Then she says softly, "I remember thinking when I hired you that the reason most of us get into this business is almost exactly the same – a love of books, a chance to spend our lives in their midst, the fate of all bookish misfits whether we are from Belgrade or Bombay."

He isn't sure what to say to this. As the Americans might say, Gabrijela does not do warm and fuzzy, and she does not do nostalgia. His lack of a response does not seem to matter, for she continues in the same quiet voice that seems to be directed mainly at herself.

"When we arrived in the UK, my parents like all refugees were determined that I acquire an education that would get me the best jobs – when I landed the scholarship to the LSE, they were overjoyed but they didn't know their daughter had already contracted a fatal disease –"

My God, he thinks, is she dying, is that why she's being so contemplative?

"Do you know the Czech writer Kundera?"

"Yes, I was just thinking about him the other day. I read *The Unbearable Lightness of Being* when I was in college and was blown away by it." He wonders whether to mention that it informed his disastrous attempts to hook up with girls for more years than it should have and decides not to.

"Umm . . . I remember reading an interview with him where he said the reason he said he was so taken with the novel form was because it concerned itself with existence not reality. It didn't examine what had already occurred – that was for historians and their like – what the novel was about was 'the realm of human possibilities.' He wanted, Kundera said, to delve into what a human being could become, he wanted to examine everything that a man was capable of. That is why he wrote novels, he wanted to be an explorer of existence, nothing less, and that was why I realized I wanted to read them. As I have never wanted to write,

I enjoy reading and thinking about what I have read too much, I realized that nothing would please me more than to spend the rest of my life working with books. Poor mama and papa, they were disappointed, not that they should have been because it was papa who turned me on to Ivo Andrić, and all the other great writers of the region . . ."

She takes a sip of her espresso. "I loved Litmus when it was really small, and everything was a struggle. But I thrilled to the fact that I was publishing some of the world's most extraordinary writers – though it was sad that I couldn't do more with them. At the time people here would only read European writers in translation if they had won the Nobel or were 'adopted' by a big name English or American writer. That is why when I had the chance to pump more funds into Litmus I didn't hesitate. My writers needed it, I needed it to be honest. William taught briefly at the LSE when I was a student, then went off and became a successful banker. When he retired and showed an interest in investing in Litmus, I grabbed the opportunity.

"He was patient as we built the company, then you found Seppi, and we made tons of money for him and the other investors, so all was well. But as I've told you, I can't hold onto him much longer. If I was any younger, I might have said to hell with him, I'll go and find the money elsewhere, but things are what they are. Morty is hell-bent on expanding his presence in the UK, and as there is very little left to buy he has turned his beady eye on us."

"I'm sorry, you know, I've been racking my brain –"

"I have no doubt you have, and I've made a few calls

myself so I am aware that there is nothing out there. But, you know, when I worked for one of the big firms, my boss, a brilliant man, once said to me that even when it seems as if there is nothing you can do, you have to do something, you can't just stand still, you have to make something happen."

"What do you think I should do?"

"I was reading the other day about the standoff between the executors of Stieg Larsson's estate and his partner, who claims to have an unpublished manuscript on a laptop. I know we talked about the Seppi estate at the board meeting but I was wondering if that was something you should follow up."

"It was one of the first things I did. I e-mailed his transla- tor. Nothing —"

"But if she and the family didn't get on she might have something hidden away that she doesn't want to talk about."

"I don't know. Also, we aren't exactly her favourite publishers."

She dismisses his objection with an elegant wave of her hand. "Look, it's worth a shot. If we spread some money around, gain the confidence of the translator, there's no telling what we might find. I don't want this done on the phone, I want you to get on a plane to Toronto ASAP."

"Are you sure?"

"Never been surer. We have to do something fast, and if Seppi doesn't work out, I'll have to go to my backup plan, which I don't want to share with you just yet."

They rise to go, he hasn't finished his latte, but he has worked with Gabrijela long enough to know when a meeting is over. As they head out the door she says, "Oh, and tell Lea to route your ticket through Delhi, I don't want the people there to feel as though they are being neglected. Ten years from now, they will be Litmus's fortune."

———

The day before he is due to leave for India, he walks down to the river late in the evening. There are many things he loves about his city: its great cathedrals and parks; its cobblestoned streets lined by buildings perpetually cobwebbed in scaffolding; the hustle of the Portobello Road market; Notting Hill before the movie destroyed the particularity of one of his favourite neighbourhoods; scruffy pubs (now alarmingly smoke free, although he has never smoked) ironed into his memory by unforgettable evenings he has spent in them with friends or lovers. But in the years that he has lived here his likes and dislikes have moved around; the only thing that has remained constant is his fascination with the great waterway. It is one of the reasons he had been looking forward to publishing Zogoiby's book, and partly why he is disappointed it hasn't turned out well.

Long before the Thames had become a part of his life it had filled his imagination; he can still remember how that came about – reading, as an impressionable teenager, Conrad's extraordinary description of its lower reaches: "The old river in its broad reach rested unruffled at the decline of day, after ages of good service done to the race that peopled its banks, spread out in the tranquil dignity of a waterway leading to the uttermost ends of the earth." He hasn't got around to visiting Gravesend yet to drink deeply of the master's vision that had so captivated him that hot afternoon in Delhi but it is a river of "abiding memories" for him all right. To get to his favourite spot he crosses the bustle of the Strand and cuts through one of the quiet streets that twist down to the river, the noise of his shoes loud on the pavement. At this time of day it is usually deserted, which is how he likes it; he wanders across to one of the benches and sits down. The dying sun lays down leaves of gold on the broad back of the river that flows so slowly along this stretch that it could be made of stone. A cruise boat and a barge of some sort are the only visible traffic, and on this bank there are few people to be seen. A jogger passes, a young woman, sleek as an otter. Barely has she passed his field of vision when he hears a rattling and sees a homeless man approaching. His hair is long and wild in the standard homeless person cut, and he is badged with the hallmarks of his tribe – several layers of ragged clothing, shoes without laces, shopping cart piled high with plastic bags and junk. Instinctively Zach tenses and prepares for a distasteful encounter, but the man has no interest in him and heads straight for a dustbin a few metres away and begins rooting through it. As he watches through the corner of his eye, he wonders how the man landed on the street; surely he wasn't born to this life, at some point he must have had all the trappings of respectability, a home, a family, ambition. When had the slide started, why had he been unable to stop it, why does he bother to keep on going? He wonders if there is a book in him, they could do an

Orwell in reverse – the tramp turned writer. Wasn't there a book like that some years ago that became a bestseller, about a homeless man and his dog? The vagrant has finished his inspection of the garbage can and rattles away. As Zach watches him go, he thinks about how lightly the man is attached to life, without any of the things that tether a person to an everyday existence, a strong gust of wind could whirl him away into nothingness and it would be as though he had never lived. Zach is no tramp and he hopes he will never be, but he and the homeless man do share one thing – an absence of rootedness.

When he was younger he prided himself on his ability to pick himself up and move anywhere, be with anyone at a moment's notice. But does his great need to get back with Julia have something to do with the fact that he is beginning to find the gossamer insubstantiality of his existence no longer satisfying, does this mean he is now ready to settle down – a phrase that has always filled him with horror in the past, conjuring up as it does visions of needy children, overbearing in-laws, and hordes of other relatives, all those people hemming him in, suffocating him. But perhaps settling down doesn't need to mean that, perhaps it could mean that he is settling into himself, anchoring himself a little bit more to this earthly plane, putting down roots, the grass becoming a tree.

And if so, where might that be? He is forty-four years old and in just a couple more years he would have spent half his life in London. Does this fact, coupled with his mother (who was more Indian than most Indians but was born in England nevertheless) and wife, make him British, or at the very least a Londoner, or is that an illusion given depth and substance by things like his job at Litmus and the fact that he lives here at the moment? Maybe, no matter where he is, he will remain resolutely Indian (he smiles to himself at the thought that in all these years he has never traded in his Indian passport, the lions for the crowns). The country of his birth has never ceased exerting its pull on him, especially in recent years as he travelled there more often to be with his ailing mother. Or perhaps nationality doesn't really matter to people like him anymore, so many millions live simultaneously in more countries than one these days, by choice or by circumstance – a twenty-first-century way of being in an interdependent world where the rising South and East are moving into balance with the North and the West.

Professionally he is excited by what has been happening in India – the wave upon wave of great writing, the burgeoning publishing scene; indeed, there had even been a time, before Litmus had absorbed him completely, when he had vaguely thought of returning and finding a job with one of the many publishing startups. When Gabrijela had decided to open an office in Delhi and given him charge of it he had been thrilled. He hasn't paid much attention to the company in India for a while now, preoccupied as he has been with the many challenges he has been facing, but suddenly he can't wait to get on the plane tomorrow. No matter what awaits him in Toronto, Litmus India should prove to be a welcome diversion. He should get going, he thinks, he should get organized for his trip, but he decides to linger, the pull of the water is magnetic. The river is silver and black with the coming of the night; as he gazes into it, another river a continent away rises in his memory, an unnamed mountain torrent on the banks of which his family and he would often picnic when he came home from school on vacation. Its steep mud banks were overhung with clumps of bamboo that sometimes attracted herds of wild elephant, and in its deep pools he would occasionally get lucky and land a fish with the primitive bamboo rod his father had fashioned for him. It was one of the totemic places of his youth; he is suddenly filled with the desire to revisit it even though he has no idea whether it still exists, but he should make the effort, perhaps he and Julia could go together. He yawns and stretches and wishes she were with him. She is the only person he has brought to this spot; it would have been unthinkable to come here with anyone else. She is busy tonight, but it won't be long before they will resume their rambles along the river, he is sure of it. He wishes he knew how to speed up the process of reconciliation, but maybe the only thing to do is leave it well alone and let things come together on their own. It is not really his style but maybe he has no choice in the matter.

3 .

DELHI

Jorge Luis Borges, no slouch at dreaming up fantastical scenarios, once wrote a story whose premise was so implausible that he thought he had no option but to situate it in India. Zach wonders what the Argentine master would have made of Delhi traffic. He had always thought the city had the least disciplined drivers in the country, but every time he has visited the capital it seems the traffic situation has deteriorated further. Their car has been immobile for fifteen minutes at a crossroad just short of the Defence Colony flyover. From where they are he can see the traffic lights change from green to amber to red and not one car of the seventy or so vehicles around them has moved. A bulky man on a scooter, engine revving madly, swerves through the tiniest gaps left in the haphazard lines of traffic and then stalls; his vehicle buzzes like an irritated wasp as he shouts pointlessly at the cars on either side. Southbound traffic, of which they are part, is all knotted up because it is meant to travel along two lanes, one for vehicles moving straight ahead and the other for cars wishing to turn right. There are now four lanes of traffic squeezed into that space, and all the cars in front have their right-turn indicators on, effectively blocking the route of the cars that want to drive straight through; further complicating the tangle are two westbound cars that were attempting to jump the lights and got caught as northbound traffic got going. Muttering "behenchod" under his breath, the driver switches off his engine; the man on the scooter, the visor of his crash helmet pushed up, is now arguing with great vehemence with the driver of the car on his left; two traffic policemen are chatting on the curb. Nothing moves, and Zach thinks of the terrifying ride from the airport the previous night when the driver of his taxi gunned his engine all through the journey to the hotel in a heavy monsoon downpour, missing other equally maniacal drivers by inches, treating red lights with contempt. White-knuckled speed and a dead stop, the way its traffic behaved could be the perfect metaphor for the new India, he thinks.

When he left the country two decades ago, it was barely stirring, although that was an improvement over everything that had taken place over the previous fifty years; now it seemed to roar ahead, stop in its tracks because of some improbable event, and then race ahead again. The newspapers this morning have been full of editorials criticizing the annual budget for this and that but the finance minister, Pranab Mukherjee, is imperturbable – India will get to and maintain a nine per cent growth rate, he declares. The astonishing thing is that nobody is willing to bet against Mukherjee. In today's India anything is possible; what a change, he thinks, from when I was a child and every ambitious Indian's eyes were trained on escape to the West.

"I have a solution for this nonsense," Apoorva Joshi says, her eyes travelling from the idle policemen to the driver of the scooter up ahead, who appears to be on the verge of a fistfight with one of the drivers beside him, with the angry honking of every other vehicle providing the soundtrack for the action. "Fine every motorist who flouts traffic regulations ten thousand rupees and give half that amount to the constable who challans the culprits. It would stop this nonsense in a second."

"You think?"

"Not really," she says with a laugh. "Each culprit will bribe the cop five hundred rupees more than his share of the fine and continue to break the rules. Everyone in India is constantly figuring out ways to beat the system, which is both a blessing and a curse."

If things had turned out differently Apoorva would probably have been born in Africa, inherited the family import-export business, and been lost to the world of publishing forever. But fate had intervened in the form of Idi Amin, and her parents had been expelled from Uganda and forced to remake their lives in Britain. When he ran into her at a party at a mutual friend's house in Hampstead, she had just completed a degree in publishing and was considering an offer to intern at a major London publishing firm. When he asked her whether she would be interested in moving to Delhi she hadn't hesitated for a moment; Gabrijela was as taken with her as he was and as easily as that they had an operation in India. Even if for some reason they are taken over he does not think Litmus India will be shut down, as Globish doesn't yet have an Indian company.

The traffic eventually gets moving again (he wouldn't be surprised if some enterprising Indian geek came up with a fiendishly entertaining iPhone app called Delhi Dodgem) and within half an hour they have skirted Lodi Gardens and are pulling into the shabby forecourt of the building where the Litmus offices are located. At the moment the company is housed in three small rooms, an office for Apoorva, another room that an assistant and a part-time accountant share, and a third that is the domain of the sales and marketing manager, seconded to them by their joint venture partner, an Indian book distribution company.

The company's launch list is due out this fall, and they're hoping to take their first books to Frankfurt to show around. Apoorva can't wait to show him covers and samples of text design. She is especially excited by a brilliant history of Kashmir she is publishing to which she has somehow managed to secure world rights. All the dejection and dullness of the past days are pushed aside as he plunges into the various processes that go into the making of Litmus India's first books. He envies Apoorva. He remembers how excited he was when, at her age, he had been propelled into the world of publishing because of an encounter with one of the world's great publishers who ran a Big Seven company with a mixture of chutzpah and sheer publishing brilliance.

He had just won acceptance to a prestigious British

publishing course, which he had decided to take for no other reason than the fact that he was bored at the advertising agency where he had spent the last three years as a copy writer. On the morning of his first day, he had found himself in a classroom that held eighty-four other aspirants to the world of publishing, mainly Oxbridge types with a smattering of foreigners, listening to a disquisition delivered by the legend, a diminutive man with a wispy beard. He had astounded them all when he lit a cigarette as soon as he got to the podium, despite the No Smoking signs prominently displayed everywhere; this was evidently a man who could not be contained by boring rules and regulations. Zach can recall nothing of the speech now, but he does remember something that happened shortly afterwards during the Q and A session.

He had always been shy, and this occasion was no different; the air was filled with the voices of aggressive English undergraduates airing their opinions and questions with the confidence bred in them by their pedigree, but the foreigners in the class were quiet; then, for reasons that he doesn't remember now, the speaker had asked the class to spell the word *millennium*; amazingly several attempts failed to get it right. He had raised his hand and spoken for the only time that morning. "Two *l*s, two *n*s," he had said; that effort had won him a brief audience with the great man, who had nodded off during the ten minutes they had spent together, woken up, apologized, saying he had just flown back from visiting his company in Melbourne, and then offered him a six-month internship with his company in London.

One of the truisms of life is that each of us, provided health and social circumstances permit, gets two or three lucky breaks; if we capitalize on these we'll be fine, if we don't things won't go as well. This was one of his breaks and it firmly confirmed him in the profession he was to follow for the rest of his life. At the Big Seven firm, despite his lowly rank as an intern, he was adopted by a group of young editors. Their days and nights were filled with talk about books, encounters with authors whom he had scarcely thought he would be fortunate enough to meet, epic drinking sessions in smoky pubs, trips to the country, and gossip about the world of publishing. Their little group was presided over by a gentle, courtly scholar, the publisher of the company, who was ice to his boss's fire. It was the best time of his life, although like his mates he was abominably paid, overworked, and without position or privilege. He hopes that Apoorva will find a similar circle of mates here, a fraternity that will enrich the profession for her and enable her to look back at this time of her life with fondness and nostalgia.

———

They work late into the evening after which she drives him to his hotel. Once there, Apoorva reviews the next day's schedule with him – they will go to meet a celebrated indie bookseller whom he has been meaning to meet on one of his trips to Delhi (especially since he has very good memories of occasionally patronizing one of the bookseller's shops as an impecunious student), wrap up things at the office, then attend a rival company's book launch. She thinks the company puts on a good show – something Litmus should be thinking about emulating at its own launch in the autumn. He wonders whether he should be telling her about the uncertainty over the company's future in London and then decides not to; Gabrijela would have briefed him differently if she'd had any doubts about Litmus India's future.

After she leaves he goes up to his room and checks his BlackBerry – of the seventy-six new messages, sixty-nine are of no consequence; there is one from Rachel in which she says she has lost an auction for a novel that A.P. Watt was conducting; one from Yanara telling him to expect a nasty e-mail soon from Sir Reginald Zogoiby's agent who is apparently appalled by their treatment of one of the UK's greatest writers; one from Julia, which he finds frustrating because of its blandness; three from Mandy, which excoriate him in the vilest way (they had fought bitterly the day he left); and one from Gabrijela giving him the name of a lawyer in Toronto whom she would like him to use if he needs to deal with any legal matters that might come up in his conversations with Seppi's translator. He doesn't usually keep scorecards but as he reviews the recent past he realizes that his score reads zero. He has not found anything that will keep Litmus safe; he is no closer to Julia than he was; and he is not as far from Mandy as he would like to be. All that the previous weeks have suc- ceeded in doing is to make the situation more vexed than it was before. His mood darkens.

He pours himself a Scotch from the minibar (company policy will not cover the expense but he doesn't care), drinks it quickly, has another a little bit slower this time, then takes a long shower, alternating between hot and icy cold, a technique to refresh himself that he has picked up from a James Bond novel. It works, and by the time he is ready to go out again he is feeling much better, not least because of the prospect of meeting the man he is going to have dinner with.

Ramesh Wadhwani is a legend in Indian publishing circles. He has worked for or advised most of the major firms and is a living encyclopedia on everything worth knowing about the Indian publishing scene. Although he is now in his eighties, and long retired from active duty so to speak, he has not lost his love of the game, and his friends pass on information and gossip about the business constantly. When they decided to open their office in the city, Ramesh was the first person Zach went to see. He declined a formal appointment to be an adviser to the fledgling firm but was only too happy to help them get started.

As always it has taken the taxi driver a fair amount of time to find the apartment building Ramesh lives in, because of the puzzling way in which buildings are numbered in the neighbourhood. As he climbs the chipped concrete stairs to his host's third-floor flat he checks his watch to find that he is already half an hour late. This does not seem to bother Ramesh, a small untidy man with a great hooked nose and bushy eyebrows, dressed in kurta-pyjamas, who greets him warmly at the door and ushers him into his living room.

Ramesh's apartment is a temple to books. Although the complex he lives in is no different from any of the other shoddy construction projects executed by a government authority in the seventies and eighties, with sloping floors, uneven walls, and leaky ceilings, he has transformed it with expensive floor-to-ceiling bookshelves made of teak and well-lit glass-fronted cabinets that hold his greatest treasures, signed first editions of practically every book of consequence published in India, and memorabilia presented to him by the numerous authors and publishers he counts among his friends. Besides those that have been shelved, books litter every surface in the apartment – piles totter on the large colourful dhurrie on the living room floor, there is a stack on the telephone table, another one on the coffee table, and Zach has no doubt there will be more in the apartment's loos, bedrooms, kitchen, and balconies. A bachelor with no real interest beyond books (that much abused description, book lover, might have been invented for Ramesh), he has poured all his savings (and a sizeable bequest from an aunt, Zach learned on his first visit to the apartment) into his col-lection. Best of all, he has a story about practically every book in the place, and an evening at Ramesh's is usually spent flit-ting from one shelf to another with the host plucking out books and spinning yarns about them.

He is in fine form this evening; he has just finished reading a well-received new novel, Neel Mukherjee's *Past Continuous*, and he can't seem to stop talking about it, its poignancy and bold exploration of homosexuality. "Just when you thought there was nothing new and exciting on the Indian literary scene along comes a novel like this that revs up the engine again. Every year, every season almost, there's something new. Last year we had Aravind Adiga, this year it's this fellow, who knows what lies in store for us in 2010?" he says, pouring Zach a large whisky. "So what do you have for me today?"

The passkey to Ramesh's world is a book and it is understood that every visitor arrives with some new offering for the host. On previous visits Zach has been able to produce a new Seppi for Ramesh's immense library but this time he can do no better than Carruthers' Cotswold novel. Ramesh takes it from him greedily, scans the first page of the opening chapter, riffles the pages until he gets to the very end, reads the last paragraph, and pronounces himself satisfied, says he is looking forward to reading the novel. "These days, when it seems anything goes, most writers forget the importance of the opening and closing chapters," he pronounces and drains his drink, indicating to Zach that he should follow suit. He shouts to his cook, who is almost as ancient as Ramesh himself, to fix them refills. Zach has been feeling a little buzzed from the two Scotches he has had before coming, and has been taking it easy with his drink, but he decides to abjure restraint and empties his glass in two swallows. He might as well make the most of this evening, especially as this is the first time he has been at Ramesh's place where he is the only guest, and the phone hasn't been ringing constantly.

An excellent dinner of kebabs, roomali rotis, rice, and a finely spiced dal that wouldn't have been out of place in a maharaja's kitchen scarcely interrupts the flow of conversation about books and publishers and authors and booksellers. Zach has heard some of the stories before but he does not interrupt his host's recollections, finding this fleshing out of a world he has only witnessed from afar utterly absorbing.

Ramesh shows him some of the rarest books he possesses – first editions of Mulk Raj Anand's *Coolie*, almost all of R.K. Narayan's novels, Ahmed Ali's *Twilight in Delhi*, Khushwant Singh's *Train to Pakistan*, Raja Rao's *Kanthapura*. Without exception, all the novels are inscribed by their authors.

His host picks up a first edition of *Midnight's Children* and tells Zach about his only encounter with Salman Rushdie. In the 1980s when Indian novelists in English were still a curiosity, Ramesh was living in Bombay, where he worked for one of the big educational publishers and witnessed the triumphant return to Indian soil of Rushdie, the first true rock star of the Indian writing and publishing scene. "The purists quibbled about Rushdie's nationality and said that he hadn't lived in the country for decades," Ramesh says with a touch of asperity, "but such criticism paled into insignificance when you considered his indelible accomplishment – he was the first writer to sing the contemporary Indian novel into its fullest being, unapologetically using Indian English and rhythms to make his masterpiece, *Midnight's Children*. Oh, the battles Salman fought and won on behalf of everyone who followed! His was the first major novel to do away with a glossary, to reject the italicization of Indian words – all the irritating colonial conventions that hobbled novelists in this country – and his fans couldn't get enough of him. Front-page headlines in all the country's major newspapers when he won the Booker, receptions and parties that lasted till dawn, my goodness it was something!

"I remember going to a reading he gave in Bombay, it was at the Taj or the President, one of the big five-star hotels, they had given the organizers their biggest event space but it wasn't enough: they had to rig loudspeakers in the hallways so those who couldn't get in could at least listen to him speak. That was some night, I tell you! Rushdie cigarette in hand, eyebrows raised sardonically, being mobbed by the cream of Bombay society – elegant women in heels and shimmering saris, distinguished old Parsi gentlemen, rotund financiers who had probably never read a book in their lives but had decided to show up for an historic occasion – I'll never forget that event."

The old cook has cleared away the plates, brought them coffee, and retired for the night, but it seems as though Ramesh could go on for hours, not that Zach is complaining. His host reaches up into one of his display cabinets, pulls out a title reverentially and hands it to Zach. "Another great milestone, Vikram Seth's *A Suitable Boy*," he says, as Zach carefully turns the pages of a beautiful red and gold hardcover book. "Open it," he says, "feel the paper, it's what they use in Bibles. That's how they managed to compress over a thousand pages into a manageable size. Quite an achievement."

Ramesh extracts a brochure from a stack next to his coffee table and hands it to Zach. "That's from the Morgan in New York City, featuring some of the highlights from their book and manuscript collection, which I finally managed to visit last year. It was a place of pilgrimage for me, Pierpont Morgan was addicted to books, and he had the means to indulge his passion. By the time he was done he had managed to amass one of the finest collections of rare books in the world, and anyone who loves books should get there at least once in their lifetime. They have three Gutenberg Bibles, the Lindau Gospels, collections from all over the world; you could spend months examining its treasures, some of the finest books ever produced by man."

"I'll try and make it, I manage to get to New York at least once a year."

"You should. Say, you've lived in the South, haven't you?"

"Yes, why?"

"Have you ever watched a farmer plowing his fields with bullocks and an old-fashioned wooden plow?"

"Can't say I have observed farmers very closely, but I have seen them, of course."

"Well, next time you come across a farmer at work look closely, because that's what the first alphabetic scripts looked like, the sort of writing you'll find on Egyptian papyrus scrolls; they ran from right to left, left to right, so alternate lines ran in opposite directions, just the way a farmer ploughs his fields. Interesting, huh!"

"I'd say."

"Pass me Vikram's book."

Zach hands the novel to Ramesh, who absently turns the pages, and says, "When Vikram decided to have his master-piece, *A Suitable Boy*, edited, typeset, printed, bound, and published in India, everyone thought he was crazy. Don't forget the Indian consumer publishing industry was only a few years old at the time. You had some excellent educational publishing, OUP and Sage and people like that, but trade publishing was more or less non-existent until Penguin India, a company created by a visionary American and a visionary Bengali, appeared on the scene. They began modestly, I remember they operated out of a small three-bedroom flat in Gulmohar Park, and were later located in a dismal office in Nehru Place, where power outages were common and the entire office park was surrounded by a giant shantytown, not the most prepossessing of sights. One editor said the office was so decrepit that for a time pigeons flew in and out of the women's toilet through a crack in the wall, until the landlord was eventually persuaded to repair it.

"So, when Vikram, in a giant leap of faith, decided to entrust the fledgling company with the responsibility of publishing his manuscript, which had sold all over the world, it seemed to be more than they could manage. And if you are to believe the stories that sprang up around the making of the novel – Vikram moving into his publisher's house to keep him honest, visiting bankers pressed into reading proofs, arguments raging across the dining table, all-nighters fuelled by whisky and masala chai at primitive typesetting establishments – it all sounds quite harrowing. It obviously wasn't easy to achieve the sort of standard that had never been achieved in the country before, but to the credit of the author and the publishing company they managed to pull it off and the result is this gorgeous book."

Ramesh shows him more of his treasures – the striking Indian hardback of Kiran Desai's *The Inheritance of Loss,* a rare edition of Arun Kolatkar's *Jejuri,* a framed cover of *The God of Small Things* that was designed in Delhi and used around the world, an almost impossible to find first edition of Rohinton Mistry's *Tales from Firozsha Baag,* beautiful folios of poetry, stunning picture books, and all the while the stories pour out of him, about the new royalty of the Indian writing scene – gifted literary novelists and world-class non-fiction writers, commercial writers who sell in the millions, and historians and biographers of distinction. Future generations of writers and readers will look to them with gratitude and awe, he says, for they are paving the way for everything that will follow.

When the evening finally comes to an end, and Zach is juddering back to the hotel in an ancient Ambassador taxi, sated with the excellent food, drink, and stories he has ingested, he thinks somewhat sentimentally, about the profession he belongs to. What gratitude he feels to be on the inside, in whatever small way, of the epic effort to create literature. And the stories behind the stories! It is the burden and privilege of publishers to be part of (even if it is only to bear witness to) the human drama that goes into the making of immortal (and very mortal) stories and poems and plays. The world knows little or nothing about the minutiae of the culture of publishing, but they are what makes it fascinating. In the more mature publishing environments, England and America, some of the larger countries in Europe, Russia, Japan, anywhere that publishing has been in existence for a while, new incidents and anecdotes are generated constantly – both apocryphal and true, although it is hard to separate one from the other. The publisher who locked his bestselling writer in his hotel room in a last-ditch effort to ensure a deadline was met, the agent who moonlighted as a dominatrix until one of her own authors turned up as a client, the publisher who offered a writer a seven-figure advance based on a paragraph, the memoirist who shot at (and fortunately missed) his agent, publishers and writers in love or in hate, novel ways of dealing with writer's block, publishers' feuds, agents at war, the politics of literary prizes . . . He finds all of this irresistible, and he is thrilled to see it beginning to happen in India, specifically in English-language writing and publishing; he does not know enough about the other great literary cultures of the country to comment about them. And what, if anything, is even more thrilling, is that everyone associated with the profession gets to see, at first-hand, the birth of a major publishing culture. In twenty years or so English-language publishing in India will be a settled and mature environment with its own orthodoxies, but at the moment it is still being born with the frenzy and missteps and wailing and gnashing of teeth and sheer bloody excitement that accompany every birth. It is fascinating to watch it come into being, and he hopes his company and he can be part of it in some small way.

———

There is a view, a minority view to be sure but one that is gaining ground, which holds that even though independent bookshops may be an endangered species, they will rise again in the not too distant future, when online bookstores become omnipresent. At this time, the theory goes, the powerful book retail chains, which are already in decline, will no longer be able to compete on price, product range, and cost, and will wither and die. This will clear the way for the resurgence of independent bookstores with carefully picked stock and knowledgeable staff. They will become a haven for book lovers as they will be able to provide the only thing the online booksellers cannot – the human touch in the form of great indie booksellers whom the community of book people in every neighbourhood will support and celebrate for their taste and insight. As Apoorva and he settle down to some serious browsing at The Book Shop in Jor Bagh, Zach hopes that this prognostication is not just wishful thinking.

Rather like Ramesh's apartment, the place reminds him of Prospero's cave – small, book-lined, and filled with magic. He hasn't seen KD, the proprietor, since his student days, but he recognizes him immediately, although he is much older now, the deep black beard he remembers turned completely white. As they enter he is laughing and chatting with an older lady who cradles an armful of books she is about to buy. The customer leaves, and he comes up to them, a smile on his face, "So, Apoorva, where have you been?"

She introduces the two men (unsurprisingly KD doesn't remember him but seems glad to be reacquainted with Zach) and in no time they are all having the sort of conversation that is all too rare in bookstores. As they talk about the great Indian novelists who have tasted mainstream success for over a decade, customers wanting KD's opinion on a book or who have just stopped in to say hello constantly interrupt them. The Book Shop offers no discounts and the bestsellers that dominate bookstores the world over get a single shelf in a corner. The bookseller asks him if he has read Mohsin Hamid and Daniyal Mueenuddin, a couple of the Pakistani writers who have captured the imagination of readers in the subcontinent. He has read one but not the other and is happy to buy a copy of his book. This is an ordinary miracle, he thinks: scarcely six months ago Pakistani terrorists had laid waste to Bombay, today the stories of their countrymen are somehow helping the healing process. And it is a place like this that fosters that process, that slows the conversation about books to exactly the right pace and rhythm so you are able to fall in love with an author you might have never heard of but for the proprietor's exquisite taste and encyclopaedic knowledge or to rediscover a writer you haven't read in the longest time. Before Zach knows it he has bought three more novels, the Neel Mukherjee novel that Ramesh was talking about, and two that he has been meaning to read – only the fact that he will be on a plane tomorrow prevents him from buying more.

When they leave the store he has some time on his hands, so he and Apoorva decide to have coffee at the India International Centre, which is not too far away. After they have placed their orders, she quizzes him about a recent book on fiction by James Wood, one of the most astute commentators on the form, especially Wood's contention that novelists will need to "outwit" what he describes as the "inevitable aging" of existing novelistic methods. Zach feels that while it is fine for writers to be strategic and innovative where technique and convention are concerned, it is not something to be unduly concerned about. The great writers of this time or any other time for that matter are not celebrated just because of the perfection of their form; they are read because of the extraordinary stories they tell, and the truths they uncover for the reader.

"I've always meant to ask you this," she says, "but how precisely did you find Seppi?"

It isn't a question he is asked much these days. At one time he had his responses down pat, so he has to think for a moment before answering.

"I didn't find him, he found me," he says.

"Did you know he was destined for greatness, is that why you published him?"

He could lie, try to impress her, but he doesn't. "No, I didn't know, I knew he had talent, but I didn't know he had that sort of talent in him. His early novels were good but not great. I have always wondered why young novelists, those who are starting out, don't write great attention-grabbing books from the outset, it's something that has always bothered me. Here they are, trying their luck at one of the riskiest professions in the world, a profession where only the top one per cent could be said to have made it in terms of commercial and critical success, yet they almost never just go for it."

"Perhaps it's because they can't," she says.

"That is the only answer which fits," he says. "I think it was Rushdie who said every writer needs to have an unpublished novel in his desk, his first attempt that drains all the irrelevant autobiographical rubbish out of him so he is free to invent, to tell stories as he is meant to, to the limits of his talent."

He beckons to their waiter, indicates that they would like refills.

"And the other thing that happens, of course, is that the more a writer writes the more confident he becomes, and the more material he draws from that mysterious place within him where stories are born."

"But Seppi," she says, "why were his first books so different from what came later?"

"He began by emulating a writer he admired, but the beauty of it is that as he was writing his early novels he was also finding his real voice."

"And the process was automatic?"

He has always refused to teach at publishing courses, he does not think the basic skill it takes to make a good publisher can be taught; every aspirant needs to develop his own taste through a lifetime of good reading and by paying close attention to the way the great books work. What he does like, though, is talking one on one with someone who has the aptitude, the knowledge, and the desire to come to grips with the essence of his profession. All such a person needs is a nudge or two in the right direction, and the sort of pointers that can arise from the stories that everyone who has been in the game for long enough can tell.

"No, I don't think there was a steady progression, but as he kept at it he was fashioning keys to unlock doors that led to his true subject matter. He told me, when I asked him why he was writing about angels, that he had always been fascinated by them – he was an altar boy, he was Catholic, he was Sicilian, and so on and so forth. However, he might never have written the books but for the oddest thing. He had an uncle, a bit of a bad seed, who had been in and out of prison. He worked for a contractor who built roads. One day there was a tragedy. His uncle was driving a road-roller, one of those ungainly, prehistoric-looking vehicles which move at about two miles an hour, and he was leaning out of the cabin, yelling to one of his workmates, when he slipped and fell under the great front wheel of the machine. He must be the only person in the history of mankind who was run over by a road-roller. Anyway, Seppi said that soon after he heard the news he had a strange dream – the actual circumstances of his uncle's death morphed into a vision of Satan falling from Heaven with the Archangel Michael standing over him with a flaming sword. He began *Angels Rising* that very night."

"What a strange story!"

"Possibly just a bit stranger than how it came to be published."

"How come?"

"Because Litmus was absolutely the wrong publisher for the books and I was absolutely the wrong editor for the books. I liked a very different kind of book, and I would have said no except I felt I owed Seppi so I took the manu-script home with me to read."

"And?"

"I think the best way to explain is to paraphrase something Kerouac wrote about in *On the Road,* I don't remember the exact words but the central character says something like all his life he has sought out the mad ones, the ones who were different from the common herd, the ones who when you encountered them made you go *Awww!* Now transpose that feeling to books, there are some books that make you go *Awww!*, that's what I felt when I read *Angels Rising* – there was no way I was not going to publish that book."

"I hope something like that happens to me one day."

"Oh, it will, just stay the course, it will happen to you; that is the greatest reward of our profession, everything else is just detail."

It is time for them to go. He has asked her not to make appointments for a couple of hours this afternoon so he can catch up with work. The hotel is only about ten minutes away, so he decides to stretch his legs, especially as his route will take him through Lodi Gardens, a lovely ordered space of flowers and shrubs woven around the tombs of an ancient dynasty. As he walks along a path lined by Ashoka trees, the dark clouds overhead spit out a short sharp shower that ends almost as soon as it has begun; the rain is warm as blood and heightens the joy he had felt at the bookstore and at Ramesh's. He is, he realizes, responding to the endless sense of possibility that India seems to offer. For the first time in over a decade he thinks seriously about returning. Not right now, there is much that remains to be done back in London, but if the opportunity presents itself he will consider it very carefully. And until that happens he will do what he can for Litmus India.

———

Before he grew up and went away to boarding school, Zach's parents would take him every summer to his paternal grandparents' house in the seaside town of Kanyakumari. Behind the house was open ground dotted with casuarinas bent by the wind. The sandy soil, evidence that all this was once under the sea, was speckled with tiny biting ants and was reputed to have a resident cobra, so he was not allowed to play unsupervised, but it was easy to give the old retainer who was charged with watching over him the slip, and he would spend hours happily exploring the tangled wilderness. From time to time travelling troupes that enacted wild, colourful tableaus and skits drawn from the epics and folklore for the children and women of the neighbourhood would interrupt his solitary ramblings. Monkeys and decorated cows were pressed into service to help the heavily made-up actors tell stories as old as time. He doubts that the itinerant players have been able to withstand the onslaught of TV and the cinema but they wouldn't have seemed out of place at the book launch Apoorva has taken him to; it is the sort of glorious spectacle that he has almost never encountered in all his years as a publisher in London. He is used to occasions where the family and friends of the author whose book is being launched gather in pubs or restaurants; the publisher makes a short speech, the author, a creature used to hiding in the shadows, responds stutteringly, and then a prolonged bout of serious drinking ensues. A variant is the launch in a bookstore where, unless the author is renowned, the event is little more than just another revolution of the carousel of that season's events played out before bored store employees and a tiny knot of the author's people.

This launch has the scale of a Bollywood premiere and the pomp of a Punjabi wedding. Giant chandeliers descend like blazing arks from the vaulted ceiling of the enormous banqueting hall of the Taj Mahal Hotel on Mansingh Road. The light bounces off glittering jewellery, burnished hairdos, and glassware polished to perfection. A blowup of the cover of the book is the backdrop to a large stage that has been set up at the front of the room; on the stage are two comfortable sofas, a low table with a massive floral arrangement, and a podium with the hotel's logo prominently displayed. Beside the stage are tables on which copies of the book, a minor maharaja's memoir, are piled up under the watchful eye of the publisher's representative. Not that anyone seems the least bit interested in the displayed books. This is a social event, and the richly caparisoned men and women from Delhi's smart set swish to and fro dressed in the latest fashions from London, Milan and Paris, chatting and laughing and air-kissing each other, between sips from the champagne flutes, wine glasses, and tumblers of whisky that sprout from their hands. Decked out in an exquisite salwar kameez that must have cost her far more than she could afford on her salary, Apoorva points out some of the notables in the crowd. Over there is a leading fashion designer with violet hair and eyeshadow, dressed in what appears to be a giant wickerwork chair; a few feet away is a captain of industry in an expensive bandh gala surrounded by a group of unctuous admirers; next to him a politician (who is temporarily out of favour) in a crisp white kurta-pyjama is being harangued by a famous TV journalist; in a corner stands a solitary man with a whisky and a samosa who has been a fixture at every book launch in Delhi for the past decade; making a lateish entrance is a much feted British author who is immediately mobbed by a crowd of socialites bright as macaws. The Page 3 photographers who have been focusing on a distinguished, pipe-smoking diplomat abandon him and train their lenses on the writer; he affects not to notice them and falls into animated conversation with a well-known book critic. Here and there, publishing folk wander, a less showy breed in dress and demeanour; a publicist fends off importuning journalists begging her for free copies of the book – the scene around them is replicated a dozen times, a hundred times, under the impersonal glare of the chandeliers. Food has begun to circulate, expensive looking hors d'oeuvres, plump prawns, and kebabs, and other things he cannot identify, and the celebrants gather them up from the circulating white-clad wait staff without breaking stride or conversation. There must be at least six hundred people in the room now. Apoorva points to the author, at the centre of a knot of people. He looks nothing like a maharaja, for he is a small, mournful-looking man dressed in an unflashy suit, although it does seem rather well cut. He is extremely well connected, Apoorva tells Zach, which is why the event has drawn such a large crowd. He still hasn't been able to spot the publisher and asks Apoorva who he is. She points to a man sheltering behind a potted palm in a far corner of the room who seems almost incidental to the festivities.

A slender woman in a sari the colour of fire that goes well with her hazel eyes wanders up, greets Apoorva languidly, is introduced to him and says, in an accent he is unable to place: "Mr. Angels himself. So tell me, sir, how do you create a bestseller?"

"If I knew I would be the most successful publisher on the planet," he says.

"Does anyone know?" the woman asks. Her perfectly pencilled eyebrows arch as she asks the question.

"There are some editors, especially in the States, who have an extraordinary ability to keep finding authors especially genre authors, repeaters, who write a book a year that with focused marketing will reliably make it to the bestseller lists. But I doubt even they would claim to have the ability to unerringly pick the next Rowling or Brown or Hosseini or Larsson –"

"Or Seppi," she chimes in, flirting in a bored sort of way. Perhaps this is how she keeps herself amused at these occasions, he has certainly sensed no attraction between them.

"I suppose," he says.

"Oh, come now, no need to be so modest," she says with mock severity.

"I don't think I'm alone in thinking that in the digital age the role of publishers is effectively over," a tall, grey-bearded man, somewhat scruffy-looking, chimes in. Apoorva had introduced him as they walked in; the newcomer's name had not registered, but he obligingly provides it again. Professor Malik. A midwestern twang. Zach wonders which university he teaches at.

"Oh, I don't think we're done for yet. Do you know the word *docent*?"

"Yes, I do, I teach literature," the professor says. He sounds irritated. Good. Zach is tired of these Cassandras who

harangue publishers at every turn as though they were inca-
pable of thinking for themselves.

"Readers will continue to look to publishers for authors
they would like to read," he says to the professor. "Formats
might change, delivery systems might change, pricing models
might change, but I doubt our essential role will change all
that much. And despite all the talk, it's not as if the world of
publishing has already changed beyond all recognition."

"You hope."

"We know – if statistics about our industry are anything
to go by. The vast majority of books are still being made,
marketed, printed, and sold as they have always been. The
industry is flat in the UK and other mature markets, but
there is no worrying decline in sales."

The woman in the flame-coloured sari has wandered off
with Apoorva. Is he to be stuck with this pedantic bore?

"Maybe so, but if the readers of tomorrow decide they
want to buy their content direct from creators what role do
middlemen like you have to play?"

"Selection, packaging, marketing, the protection of copyright –"

"Which online companies can do just as well as you can.
Amazon Books. Apple Books. Why not? They pay better
royalties than you guys, and when the majority of readers
begin to read digitally –"

"There is no reason why we can't add newer skills to the
ones we possess. We already produce digital versions of our
print editions, we're beginning to figure out how to repur-
pose content in new and exciting ways, we're learning how

to market direct to consumers, we will just need to keep pace with the changes in the way people buy, read. And to answer your question about Amazon starting to publish, as you know they already do so, as do some of the other big retailers, but that's not what is encoded in their DNA at the moment. That might change, the world of business is not static and companies will slide up and down the value chain depending on changes in the environment and their own strategic imperatives, but at the end of the day in the book business, just as in every other business, each link in the chain will need a specific focus. The brand names might change, certain companies will disappear, others will replace them, but publishing will not die."

"Or maybe, two decades from now, no middlemen like publishers or agents will be required," the professor responds. "Authors will sell work directly to their fans, just like in India and elsewhere in the civilized world a thousand years ago, when wandering storytellers and bards and minstrels communicated directly with their audiences. Nobody taking a slice off the top."

"I think that's a simplistic view. You forget that publishers support writers with advances –"

"– and make off with the lion's share of the profit," the professor cuts in querulously.

"A common misconception. Most books don't make their money back. And, contrary to what people think, the majority of publishers feel that they have had a successful year if they have made a profit of ten per cent, which is less than what successful authors make."

"That may be so but in the digital age it will be possible for authors to go direct to their readers and keep most of the value that has been attached to their work."

"Sure and there will be a few authors who will do that, especially those who have made a name for themselves, but don't forget that most authors only become famous because publishers have taken a gamble on them, and nurtured them through the years when they weren't as well known. For the few who decide to take the self-publishing option there will be hundreds of thousands of others who will want to do nothing but continue with what they are best at, which is to write and create. All these writers will be happy to leave the editing, marketing, selling, and safeguarding of their work to publishers. I doubt that that is going to change any time soon."

"Really?"

"Yes, really. There must be a reason why even writers who have uploaded their work to popular online publishing sites like Wattpad rejoice when their work is picked up by a regular publisher."

The conversation is beginning to exhaust him; he can't wait for the event to start. He reaches for a refill from a passing waiter.

Screeching noises from the microphone. A young woman in a green sari, a PR lady from the hotel, waits for the static to die down, asks everyone to take his or her seat as the event is about to begin. Nobody pays the slightest attention; the laughter and the conversation continue to rise up to the ceiling. Various other people take their turn at the mike, the publisher, an important hotel functionary, the harassed publicist, the PR lady again. While the concerted effort manages to shake loose a few people at the fringes of the gathering who drift towards the chairs, everyone else is too busy eating and drinking and having a good time to budge. Finally a chunky-looking man, who may or not be connected to the organizers but who has the air of someone who must be listened to, strides up to the microphone and roars at the audience to sit down. Unhurriedly people begin looking for seats.

"Zach, Professor Malik, this way please, I've reserved seats for you," Apoorva beckons. The professor leads the way and she whispers to Zach, "I'm trying to get Professor Malik to give us his next book, a novel." Despite himself, he says, "The professor doesn't seem to think publishers are necessary." She grimaces and shrugs; it is obvious she has heard the man's rant before.

They have seats near the front. It takes another blast from the tubby man before the rest of the audience is seated.

"How on earth can publishers afford all this?" Zach asks Apoorva.

"They can't," she replies. "The hotels comp all the expenses, they have a cultural budget for these things, publishing events are hot, get them tons of free publicity. And I hear for this party the author provided a few crates of Black Label."

There are three people on the dais, the author who is talking to the junior minister who will launch the book, and the publisher who is going through his notes. The PR lady at the microphone announces the publisher and leaves the stage.

At this point, he switches off – he knows the drill, and he has no interest in the author (Apoorva has told him she has heard rumours that he intends to buy back five thousand copies from the publisher). The publisher introduces the book, the author, and the minister, and disappears, whereupon the minister, a lean, wolfish-looking man, begins to make a speech that can be barely heard above the background noise. Zach's mind begins to wander. Small wonder, he thinks, that some of the world's greatest novels have featured social gatherings like this one. Hundreds of beautiful, famous, successful people gathered together in one place, all apparently having a good time, but at what cost? For the novelist what is fascinating is the price of admission to events like this, and he is not thinking here of the fancy pieces of cardboard that are nominally the means to get in; no, what is of interest is the tough journey that every one of these people, whether high born or low, has had to make through life to get here. The youthful ambition and self-regard, the early successes and defeats, the constant struggle and effort, the disappointments and the wrong turns, moments of brilliance and moments of compromise, acts of selfishness and sensitivity, incidents of duplicity and honour, the courage and the pathos of their endeavour, the ruthlessness and the betrayals they have had to take in their stride . . . Told by someone with the requisite skill, the stories of many of those present here today would make compelling reading.

The minister's speech begins to wind down. When at long last he finishes to polite applause, the author's speech seems more like an afterthought. After it is over, the minister unwraps a copy of the book, which the author and he hold up to the cameras, and the formal part of the evening comes to an end. At least a quarter of the audience has paid no attention whatsoever to the proceedings.

Apoorva, the woman in the flame-coloured sari whose name turns out to be Mandira (and who, he gathers, lives in Berne – do none of these people live in Delhi?), and the professor decide to repair to the bar upstairs for a drink. He is conscious that Apoorva would like to publish both of them, so he resolves to be as helpful as he can, although he hopes never to see Professor Malik again.

Fortunately for Zach, the professor, who has been throwing back large glasses of rum all evening, seems to have lost all interest in him. He speaks earnestly and drunkenly to Apoorva, and Zach is left to amuse himself with Mandira (he still does not know whether she is a novelist or poet or celebrity chef). She is witty and coolly intelligent, and he is beginning to thoroughly enjoy her company when Apoorva cuts in to say that he should probably be thinking of getting back to the hotel if he is going to make his flight early in the morning.

The professor beams at him drunkenly. "The crash will come, buddy, never fear, it will come."

"Not for a long, long time," he says. He smiles insincerely. "Apoorva tells me you are writing a novel, which I can't wait to read. And when it's ready you must give it to us. We'll do a great job of publishing it."

"Oh, it will be a few years before it's done. By then who knows whether or not you guys will be around?" The professor aims a wink at him but doesn't quite pull it off, ends up blinking like a mole in the harsh light of the lobby where they are gathered as they wait for their cars.

"As long as people tell stories and people consume stories there will be a role for all of us," Zach says quietly. "I think it was Forster who said that we would only need to worry when human beings no longer had any need for stories and had begun to regard themselves in ways that were new and quite inconceivable from our present vantage point. It was true when he said it, it is true now, and I hope for everyone's sake it will be true for some time to come."

4 ·

TORONTO

There are as many theories about how to deal with jet lag as the Inuit supposedly have names for snow and Zach knows all of them, and believes not a single one. He doesn't know if it is worse outward bound or returning home, melatonin has never worked for him, sleeping at the same time you would at home in whichever new time zone you are in doesn't help in the least – all he knows is that it is one of the things that irks him most about long-distance travel. Morosely he watches the brightening horizon from his hotel room, the CN Tower like a weirdly shaped pipette presiding over the downtown high-rises, and thinks about his meeting in the evening with Seppi's translator. When he had called Caryn Bianchi from London to set up the appointment she seemed pleasant enough, which was a relief, but she was noncommittal about what she might have for him when he explained the purpose of the visit.

He still believes he is wasting his time but Gabrijela

thought differently and so here he is, the excitement of the visit to Delhi already receding. What if anything might Caryn have in her possession? He racks his brain to think if Seppi had ever mentioned to him that he wrote short stories, but he doesn't think so; perhaps an unpublished first novel, surely every novelist has one of those, or maybe an unfinished draft of something that he had been working on at the time of his death. Zach has gone over all the possibilities a hundred times, a thousand, and he knows nothing, will know nothing until he meets Caryn.

Perhaps he will have a marlin moment. When he had spoken to Julia from Delhi, intending to quarrel with her over the blandness of her e-mail, she had disarmed him by hoping he would have a "marlin moment" in Toronto, her way of describing a welcome surprise that came out of nowhere, which had its origins in the only other real holiday besides Bhutan that they had taken together. Over his usual reluctance she had booked a trip to Cuba. Their first week on the island, which they had spent at a beach resort, had been awful. He wasn't a beach person and the combination of salt, sand, mugginess, mosquitoes, and unattractive bodies in string bikinis and Speedos had driven him crazy. His constant complaining had upset Julia, but fortunately before they had begun flinging mojitos at each other they had moved on to Havana, which Zach had loved — the ruined old city, its walls washed with the colours of the summer sky, the music and dance that greeted them at every turn, the ghosts of its past, and the astonishing beauty of its young: the men with the liquid grace of boxers or matadors and the women with eyes of mystery and fire. The enthusiasm and zest with which the Cubans went about their daily lives, especially when they had to make do with so little and deal constantly with the heavy hand of the state, had at first intrigued him and then caught him up in its optimism and energy. He had stopped grumbling and their last few days in Castro's socialist paradise had drifted by in a haze of cigar smoke, Cuba libres, mojitos, snatches of "Chan Chan" sung and played with various degrees of competence and enthusiasm, and dancing in a variety of styles, with the only constant being the hip-swinging sexuality that the locals managed to infuse into every performance whether staged or impromptu. The day before they were due to return they had hired a boat and decided to try their luck at deep sea fishing, which neither of them had ever attempted before.

Ernest Hemingway had been a boyhood hero of Zach's, especially during his shikari phase, but when his tastes grew more literary he had abandoned the maestro of two-fisted prose for authors who better fit his idea of the literary writer. However, just before they had taken off for Cuba he had suddenly been seized with a huge desire to reread Hemingway, and had bought himself a copy of *The Old Man and the Sea*. When he finished the book he understood the writer's literary genius for the first time: the ability to bring a character alive with a phrase or two, the sentences of burnished steel, the extraordinary insight and, most of all, the power of his storytelling. An unexpected by-product of this new appreciation of the American novelist was a desire to experience for himself the thrill of bagging a great game fish; as a boy

he'd tried to emulate him with a gun, now he would give it
a go with a rod and a line.

Julia hadn't been too interested in the idea but had given
in with good grace when she had seen how keen Zach was;
it helped that they hadn't fought once in all the time they
had hung out in Havana. On the morning of the fishing
expedition they were both seriously hungover, and the prospect of spending five or six hours on a small boat in deep
water hadn't been appealing. They had almost decided to
cancel when Zach, summoning up his last reserves of enthusiasm, had managed to get both of them into a taxi in time
to catch the boat they had booked the previous day.

Propitiously enough the marina they set out from, into
waters that seemed to have been plucked from the heart of
a sapphire, was called the Marina Ernest Hemingway, but
that seemed to be the only bit of luck they were going to
have that day, for three hours later they hadn't caught a single
fish. Indeed the only sign of marine life they had seen was a
barracuda swimming at great speed away from the four lines
that trailed in the water behind the boat. It was hurricane
season and though the island itself had been untouched, a
vicious tropical storm offshore had left the ocean roily, and
as the boat rose and fell on the choppy water their outlook
towards their little expedition worsened. They felt too ill and
too tired to quarrel about it, however, so had just sat quietly
looking out at the distant shoreline of Havana and hoping
their stomachs would not revolt. Just then one of the fishing
lines on the port side had begun to flow out with great
vehemence, and all their misgivings were shoved aside; the

captain throttled back the engine, the first mate led Julia
(who demurred but Zach had insisted) to the fighting chair
in the stern, the rod was locked into place, the first mate gave
her some tips on how to play a big game fish, when to let the
line out and when to reel it in, and battle was joined.

Sleepless in his Toronto hotel room, he can see the events
of that morning as clearly as if they were unfolding before
him right now – Julia tiny against the vastness of the ocean
but determined, gripping the rod tightly and grimly following the shouted commands of the first mate, while unseen
below the blue water her quarry fought to escape. A little
while later it was over. They saw the fish for the first time,
about twenty metres astern, long and lean and astoundingly
beautiful, its skin the colour of crushed emerald. All the fight
had gone out of it. The first mate had sprung into action as
Julia hauled the fish up to the boat; it was dispatched swiftly
and stored away. "Mahi mahi. Good eating," the first mate
had said, a smile lifting his grizzled mustache. Zach had
hugged Julia, he was delighted for her. For her part she
seemed a little shaken; the thrill of the battle had been exhil-
arating but the death of the mahi mahi had disturbed her, he
could see that. But he was excited now by the prospect of
landing his own fish. The adrenalin pumping through his
veins, he had scanned the heaving water alertly, almost as if
he expected squadrons of tuna and sharks and sailfish and
marlin to spring forth and impale themselves on the wicked
hooks that bobbed in the wake of the boat.

Two hours later, with the sun directly overhead and their
time up, their splendidly named captain, Alejandro Cordero

Garcia, had come down the stairway from the upper deck and told him he was turning for home. Grumpily, Zach had agreed. The boat had described a wide circle in the water and begun to slam through the surging seas in the direction of the marina. Julia was dozing fitfully by now but Zach had remained awake, looking out through a cloudy porthole. In Hemingway's great novel, the old fisherman had dreamed about lions in Africa, but Zach could think only of schools of marlin cavorting in the depths, laughing through their pointy noses at his fantasy of hooking one of them. Tiny flying fish skimmed above the surface of the water. Showoffs, he had thought, why couldn't they swim through the water like regular fish! The first mate had been sympathetic; it was rare to get a marlin, he said, none of the boats in the marina had caught one for days, and he knew of groups who had spent weeks on the water only to come up empty-handed.

Zach's despondency had grown as the shoreline had become more distinct. He had been hoping against hope that a fish would strike but knew that it would be unrealistic to hope anymore, best to roll up his fantasy and stow it away. He had uncapped a bottle of the local version of Coke, taken a long swig of the sickly sweet drink. He should get seriously drunk tonight, if he was hungover on the flight home he would just have to deal with it, no matter how unpleasant it might be.

And then, gloriously, his marlin moment was upon him. The aft starboard line had begun to chatter out into the water. Instantly the engine note changed as the captain began to slow the boat down, bring it around, to impede the headlong flight of the fish. Zach had been tied into the fighting chair, the rod had been slotted in, and he had been told how to play the marlin (for the captain and his assistant were certain that that was what was on the end of his line): pull back the rod and reel in the slack whenever he could, pay out the line whenever it made a run for it, keep the line taut at all times but not so taut that it could break. Half an hour later his arms were aching from the strain of hanging on, his T-shirt and red baseball cap with the iconic image of Che were sodden with sweat, and they still hadn't caught a glimpse of the fish. The line was far astern, his quarry had shown no signs of tiring, and he had begun to wonder if he had it in him to land his trophy. The first mate had offered to spell him but he had refused. This was his fish, he would either bring it in himself or it would get away, it was unthink-able that there could be another option.

And then, without warning, the marlin had smoked out of the water like an express train. Up, up, up, it had flown, its tremendous blue-black body arched like some godling's bow against the sky, the coastline, and the wave-tossed sea. It was a sight he would never forget, his marlin moment, that instant in which enchantment had burst upon him when he had least expected it.

No question that he needs something like that now, he thinks, but he is not at all hopeful. Best to temper his and Gabrijela's expectations; Caryn is not a magician, she cannot be expected to conjure up something for them just because they are desperate. He decides to go for a walk, there is no point being cooped up in his room alone with his unproductive thoughts. When he emerges from the air-conditioned lobby of the hotel onto the street he is surprised by how hot and humid it is, it could be Madras in the late spring. He wanders around aimlessly for a bit, then gets bored and ducks into a Second Cup coffee shop and gets himself a latte, flips through a day-old newspaper, then, still restless, decides to return to the hotel and catch the morning news on TV.

Showered and shaved he is about to leave the room for a meeting with Michael Levine, the city's top literary agent, and one of the few people in the publishing community who isn't already on vacation, when the phone rings. It's Sally, the freelance publicist whom they have used for all the Seppi events in this country; she is calling to remind him about lunch with the editor of one of the city's trade journals. Zach groans inwardly; he had forgotten he had agreed to the meeting. Chronically media-shy, the last thing he wants to do is be interviewed by the editor of *Bibliomania*, but Sally has been a rock throughout the Seppi years and she has made it clear in her gentle way that she is calling in a favour. She gives him the name of the restaurant, makes sure he writes it down, then rings off.

———

Several blocks away, Simon Prescott, the editor Zach is so reluctant to meet, gets on the streetcar he takes to work every day. Simon is a modest man, even his fantasies are homely. This past month he has dreamed off and on of being the driver of the streetcar; he thinks it would be cool to put on the uniform the Toronto Transit Commission provides, wedge himself into the driver's seat of the vehicle, and let her rip at forty kilometres an hour. He has never possessed a driver's licence, so he understands this fantasy is beyond his reach but it is pleasant to dream about sliding along the rails at a sedate pace.

This morning, however, as the streetcar rolls towards the tiny office of *Bibliomania* in Queen West he does not think about his fantasy, because he is excited by the prospect of conducting what could well be his biggest interview of the year. As editor-in-chief of *Bibliomania,* the country's sixth most important magazine about books, Simon has long accepted that Canada's leading publishers and writers will routinely rebuff him. In his first year as editor-in-chief, a position he had ascended to as the longest-serving member of the magazine's staff of four, after his predecessor who had joined as an intern seven months earlier had resigned, he had tried hard to improve the quality of the magazine's stories but had given up in the face of the indifference of the industry he was covering to his magazine's place in the general scheme of things. Matters weren't helped by the modest budget that the magazine was expected to survive on, despite the stream of applications made to the Canada Council begging for it to be increased. However, his survival as editor-in-chief was testament to the fact that he did possess certain qualities that made him perfect for the job from the point of view of the owners of *Bibliomania.* Among these were the ability to live on a salary slightly above minimum wage with no benefits, the knack of persuading publicists to keep sending him free copies of books that had just been published, arranging interviews with authors no one else wanted to cover, and getting college students and other would-be writers to write book reviews. Once or twice a year Simon got lucky and landed a story that was big by *Bibliomania*'s standards, usually an interview with a prominent visiting author, jet-lagged and bullied by his publisher into repeating the story of his genius yet another time.

Simon did not have an expense account, but this was usually not a problem because the publicists that his well-being depended upon would often pick up the tab. Today, however, he had miscalculated, for the man he was going to interview would not be accompanied by a publicist; Simon hadn't thought of that when he had arranged to meet Zachariah Thomas for lunch at Yonge Izakaya, a Japanese restaurant near his office that he frequented because he had long been infatuated with the restaurant's maître d' or hostess or whatever the Japanese equivalent was. To be on the safe side, Simon had borrowed twenty dollars from his deputy, but hoped he would not have to use it – perhaps Thomas would pay.

Simon did not know much about Japanese food, and it was quite by chance that he had eaten at Yonge Izakaya for the first time – a publicist had asked if he would mind eating Japanese as her author was dying for good sushi. Simon did not mind, although his acquaintance with sushi was limited to the platters that were sometimes served at book launches. Any doubts that he might have had about the publicist's choice of restaurant had disappeared when Sachiko (this wasn't her real name but to Simon's frustration none of the wait staff at Yonge Izakaya wore a name tag; he was too shy to ask her name so he had given her a name he had Googled – it meant bliss) greeted them and led them to their table. She was, without a doubt, the most beautiful woman he had ever seen – tall, slender, her ivory-white complexion set off by the very dark lipstick she wore.

Since that first encounter he had eaten at the restaurant eleven times, spending exactly eight dollars and fifty cents each time on the Gold Dragon Sushi Special (cucumber and avocado with shrimp tempura topped with salmon). To his dismay, Sachiko who had a smile that heightened her remarkable looks had stopped using it on him after he had lunched at the restaurant a couple of times. Despite the setback, he had continued to visit the restaurant because he was hopeful that his persistence would be rewarded.

————

Zach arrives at the restaurant extremely frustrated. Neither agent he met this morning had anything that would work for him, and unless Caryn is about to spring a welcome surprise this evening the trip will be a bust. He hopes his lunch companion is well informed about the local publishing scene, maybe he will be good for a tip or two about the next great Canadian phenom. He doesn't expect the interview itself to be much of a problem, Sally has briefed him well – all he will have to do is come up with a few anecdotes and quotes about Seppi and say a few nice things about Canadian writers, which he will be more than happy to do, he has read many with genuine pleasure: the great ones like Alice Munro, Alistair Macleod and Margaret Atwood of course, not to mention Robertson Davies, who was the first Canadian novelist he read with something approaching awe. And he also admires quite a few of the younger and more adventurous ones who seem to display an almost preternatural skill at getting into the skin of other cultures – indeed, he would publish some of them in a heartbeat if they ever came free of their existing publishers.

Unfortunately, though, the meeting is turning out to be much worse than he had expected. It had started out all right, he had found Simon Prescott to be as pleasant and polite as every Canadian he had met on his three visits to the city (this was even true of the immigration officials at Pearson Airport, which filled him with something approaching wonder). But it had gone rapidly downhill from there.

"Nice restaurant," he'd said on arriving.

"That it is, in no small part because of my girlfriend, Sachiko, who is the manager, I mean the maître d'."

"Oh, excellent, was she the one who showed me to our table? She's a stunner." It was true. He is no expert on the Japanese ideal of feminine beauty, but the hostess who had greeted him and led him to his table was exquisite. Taller than the average Japanese woman. Heart-shaped face. Electrifying smile. Black lipstick.

"So where did you guys meet?" He thinks that he is spending too much time on Simon's personal life, but his lunch companion's face is lit with pride and he obviously wants to dwell on the subject.

"Here, I'm a regular."

The subject of their conversation comes up, heels clicking on the wooden floor. She says brightly: "Hi, your server will be with you in a minute, meanwhile may I get you something to drink?"

"Sure, Sachiko. Simon has just been telling me about you."

Her forehead creases for a minute in the tiniest frown and he almost expects her to say, *What the fuck has this jackass been saying to you?*

"My name is Megumi, and I'd be very pleased to get you gentlemen something to drink."

There is silence at the table for a beat. Zach dares not look at Simon, but recovers first to mumble, "Just some green tea for me, please."

Simon does not say anything. Megumi says pleasantly, "How about you, sir?"

Simon's face has gone red; Zach thinks that one of the benefits of having a darker complexion is it helps you cover up embarrassment better. Simon shakes his head miserably.

"Your server will be here in a minute," Megumi says with a smile as she turns and clicks away.

The server comes up – she looks Middle Eastern – takes their order, the Premium Sashimi plate for him, the Gold Dragon Sushi Special for Simon, and silence descends upon the table again. After the frustrations of the morning Zach is not exactly filled with fellow feeling, but he feels he must do his bit to help Simon out.

"So how many issues of *Bibliomania* do you publish every year?" he asks cheerfully.

Simon says in a voice that is barely audible, "We have an annual print edition, and the rest of our content is online. We'll be completely online next year."

"Tell me, what's hot and happening on the Canadian publishing scene?"

"Not much," Simon says, toying with his wooden chopsticks.

Come on, snap out of it, guy, he wants to say, there will be other women. Look for someone who is more in your league. He silently curses Sally for setting this meeting up.

"OK, what would you like to know from me?"

"You're the editor of the *Angels* quartet – could you tell me how you discovered Seppi?"

"Sure –"

"But before we get to that, could you give me plot summaries of the books? *Bibliomania*'s readers would like to know what they are about."

He has been feeling sorry for Simon, now he is seriously irritated by him. Although everyone he knows in the world of books has horror stories about mediocre literary journalists who don't prepare for interviews or are too lazy to get their facts right, this guy is in a class by himself. Did he really want to be given a précis of each Seppi book? Even if he hadn't read them – and he must have spent the last decade under a rock to have not done so – surely he could have looked up the book descriptions online?

"Why don't you look them up on Amazon?" he says.

The muddy-green eyes look up from the pad over which his pencil is poised. "Don't you have a press release?"

"Look, mate, I flew in last night from Delhi, specifically to meet with writers and agents, and I only made room in my schedule for you to accommodate Sally's request. If you haven't taken the trouble to research Seppi's work, I'm sorry but I don't think we're going to be able to do an interview that's worth anything."

The clicking of heels, Megumi's voice asking brightly, "I hope everything's satisfactory, gentlemen."

Fuck, how long has she been here? Has she heard him berating Simon? He looks up at her, smiles and nods, she moves on. Their food arrives and he forces himself to calm down. He rattles off one-line plot summaries of the four books between bites of his sashimi, which is excellent. Simon takes down everything he says laboriously, but the atmosphere throughout the rest of the meal is chilly, and he is relieved when the bill comes. As they are leaving, the staff of the restaurant bid farewell in a loud voice. Megumi joins in, favours him with a smile and ignores Simon. Despite his irritation, Zach feels for the man, I hope your romantic life gets better, he thinks, not that he's anyone to talk!

———

Caryn Bianchi looks different from when he last saw her; he isn't sure whether it has to do with the way she has styled her hair or whether the lines of her face have softened in some way, but the rather severe-looking woman he remembers somehow looks much more approachable. She hadn't said much at their last meeting, and she doesn't say very much this time either. Now, as then, Seppi is the third person at the meeting. It is very hot in her small office. The ticking of a clock with large numerals on its face fills the silence. Bookshelves line the walls but all they seem to contain are multiple editions of the quartet in all the languages it has been published in. The office is only big enough for a desk and two chairs for visitors, and he sits in one of them. From where he is sitting he is able to make direct eye contact with an enormous framed black and white picture of Seppi looking like the famous photograph of the young Kafka. The other walls have posters of the *Angels* movies.

Once they get past the social niceties, Zach comes to the point. Is there any unfinished work by Seppi that Litmus can acquire and publish, he asks? Work that belongs to the *Angels* line would be especially welcome, but he would be glad to consider anything publishable.

"You are the seventeenth international publisher to ask me the question. Every Canadian and Italian publisher has asked the question as well. My answer has always been no."

His spirits deflate, although he had never really expected to find anything in this tiny office in North York. There is no more business to transact, it is time to go. But Caryn doesn't seem anxious to conclude the meeting. They have had their differences in the past, but he knows how much he owes her, so he curbs his impatience to get going, waits for her cue to rise. As his gaze takes her in, the sensible haircut, the brown hair now flecked with grey, the grey business suit, the unexpectedly jaunty green T-shirt beneath the jacket, the

giant face of Seppi over her shoulder, he thinks about what
she must have had to live through. He knows what it is like
to lose someone who is a part of you, and he empathizes
with her. On the scale of human sorrowing he thinks the
loss of someone on whose life and work your own was
predicated could only compare to the loss of parents, a
much-loved partner, or children. Sure, he had mourned
Seppi's passing, but he was one of several authors Zach had
worked with. What Caryn had to deal with was the sunder-
ing of one of those exceedingly rare partnerships that was
closer than most blood relationships in which the creative
soul of the translator is bound up with that of the writer, the
better to create the work anew in another language. He
remembers speculating about the relationship between Seppi
and this woman; it would have been in keeping with the rest
of their relationship, he thinks, if they had been lovers: the
quiet serious writer, with no life outside his work, who had
somehow managed to pin the gargantuan, blaring lives of
angels to the page, and the quiet, serious translator, with no
life outside Seppi, who had devoted herself to absorbing his
art before recreating it again in a way that was true both to
its creator and to the new voice with which it was expected
to speak. The glory and gain were the author's and her only
reward was the work itself, before Seppi's generosity had
kicked in and he'd given her enough money to live the rest
of her life in comfort. But he guessed that wouldn't be
enough to make up for her loss.

Her voice cuts into his reverie.

"I said no to all the others who enquired, and I said no to

you when you wrote me because that was the way Massimo would have wanted it," she says softly. It sounds strange to hear the author he has always thought of as Seppi called by his given name.

"There were only two people he trusted with his work besides me," she continues. "His first publisher in Palermo, Vittorio, and you. Vittorio died three years ago. One of the last things Massimo said to me before he slipped into a coma was how grateful he was for the money you paid him for the quartet even though his first two novels had earned him just under eight thousand dollars. He knew just how hard you must have fought to keep publishing him." She smiles for the first time since he has entered her office.

The best twenty thousand quid I ever spent, Zach thinks to himself. He has no idea whether he will ever come into such good fortune again – but you never know, publishing has its own mad logic and those who know the least about it are publishers themselves.

"Do you mind if I tell you a bit about myself, Mr. Thomas?"

"Zach, please. Sorry I should have asked earlier, are you free for supper?"

"Supper – I love the fact that you English still use that word. Language is turning flabby and inexact, don't you think, soon we'll call all the meals we eat dinner irrespective of when we actually take them."

She locks up, and they walk in silence to a French restaurant nearby. It is deserted at this hour, and after they have placed their orders Caryn returns to her story at the same place she left off.

"I was talking about how the fidelity of language is being given short shrift today, Zach, because that is one of the things that I have obsessed about all my life. I suppose I wanted to be a writer once, but fortunately after three failed attempts I realized that I wasn't good enough. Then, for a lark, I translated the first chapter of *The Leopard*, Massimo's favourite as I would learn."

"Yes, I know, he told me it was that novel which inspired him to write his early work."

"The experience of sinking into the voice of a great writer and then playing with words and concepts to come up with a faithful but new creation satisfied my longing to be a writer, even though I suppose it was at one remove. I then wrote to every Italian writer I admired, attaching a copy of my Lampedusa translation, and asking if I could work with them. Massimo, who was working on his second novel at the time, was the only one who replied. Soon after, he fired the translator of his first novel, and I worked with him for the rest of his career."

"Did you know he was working on the quartet when you signed on?"

She shakes her head. The waitress brings the food; she waits for it to be served and then does that thing he had remarked upon to himself – picking up the conversation exactly where she had left off.

"Massimo was very particular about the way he wrote. Every book went through four drafts, and he wouldn't show a word to anyone until the last draft was edited to his satisfaction. Except for me. Did you ever wonder how it was that you received the English translation of his latest novel at exactly the same time his publisher in Palermo received the Italian version?"

"I did wonder, yes," he says.

"When he finished his second draft, Massimo would e-mail it to me and I would begin translating it as he began to work on the third draft. As you know no good translation is precisely literal. And because Massimo's second drafts were so close to the final version it was not difficult to get the translation going. He would let the third draft sit for three months, and that was all the time I needed to make a first pass at the translation, which he and I would then discuss. It worked very well," she says, a wistful note in her voice. He wonders again if there was anything more to their relationship, and as if reading his mind she provides him with the answer.

"Massimo and I were never more than friends and collaborators." She pauses, takes a bite of her steak tartare. "I hope you do not think I am giving you too much information?"

"No, no, not at all," he says hastily.

"I thought I should tell you," she continues, "because I want you to know exactly what my relationship with Massimo was. We were not lovers but we were if anything closer than lovers. He lived for his work, the *Angels* quartet in particular; in fact he often talked about repudiating his earlier novels, except you publishers wouldn't permit that" (she says this with a little smile to take the sting out of the rebuke), "and I shared his absolute commitment to the work. In fact, I often thought the translations went so well because we seemed to be drinking from the same fount of inspiration.

"Anyhow, I was his sole confidante and this is why what I am about to tell you, Zach, will be the first time that anyone besides Massimo and I knows that he was on the verge of completing a fifth *Angels* book when he passed away. He had completed the second draft and had begun revising it before he became too ill to continue. The novel was under contract to no one, and he left all rights in it to me in a note he wrote by hand in his final days. You see, Zach, Massimo was extraordinarily correct in everything he did, correct to the point of absurdity. This was why he was not very keen about demanding a greater share of royalties or removing territories or rights that you were not doing very much with. For him a deal was a deal. In the same way, he felt obligated to leave his millions to his cousin Giuseppe, who did not care about him at all, the only blood relative he kept in touch with after his mother died." Her tone has sharpened, is bitter.

"I would get a bequest and no more, not that I am complaining. He bought me the house I live in and use as an office, and set up an ironclad trust fund that would provide me with an income of two thousand dollars a week for the rest of my life with provisions made for hospital care and any expenses that would need to be met after I was gone. It was a very thoughtful and handsome bequest, although it was a tiny fraction of his fortune." Her tone is still laced with anger.

"But that is not very material anymore. What is, is the fact that the fifth book was his gift to me, to our lifelong collaboration. I have it here." She holds out a flash drive. "And according to Massimo's handwritten addendum to his will I was to allow you to read it if you came to Toronto to meet with me. You are not allowed to make any copies, you are not allowed to share it with anyone, and once you have read it you are allowed just one opportunity to make an offer for all rights except Italian rights, which I am to sell direct to the son of his Italian publisher if we are able to agree terms. I would like to tell you, Zach, that I tried very hard to dissuade Massimo from selling all the rights to you but his punctiliousness and stubbornness won the day. All I was able to wrest from him was the agreement that if you failed to make an offer that matched the one he thought was appropriate I could go elsewhere."

Zach is stunned into silence by Caryn's revelation and then his mind starts racing with questions. He manages to say, "We will pay you whatever you want!" And of course they will – even if he and Gabrijela need to sell themselves as sex slaves to raise the money.

"I am sure you will, Zach," she says smoothly, "but Massimo was very clear that your offer could only be made after you had read the manuscript. If you genuinely liked it I am at liberty to sell it to you but, as I've said, only if your offer was within ten per cent of the number he had in mind."

"Anything you say," he says, eyeing the flash drive in her hand. He wants to leap up and hug her, kiss her even, but his Indian and English propriety militates against such an unseemly display. He stays seated, says, "This is perfectly extraordinary, how very exciting!"

"It is, Zach," she says. "What does the date 21 December, 2012 mean to you?"

"Isn't it associated with doomsday scenarios?"

"Exactly. According to the Mayan calendar the world will end on that day. The Book of Revelation says something that's close enough, and other major faiths have cryptic messages that could be interpreted to mean the same thing. Massimo's final book in the quintet starts and ends on 21 December, 2012."

It was perfect, how could the concluding book not be set during the Apocalypse? They could run a year-long marketing campaign that would start as soon as they had acquired the book, that would cleverly interweave doomsday prophecies along with teasers from the book – but he was getting ahead of himself, first they had to acquire the book.

"The book is called *Storm of Angels,* and for the first time God makes an appearance along with the four archangels from the previous books. Their mission this time is to save the human race not from catastrophe but from itself."

"Judgment Day?"

"Correct, and it is a book unlike anything that has been written before on the subject – whether gospel or secular literature. In it, finally, Massimo was able to fuse his love of storytelling, his faith, and a high literary style. Do you recognize this line, Zach? 'It was a cold, clear day in April, and the clocks were striking thirteen.'"

"Orwell, *1984.*"

"Indeed. Massimo thought that was an extraordinarily perfect first sentence, especially for the sort of mood Orwell was trying to create, and the first line of his new book pays homage to the master – 'It is a cold clear day in December and in every capital in the world the clocks are striking twelve.' Naturally chaos ensues but I'm not going to take away from your pleasure in discovering the treasures of the book for yourself." She hands him the flash drive.

"Would you like some dessert? Coffee?" he asks.

"I am sure you have more important things on your mind than hanging out with me, eh," she says with a mischievous smile.

———

He finishes all 797 pages of the novel at 3:48 A.M. by the bedside clock in his room at the Empire Suites Hotel on King Street. The late hour barely registers, he has read without stopping, fuelled by more cups of coffee than he has been able to keep track of, and the combination of caffeine, engrossing storytelling, and the massive flow of adrenalin that is released when he is on the verge of a major acquisition has rendered him almost incoherent with excitement. He phones Gabrijela, it's about nine in the morning in London. She picks up her phone on the first ring, it's clear she has been waiting by the phone ever since he e-mailed her with news of his meeting with Caryn.

"So?"

"It's astonishing. The style is somewhat different, but it's quite amazing. It's got a tremendous amount of stuff in it that people can relate to because it's so contemporary: we are in the last years of Obama's first term, the Afghan war is escalating, India and Pakistan are on the brink of nuclear war, Iran and North Korea announce within weeks of each other that they have test-fired intercontinental nuclear missiles, China decides to the consternation of the G8 that its currency will no longer be pegged to the dollar –"

Gabrijela cuts in, "What about the archangels, Zach, we're not talking about a current events book here."

"Oh, I was coming to that, they are here all right, and for the first time we're also able to see the face of God. It's quite remarkable, I tell you. The narrative style is a bit more ornate than Seppi's other books but it fits the subject matter like a glove. My feeling is that this will be the biggest book of the series by some distance –"

Gabrijela interrupts him again. "What do you think she wants?"

"I said we would give her anything she wanted, but she was really specific that we should make an offer that meshes exactly with what Seppi thought the book was worth."

"Well, I've had Olive run some numbers, and he has earned around twenty-four million pounds from the four books to date, which makes it approximately seven million quid per book. What if we offered her ten million?"

That is five times his annual advances budget, he thinks. "We have to be sure that our offer is within ten per cent of the number he had in mind, give or take," he reminds her.

"Is there anything that he might have said to you, which she might have let drop yesterday, that can make us zero in on the figure?"

"Not really. I was wondering if we should work on a multiple of the 20 K we paid him for the quartet?"

"Two million, twenty million, is that what you were thinking?"

"Sort of. And I think we should probably be thinking in terms of Canadian dollars, not pounds, both Seppi and the translator were probably thinking in terms of dollars."

"Quite so."

"I'm not sure about the multiple of our first advance though."

"Fine, what about a figure based on the number of words then?"

"It's a little over 250,000 words long."

"So that gets us to two-and-a-half or twenty-five –"

"I'm not sure, Gabrijela, it's just seems too round a figure."

"So, what do you think?"

"I wish I knew. No, actually wait, you know the central conceit on which the novel is based is the day of the Apocalypse."

"Which is?"

"The 21st of December 2012."

"Which would make it 21,122,012, twenty-one million dollars and change."

"Don't the Canucks write the date the American way, with the month first?"

"I think they do which would make it 12,212,012, a tad over twelve million dollars."

"Maybe that's what he had in mind."

"Well, make the offer then, the P&L should hold it easily. I'll confirm that by e-mail in just a second, and if for any reason it's off the mark, beg, threaten, seduce, do whatever is necessary to make her sign on the dotted line. By the way, are you sure she controls the rights?"

"She says she does, apparently she has a handwritten letter or something."

"Make sure she shows it to you. I'm not going to drop twelve million dollars on this book and then find we don't have the right to publish it. Take her and whatever documentation there is to the lawyers I told you about, and make sure everything is in order before you head home. Oh and, Zach, don't get on that plane without closing this deal, OK!"

He hears her chuckle.

———

When he phones her, Caryn suggests they meet at a Tim Hortons across the street from his hotel in an hour's time. When they meet she orders a double-double for him so he can experience coffee the way Canadians like it. As they begin to sip the sweet, creamy brew, he hands her a folded sheet of hotel notepaper on which he has written down the figure that Gabrijela and he have agreed upon. The sheet of paper has no other writing on it. She opens it, stares at the number for what seems like a very long time. The tension is too much for him to bear; he takes a gulp of the coffee, scalds his tongue, winces, and almost misses the slight nod of her head. Her smile is unmistakable though.

"Seppi was right to trust you," she says simply. "You knew him better than most. The book is yours."

———

In preparation for his visit to the law firm that Gabrijela had recommended, Zach has put on a suit and he regrets it as soon as he steps out of the air-conditioned lobby of his hotel. They have decided to walk to the offices of Manning & Charles LLP, but within minutes of setting out he is sweating, the heat and the humidity of the day magnified by the pollution of the traffic-clogged streets. Fortunately they do not have far to go and are soon at the great steel and glass Bay Adelaide Centre in which the law firm is housed.

Their arrival is announced by a receptionist, and within minutes a tall pleasant-faced lawyer dressed in pinstripes takes them through a warren of cubicles to a boardroom that overlooks the lake. The room's arctic chill quickly dispels the discomfort Zach felt while walking to the appointment. Douglas Manning, who turns out to be one of the founding partners of the firm, offers them refreshments, then takes a legal pad from his briefcase and asks how he can help them.

Zach quickly sketches out the circumstances that have led Litmus to seek the firm's advice: the new manuscript, the provisions of the main will, and the addendum that gives Caryn ownership of the manuscript. Manning scribbles on his pad and does not interrupt him while he is talking. When Zach runs out of things to say, Manning turns his attention to Caryn and asks to see the letter. It is a brief scrawled note on an A4 sheet with a somewhat crabbed signature at the bottom.

After reading the note Manning asks, "Ms. Bianchi, is the signature on this document the late Mr. Seppi's?"

"It is," she says.

"Do you have any supporting evidence to prove that it is authentic? Samples of Mr. Seppi's signature, for example?"

"I do," Caryn says, and to Zach's surprise and covert admiration, she pulls out a letter and a photocopy of a cheque that Seppi had signed. An organized woman, he thinks, but she would have to be in order to be effective as Seppi's agent and literary executor. The lawyer takes the proffered items, examines them, and puts them to one side.

"These seem in order, Ms. Bianchi," he says, "but, meaning no disrespect, I am no handwriting expert and they will need to be authenticated should we find it necessary to approach the courts. I don't wish to alarm you, but the fact that Mr. Seppi's addendum was not notarized by *his* lawyer or witnessed may pose a problem. Further, there might be a conflict of interest as you are his literary executor."

He purses his lips, looks out of the window at the lake glittering in the late morning sunshine, its surface stubbled with sails, then turns back to them. "Who else could lay claim to ownership besides Mr. Seppi's cousin?"

"Nobody I can think of."

"Are you friendly with Mr. Seppi's cousin?"

"No, not really, Giuseppe and I are civil to each other but I wouldn't say we are friendly."

"Is there much money at stake here?"

"Yes," she says crisply, "potentially over ten million dollars."

Manning gazes out of the window again.

Zach chimes in. "Do you think there might be a problem?"

"Again, I have no desire to be alarmist, but when there is

so much money at stake, the potential for other interested
parties to make a claim always exists. If I might make a suggestion, perhaps Ms. Bianchi could get in touch with the
cousin and see if she could come to some sort of arrangement with him. He might not make a claim if that were to
be so."

Caryn is beginning to remonstrate but Manning calms
her down at once by saying that all he is doing is making a
suggestion – if she doesn't want to take his advice that is up
to her. But he is quite clear in his view that without a settlement she might be in for a long, expensive court battle
without a guaranteed verdict in her favour.

They discuss the meeting at the lawyer's office over coffee at
his hotel's lobby-level restaurant. Caryn is upset by Manning's
opinion, the prospect of negotiating with Seppi's cousin
makes her tremendously uncomfortable, but as they continue to discuss the situation it becomes clear to both that
it's the wisest thing to do. He offers to go with her to the
meeting. She pulls out her cellphone, calls a number, and
after a conversation that is conducted more in Italian than in
English sets up an appointment for the next day. After Caryn
has gone he phones Gabrijela and brings her up to date on
the day's events; she wishes him luck at the meeting with the
cousin and tells him to call her at any time should her help
be needed with the negotiation.

Jet lag gets him up early the next morning. He is ready

well before the appointed time and prowls around his room restlessly. Three days ago he was in London fretting about the future. Now he is in the midst of lawyers, negotiations, and possibly the biggest deal of his life. Swing it, and he can already feel the applause, smell it, hear it.

When they reach their destination, a handsome detached two-storey residence that he recognizes from his previous visits to see Seppi, Caryn parks her little VW a few doors down, and then to his surprise buries her head in her hands and begins to weep noisily. He hesitates, puts his hand on her shoulder.

"It's OK, the meeting will go well, I'm sure."

He doesn't know what else to say. A few minutes later, her sobs subside, she finds a tissue in her handbag, wipes her face, blows her nose, and turns to him, saying, "I am sorry. This is my first visit to the house after Massimo's funeral."

But, of course, the first thing the cousin would have done is move into his fancy new home. When they ring the bell, there is no evidence of her recent breakdown. Cousin Giuseppe opens the door; he is a large man, a pendulous belly overhangs his jeans.

"Ciao, Caryn," he says.

He turns to Zach. "And you are Massimo's publisher. Welcome."

He leads them to the family room that overlooks a back-yard messy with junk – a rusting lawn mower, pieces of pipe, a half-assembled bird feeder. Ugly black squirrels dart around the lawn, chittering and squeaking. The disorder outside is of a piece with the untidy rooms of the house. This was not how things were on a previous visit when the room Seppi,

Caryn, and he had met in was neat and orderly. Caryn sits on the edge of a handsome wing chair and tells Giuseppe why they are here in the mixture of Italian and English that she used when she spoke to him on the phone. Giuseppe scratches his belly under the T-shirt, yawns, and busies himself in the adjoining kitchen, making the coffee that he offered them. Once that's done he launches into an animated mono-logue, delivered entirely in Italian.

When he has said his piece Caryn says sharply, "That is unfair, Giuseppe, you know Massimo would never have stood for it." She has spoken in English for Zach's benefit.

Giuseppe shrugs, massively indifferent, and says in English, "He was my family, you were a business associate. If you don't think my terms are fair, let our lawyers talk."

She remains composed, though her colour has risen, "Very well, then, let Mr. Thomas and I discuss it, and we will get back to you."

"I'm in no hurry, Caryn."

"But we are. Mr. Thomas needs to carry word back to London about our decision."

"I'm being generous, Caryn," Giuseppe says with a smile and a wink at Zach when he thinks Caryn isn't looking. Zach doesn't let any emotion show, wonders what this gross ape has proposed. They leave without drinking their coffee. When they are back in the car, Caryn shrieks in frustration and then says, "It's unbelievable, that greedy bastard wanted ninety per cent of the advance and all future revenues."

"That's ridiculous! What did you offer him?"

"Half."

"Which is really generous, I'd have started with a quarter myself."

"So what do we do now?"

"We'll go back to Manning. Perhaps the lawyers can talk and work out a more reasonable division of the money."

"I hope Manning is tough," she says grimly. "Giuseppe's lawyer is a nightmare – you know, one of those sleazy, ambulance-chasing creatures out of central casting."

———

The negotiations drag on for two days, and Zach begins to understand that a prolonged legal negotiation is much like attending upon a critically ill patient. A lot of their time is spent worrying and waiting, getting their hopes up as bits of half-baked information leak back to them, only to have them dashed again a few hours later. The oppressive heat of the past few days has subsided, so instead of being cooped up in the hotel, they go on long walks through the city. Although the tension he is gripped by doesn't allow him to properly appreciate its many virtues – leafy ravines, well-tended neighbourhoods, a profusion of parks and flower beds, the bustle of Yonge Street and Chinatown, all of this flowing down to the dark eye of the lake – he can see why Toronto attracts so many immigrants, and features high in quality of life rankings.

The attractions of the city aside, the time spent with Caryn makes him warm to her. What a price a life spent in the service of literature can sometimes exact, he thinks, all those years of dedication to Seppi only to end up at the mercy of a greedy philistine! They are eating lunch in a cavernous dim sum restaurant in the heart of Chinatown. After instructing him in the art of eating chicken feet, laughing with delight as he gingerly begins to suck the skin and flesh off the greasy claw, she finally begins to open up about herself.

He discovers that she is a native of Montreal, and formed part of the great anglophone exodus from what was then Canada's cultural epicentre during the political disturbances of the 1970s. She had found that her master's degree in linguistics from McGill was useless for anything but a career in teaching or research, neither of which had interested her, so she had taken off to Europe where she eked out a precarious existence teaching English, waitressing, taking secretarial jobs, while making the translations that would come to dominate her life. Then the connection with Seppi came about, and she had returned to Canada and to Toronto, a city she barely knew, having lived in it only briefly before her European sojourn. She had no real friends except Seppi but returning to Montreal had not been an option. She hated how provincial it had become (although its bakeries and patisseries put Toronto's to shame), her parents had split up, and she had no lasting connections with her extended family or friends. She had stayed on in Toronto and toughed it out (she makes the merest mention of an unhappy romantic entanglement) until at long last the angels had alighted and her life had entered its happiest phase. With Seppi's death, Caryn's existence had grown unsettled again, but he hopes *Storm of Angels* will calm things down for her, assuming cousin Giuseppe doesn't play spoilsport. The next morning Giuseppe finally comes around, accepting a 75:25 split in his favour. Zach books his ticket home the same evening, thrilled with the way things have gone. Caryn, who has found a way to a grudging acceptance of the deal, drives him to the airport, and they have a drink at the bar to celebrate. The onrush of positive energy that accompanies the successful culmination of a deal is one of the highs that publishers and writers share unreservedly. Together they toast Seppi, themselves, and the future of their book. When it's time to go he gives Caryn a hug (any distance that existed between them has disappeared), and makes his way to the boarding gate still wrapped in a soaring sense of well-being. Onwards and upwards, he thinks, onwards and upwards, and the thought stays with him as the plane floats free of the blaze of light that is Toronto and points for home.

PART TWO

Always in your mind keep Ithaca
To arrive there is your destiny.

– from "Ithaca" by C.P. Cavafy

5.

FRANKFURT

M ortimer Weaver fishtails ineffectually above the heavy-haunched publisher of Globish's New Woman imprint in the bedroom of his suite at the Hessischer Hof. Ever since he had a quadruple bypass operation two years ago, despite his doctors' assurances, he hasn't been able to perform as he once was able to in bed, but like the muscle memory of top-flight athletes his sexual instinct remains undimmed. One of its manifestations is the revolving door of women in his life, especially at the Frankfurt Book Fair where, safe from the prying eyes of his colleagues in New York, he has conducted a variety of sexual adventures.

After a while he stops flopping around on top of his partner, says with as much remorse as he can, "Sorry, my dear, jet lag is the very devil," and clambers off. As she is getting dressed a famous line from an Allen Ginsberg poem pops into his head, and he wonders in how many other hotel rooms in the city this scene is being repeated, hopefully with more satisfactory result. The well-known cliché about Frankfurt – that its whores go on holiday when the book fair comes to town because all the publishing folk are busy fucking each other, both literally and metaphorically – is based on more than just industry folklore.

After his colleague has left for her own room, Mortimer sprawls on a sofa and turns his attention to his first appointment tomorrow, a breakfast meeting with an old flame and the current CEO of Litmus, a company that has been in his sights for almost two years now. The problem is Gabrijela will not sell unless her hand is forced; what she does not know is that her chairman, Sir William Boyce, is on the point of capitulating, and once Mortimer has a majority shareholding it will only be a matter of time before Globish will be able to ingest all of Litmus. The fact that Litmus has just acquired a new Seppi is both good news and bad news – he will have to raise his offer but he can reassure Globish's board, and especially his boss, Greg Holmes, the majority shareholder of Globish's parent company, Amadeus Inc., with the news that he will be bringing one of the hottest properties in the publishing world into the Globish fold.

He will make the usual promises to Gaby – that she can stay on as CEO, that the company's independence will be guaranteed and so on – none of which he will be able to keep, and if she is smart she will know that. Inevitably the time will arrive when with a genuine show of sadness (even he is surprised by how sincere his insincerity can often seem) he will fire her, sweep the parts of the company he no longer has any use for into the trash can and fit the remaining bits into the increasingly bewildering patchwork that is now Globish Inc. The acquisition of Litmus should see him well on his way to achieving his goal (and also, it must be said, that of his boss) – overtaking all the companies that are bigger than his own – Macmillan, HarperCollins, Simon & Schuster, Penguin, Hachette, and Random House – until he stands alone on the summit.

For a fleeting moment he thinks that once he would have hesitated to press home his advantage – after all, he thinks of Gaby as a friend, and they have shared a bed – but he thrusts the thought aside ruthlessly. Loyalty, he had decided decades ago, was an overrated virtue. The time when publishing was a business conducted by gentlemen was long gone. Authors weren't loyal to agents or editors, agents weren't loyal to editors or publishers, publishers dumped authors, and chief executives dumped colleagues. No big deal, it was all part of doing business.

Mortimer might not have been as cynical in his view of the world if he hadn't been at the receiving end of treachery early in his career. He had always known he would make something of himself. His father was a successful executive at an insurance company, and Mortimer and his three sisters had grown up in an affluent neighbourhood on the south side of Glasgow. He had been sent to an expensive public school not far from home, which he had hated for its insistence on swims in icy lochs and rivers and other activities designed to toughen its students (he had never been especially athletic). He had also been humiliated on more than one occasion by the upper-class toffs and minor royalty who were the ruling elite at the school; a clever and sensitive boy, Mortimer couldn't wait to see the day when he would leave them all far behind. After passing out of school, he had fled to America, where class and lineage were not prerequisites for success, and managed to obtain an MBA in marketing from Harvard Business School, the only springboard an ambitious young man needed at the time to launch himself into the corporate world. He was soon earning an excellent salary with a securities firm on Wall Street. He met and married the first of his three wives, a Korean-American woman called Barbara Chang, a colleague at his firm, and seemed set for a comfortable if undistinguished career in the corporate world. He began to think of himself as Morty, an essential first step in the process of Americanization, although he was too smart to become a parody of himself like the upper-class British twit in Tom Wolfe's *Mid-Atlantic Man*.

Two years later, his father had died of a heart attack and his wife had left him (the events were unrelated), and Mortimer found himself back in Glasgow sorting out his family's affairs. He landed a job with a bank in his home city, married again, a Glaswegian this time, and his life seemed to have recovered its stability. Soon enough, though, Mortimer was bored. Glasgow was too small to contain his ambition; he found his wife, Mary, provincial and dull; football and beer bored him. After a few years of trying to settle down, he threw over both wife and job for yet another fresh start, this time with a leading entertainment company in London, where he soon rose to head a TV channel. He was thirty-four years old and headed for the big time. He loved the energy and unpredictability of the TV business, and the creative people he associated with (during his time at public school he had distinguished himself in elocution and debating competitions and had toyed with becoming a writer, although he discarded the idea when he realized that success wasn't guaranteed). He was also delighted that he was one of just two candidates for the top job at the group's TV division when the incumbent retired. His competition was his best friend at the company, James, who headed the international sales and licensing department. The public school he had attended, despite his dislike of it, had instilled in Morty a very strong sense of fair play, and although he competed vigorously with James every move he made was above board.

"Treachery" is derived from the Old French *trecherie*, which means to cheat or deceive, and it is something most of us experience in one form or the other at some point in our lives. If we are lucky, the consequences will not be too extreme and we will pick ourselves up and keep going with only the tiniest scar, but sometimes betrayal can have a cata-strophic effect. We cannot guard against treachery because it is *always* perpetrated by someone we trust, and so when James accused Morty of diverting a substantial amount of money from a business deal to his own bank account, he was taken completely unawares. He was so shocked by his friend's perfidy that he didn't put up a fight, but from that point onwards Morty would never completely trust anyone again – especially at work.

He resigned his job, obtained a position with a publishing company, and it was at this time that he met and became infatuated with Gabrijela. Their affair was intense but brief; they were both much too aggressive and competitive to make a go of it, although they continued to be friends after a fashion. A year before his fortieth birthday, Morty decided that if he needed to make his mark he would need to accelerate his climb up the corporate ladder. He quit his publishing job and over the next decade he zigged and zagged through the management jungle. He learned to play the corporate game to perfection – forming necessary alliances, surrounding himself with loyalists, sucking up to those above, dealing with threats to his pre-eminence ruthlessly, changing jobs every three years on average – with his eyes always fixed on his goal of getting the top job at a major global corporation, ideally in one of the creative industries (movies, TV, books, or media) by the time he turned fifty. He missed his target by two years, but at the age of fifty-two, Mortimer Weaver became President of Globish Inc. He married again, this time picking his spouse, Madeleine, an Englishwoman, for her social connections, but when that marriage began to come apart at the seams after seven months, he abandoned all notions of leading a settled life on the home front.

Now his only ambition was to make Globish the largest and most powerful company in its field. When that happened he would finally be where he wanted to be. And if there were ever a place he would want that coronation to take place it would be Frankfurt. He loved everything about the Frankfurt Book Fair. The fact that it was over five hundred years old. Attracted almost three hundred thousand visitors over five days. Held over three thousand events. Hosted more than seven thousand exhibitors from over a hundred countries in 170,000 square metres of space spread out behind the familiar landmark of the "Hammering Man." And although Turin and Calcutta might claim more visitors, no book fair was bigger, more important, and more prestigious than Frankfurt.

Statistics aside, Frankfurt was where Mortimer felt most acutely his Master of the Universe status, it was where his keen mind ticked even more keenly, the spring in his step belied all the infirmities and reverses that the aging human body was prone to, and his predatory instincts were sharpened to the point where he knew that every time he went for the jugular he would not miss the mark.

———

On the first day of the fair he shaves his round head carefully. Once upon a time he had felt acutely the lack of a distinguished mane, but that is no longer the case – his natural arrogance asserted itself soon enough, and he now holds his distinctive head high. Having satisfied himself that his pate is bald and gleaming, he admires it for a minute or two in the mirror. How magnificently it sweeps back from his forehead; smooth, without any knobby bits, his is a head to inspire awe and envy. It even makes up for his lack of inches – what a presence he would have been if he'd only been taller! He towels off, brushes his teeth with care. He runs his fingers over the raised scar on his chest, lasting evidence of his heart operation; he had initially felt diffident taking off his shirt while making love to his various lady friends but he has got over that too. The scar is one more piece of evidence that Mortimer Weaver can overcome anything that's thrown at him.

He puts on his Brioni suit, expertly knots his Hermes tie, give his Lobb shoes a quick wipe with a shoeshine cloth to make sure they gleam even brighter – these details are important to him, symbolizing as they do his reinvention of himself from an upper-class Brit in ill-fitting suits, unshined shoes, food-speckled tie, and socks without elastic into a sharply dressed American executive. Encased in his armour, Mortimer strides out of his suite to do battle with Gaby. He has magnanimously agreed to have breakfast with her at the Marriott where she is staying; no longer seeking the home turf advantage when it comes to business dealings, he doesn't care where he fights.

At the hotel coffee shop, which is filled with assorted publishing types whom he affects not to know – the elite gather at the Hessischer Hof and the Frankfurter Hof, and the rest simply do not count – he spots Gaby sitting at a table by the window. He is faintly annoyed that she is not alone. He gets to the table, pecks her on the cheek (he feels a slight twinge of desire when he notices that she is looking good, the short haircut suits her, as does the classically cut navy blue dress with just the merest hint of cleavage), and discovers that the man with her is her publisher, Zachariah Thomas. Mortimer has never met him, but knows him by reputation as the editor behind the *Angels* phenomenon. Maybe it is not a bad thing he is here, Mortimer thinks: if he does manage to acquire Litmus, the publisher will be one of the assets he will be looking to keep, especially if he has any more Seppi titles up his sleeve.

Scarcely has he taken a bite of the croissant he has ordered than Gaby in her forthright way, a trait he admired about her when they were together, says that he can forget about adding Litmus to the Globish empire. She is about to issue a press release to announce the acquisition of a brand new *Angels* title to which they have world rights and which they intend to crash out in a couple of months – the company's 2009 top line, bottom line and cash flow are all assured, and he can forget about wooing any shareholders into parting with their holdings.

Mortimer has known this for months (it is hard to keep anything really quiet in the world of publishing, especially to someone with his resources), but he pretends he does not know, and says with just the slightest hint of disappointment showing on his broad face that he is delighted for her and for Litmus. He adds that he would even be content to be a minority shareholder; he thinks it is part of the corporate responsibility of bigger companies to encourage small independents to survive.

"We are not a small indie, Morty," Gabrijela says tartly. "And if I were you I would worry about your own company; in these changing times, I think its vast, bloated companies like yours that are at the most risk."

His smile grows broader. "Oh, we're in better shape than ever," he says mildly. "Our results this quarter are our strongest in ten years."

"I'm sure they are," she says sweetly, "I know how you guys manipulate your balance sheet and forecasts."

He loves the way she is utterly unafraid to do battle with him; if only the circumstances had been different, perhaps they could have made a go of it. He holds the thought for a moment, luxuriates in it, and then regretfully lets it go. He is unusually congenial for the rest of the breakfast and even deigns to have a word or two with the publisher, whom he had barely glanced at when the meeting had started. When breakfast is over he kisses Gaby on the cheek, nods to Zach, and strides off towards the Globish booth.

"So, what did you think?" Gabrijela asks as they watch Mortimer's broad back recede.

"He didn't seem to notice I was around," Zach says.

"Typical Morty," she says. "He's the ultimate starfucker. Likes to hang out with the rich and famous and powerful, but of course he has to occasionally tolerate us plebs. He can turn on the charm when he wants to, but otherwise you're part of the furniture so far as he is concerned."

"He didn't seem to be put out that you had the new Seppi."

"That means nothing. Once Morty has set his heart on something, he'll keep trying to get it – it's one of his few weaknesses, he hates being thwarted. Oh no, he'll up his price, keep working on William and the others. I don't think we've seen the last of him."

"Aren't you concerned?"

"Of course I'm concerned but there's not a whole lot I can do, beyond what we're already doing. Keep on fighting, keep the company healthy and prosperous, and hope we can maintain a united front."

"And if he succeeds despite everything?"

"I'll be out of a job, that's for sure, but I think you'll be fine: he will have the good sense to realize that if he is acquiring Litmus it's not just for Seppi and the other authors he wants, it is for those who found them in the first place. Anyway, let's not worry about any of that now, let's get to our stall, I'm dying to see our angels."

———

The nerve centre of Frankfurt Book Fair, the place in which the most lucrative deals are struck, is Halle 8, where the US and UK publishers are located. In the warren of stalls, the spots where the Big Seven publishers have pitched their tents are vast, spreading oases of opulence. While the smaller fry have to make do with cramped stalls, and indifferent food and drink purchased from surly wait staff at the food stations dotted throughout the hall, the big companies have gourmet sandwiches and food served to staff and their guests, a functioning office, and dozens of tables arranged throughout their acreage at which business is conducted without pause. Shelves are filled with top-of-the-line bestsellers, life-sized posters display the faces of star authors, and enormous blowups of their logos proclaim their might to every passerby.

When Mortimer walks up to his stall, the sight of the Globish logo, a cougar looking over its shoulder, fills him with pride, and the furious activity taking place within the stall touches a chord within him. He loves the sight of the "little people," as he refers to them privately, scurrying around and swelling the coffers of Globish Inc. with their labours, insignificant though they may be. (When he makes his speeches at company gatherings or addresses them in the letters he writes to all employees every month, these lowly employees are transformed into "valued members of the Globish family." He is only too aware of the irony given the mess he has made of his own personal life, but he knows such hypocrisy is another aspect of the corporate game he has to play.) He feels genuinely choked up for a moment – *they are doing all this for me!* – briefly forgetting that he thinks every one of the people he employs is eminently disposable. This is not unusual, for one of Mortimer's greatest assets, built up over the years, is his effortless ability to reconcile the various contradictions that make up his psyche. He is entirely sincere when he tells a young executive receiving a promotion that he "will be CEO one day," and he is just as sincere when he informs the same manager a year later that he has no option but to get rid of him because he has to lay off ten per cent of the managerial cadre.

He makes his way to his table at the centre of the stall and beckons to one of the hard-pressed women at reception to send in his first appointment of the day, an eminent Korean publisher. The fact that they do not have a language in common is nothing more than a minor inconvenience; he likes Mr. Park and is generally approving of the way Asian CEOs conduct themselves. There is no pretence at egalitarianism, they accept the bowing and scraping that their exalted position entitles them to, and there is none of this nonsense about pandering to the needs of subordinates. He remembers his visit to Mr. Park in Seoul, the ceremonial feast that was held in his honour, the army of formally dressed subordinates who sprang to carry out the slightest wish of the chairman – he can quite easily imagine himself running a company in Seoul. They chat for a while and then Mr. Park leaves after some confusion: Mortimer bows and his guest sticks out his hand, and then they reverse their greetings, before finally managing to grasp hands in a desperate gesture of farewell. A Norwegian publisher takes his place, followed by German, Japanese, and British publishers in quick succession. Their conversations are vague, for the truth is that Mortimer's presence at the stall is wholly unnecessary – he is a showpiece, he is not a worker like the others; he is here to bestow a lordly gesture upon some unctuous underling, or smile benevolently as a visitor rattles off some incomprehensible request in Croatian or German.

When he first arrived at Globish, Mortimer drove his vice presidents and other subordinates crazy by insisting on doing actual work, before he realized that his role was not that at all – he was expected to come up with big-picture strategy, get on planes, make well-crafted speeches, look grave (but remain silent) when serious business matters were discussed, and be an equally silent spectator to the strings of e-mails that he was copied on every single minute of the day. When he was pressed for a decision, he had learned to say, "I will get back to you." If the matter was unimportant it would soon be forgotten; if it was important, somebody else should be seen to be making the decision so that he could shrug off all responsibility if it turned out to be unworthy or unwise.

Just after the last visitor of the morning departs, a harassed-looking girl comes up with a message that his limo is waiting to carry him off to lunch with the director of the Frankfurt Book Fair, and Mortimer leaves Halle 8 for the day.

———

Two rows away from the Globish stall, in a much smaller, far less opulent space, Zach has had hardly a moment off, as an unending stream of visitors flocks to his table, galvanized by news of the fifth *Angels* novel. Few rights are left unsecured: they have sold the book to every one of the forty-eight publishers who have published the previous novels, in keeping with Seppi's wishes; he has left it to his rights director to sell any further territories in which there has been interest and she has already sold Farsi and Vietnamese rights, and is negotiating with a Serbian publisher.

He snatches a sandwich and a Coke between appointments and settles in for a long day of repeating the same story over and over again. Although this becomes deadly dull after the first few repetitions he doesn't mind, this is what every publisher dreams about, to be at the very centre of the excitement that sweeps the world when a book begins to command an extraordinary following. His next appointment is with Kaisa, the Finnish publisher of Seppi whom he had channelled momentarily during his holiday in Thimphu. She is a dark-haired, whip-smart woman with violet eyes, a startling hue that he thought was unique to Liz Taylor. She brings up a subject that many of the publishers have discussed with him – the thematic shift and striking change of style in *Storm of Angels*.

"Does the content concern you?" she asks.

"Not at all," he says. "It is more political than its predecessors because it is the only one of Seppi's novels to be set in our times, and it cannot have been otherwise. If the others weren't historical novels you might have considered them to be rather more political than they seem to be."

"And the style?"

"Well, it is a second draft that his translator tidied up and made ready for publication, so it didn't get the repeated revisions that the other novels had. Besides writers' styles do change over time –"

"So, you have no concerns there?"

"Umm, no . . . Caryn had more input than might have otherwise been the case but you shouldn't worry."

"No, I'm not worried, not really," she says doubtfully.

After she leaves, he looks at his schedule, sees he has a few minutes for a quick bathroom break. He hopes the queue won't be too long and is just about to get up from his table when a voice hails him cheerfully from behind.

"Zach, hi, hope you have a moment – I won't take too much of your time." He recognizes the voice and steels himself. No Frankfurt is complete without a meeting with Arthur Blayney, although Zach has never set up these appointments. Unfortunately, the Welshman is a published writer who is not literary enough nor commercial enough nor high profile enough to have made a breakthrough in commercial or artistic terms. To make matters worse, Arthur insists on coming to Frankfurt every year, with his sling bag stuffed with paperback editions of his published books, folders of clippings, a laptop with the scripts of his next two books that have been turned down dozens of times, in the forlorn hope that he might be adopted by some kind publisher or agent, despite the fact that for as long Zach has known him he has met with no success whatsoever. But it's not just unsuccessful writers like Arthur who should stay away from Frankfurt, thinks Zach. He is of the view that no author should *ever* visit the fair, unless he or she belongs to the hallowed one per cent who are the toast of the profession. He cannot think of a place more disheartening or inhospitable to the average writer. Tens of thousands of people working themselves to the bone ostensibly in the service of authors, but when you come right down to it unless you are a VIEW, or Very Important Eminent Writer, the words *author* and *writer* are mere abstractions in the context of Frankfurt. Here, all the soldiers and generals of the publishing corps are engaged in the serious battle of books as a business, and the talent is at best a distraction, at worst an irritant.

Writers like Arthur who belong to the dead zone of once-published midlist authors should come no closer to Frankfurt than the airport for all the difference their presence makes. Zach suppresses his irritation and listens as the large, shambling man, with his round face, sad, brown Labrador eyes and unctuous smile, delivers his familiar litany of woe — indifferent publishers, vicious reviewers, unaware readers. He has heard this all before, you don't get to be a publisher without having had to deal with writers who feel under-appreciated, but most of the writers he deals with are not like Arthur – twenty years after he was first published the man still doesn't seem to get that there isn't a vast conspiracy working against him and his effulgent genius.

"Did you know," Arthur is whining, "one publisher said of *Lolita,* 'I recommend it be buried under a stone for a thousand years.'"

There are a number of obvious things he could say to this. First, Arthur Blayney is *not* Vladimir Nabokov. Second, there are other equally impressive stories of publishers' idiocy – Stephen King, John le Carré, John Grisham, J.K. Rowling, Anaïs Nin, Joseph Heller were all rejected by publishers at the beginning of their careers – but it doesn't prove a thing beyond the fact that in a notoriously subjective and inexact business mistakes will sometimes be made. Third, for every story of ignorance and bad taste there are hundreds of thousands of stories of writers who might have remained unsung if they hadn't been published with diligence, devotion, and vision.

He chooses to say nothing, because to say anything would be to prolong the conversation. He manages to slip away eventually when Apoorva turns up at his table, even though he knows that upon his return to London he will be inundated by self-pitying e-mails and Facebook posts. Arthur's problem, not mine, he thinks.

———

As this is Apoorva's first fair he has promised to take some time off to walk around Halle 8 with her, give her a feel for the place, introduce her to people she might find useful. Not that he thinks his support is critical; he has caught a glimpse of her from time to time passionately espousing the cause of her launch list to the people she is meeting with and is impressed by how confident she seems. As they walk along, peering into stalls, stopping for impromptu meetings with friends and colleagues in the hallways, he thinks that this Wordsworthian ramble through the publishing countryside, where every form of creativity is on display, from the striking photo books of Taschen and Thames & Hudson to the latest offering from hallowed imprints like Faber and Knopf, is the part of the Frankfurt experience he likes the best. If you're a publishing professional, no matter how tedious the business of selling and buying rights can be, you cannot fail to be energized by the power of the industry you are part of at a place like Frankfurt – if the book is dead, if publishers are history, you wouldn't know it here. Everywhere you look there are dozens of publishing people, Poles, Australians, Egyptians, Indians, Canadians, Japanese, and other nationalities that he can't even begin to guess at, all with one goal: the dissemination of books and literature. What other business can even begin to compare with publishing, its richness, its variety, and its place at the very core of humanity's cultural soul.

Only the previous week he had spent an exceedingly drunken evening with one of his novelists who had been shortlisted for a minor award. At one point, tears leaking from his eyes, Charlie had leaned over and said to Zach how fortunate he felt to be a novelist, the most recent in a long line of writers dating back to Shakespeare and even further beyond to when the first stories were told, each generation handing down its custodianship of the story to the next generation. As he thinks about his meeting with Charlie, in the middle of the organized chaos that is Frankfurt, Zach has an epiphany. He sees a river of stories, its headwaters stretching all the way to a time before time, to the beginnings of the human race when the first stories were told to a small band of listeners. Over the ages the river swelled and split off into hundreds and thousands of tributaries, and as it did so there came into being a group of people who were charged with channelling the flow to readers, removing obstructions, plugging leaks, filtering out impurities. And in the future, as the Internet really comes into its own, into being the ocean into which all these rivers would eventually flow, the need for publishers to regulate the dispersal of humanity's stories to readers would only grow.

He has read somewhere that it is estimated that something like 146 million books have been published since records started being kept, and every year a couple of million more are added. If you added in all the people who write in the online space, the ocean of stories would become a tidal wave, a tsunami that would drown its intended audience without dedicated publishing professionals to tame it, make sure it got to consumers in a way that best suited them. He recalls the argument he got into with that obnoxious professor in Delhi (so much has happened since that encounter that it seems a very long time ago, although barely three months have passed). He thinks, as he did back then, that Malik had got it wrong. Zach has no doubt that as time goes by the boundaries will become blurred, with retailers, agents, publishers, all those who purvey the work of those who create it, evolving into different versions of themselves but there will still be a role for them.

Just then they run into the Archangel Gabriel. Eight feet tall, with golden wings, and balls of fire shooting from his hands, he looks spectacular. There are three other archangels wandering around the fair. The walkabout signals the beginning of an ambitious marketing campaign for *Storm of Angels* that will cover every possible marketing channel – print, television, online, digital downloads, movie screens, outdoor, transit, video streaming and bundling, in addition to bookstore promotions. The "Reach Out and Touch an Angel" campaign will revolve around the four archangels (in keeping with the book's premise, God will be known only by his absence until the moment of revelation). And here is where it has all begun, with these four stilt walkers from a circus in Hamburg, covered in non-toxic gold, silver, bronze, and emerald body paint, handing out goody bags containing an *Angels* T-shirt, a halo, a sample chapter, and for twenty-five lucky customers a day a Kindle loaded with the first five sections of the twenty-five-section tome. He watches Gabriel make his stately way down the aisle, then catches sight of his watch, bids Apoorva goodbye, takes a quick bathroom break – to his good fortune the queues aren't long – and heads for his appointment with Julia at the agents centre in Halle 6.

The Literary Agents and Scouts Centre has the best security of the fair. Uniformed guards ask Zach to show his ID and to state his business, with precise details as to with whom he has an appointment. Needy authors like Arthur Blayney do not stand a chance of gaining admittance. These days it is inordinately difficult to secure a good agent; you can always self-publish, but as publishers cut back on their lists, the only way to secure a triple-A publisher is to find yourself an agent who can deliver the sale.

The centre is a vast barnlike space with tables arranged in horizontal rows. There are no walled-off cubicles or stalls as in the publishers' halls, and every agent can look around and see which of her colleagues is having a successful fair and how she stacks up against the rest. He is early for his meeting with Julia and when he sees she is deep in conversation with two serious-faced Dutch publishers – he knows them slightly – he goes for a stroll around the place, reading the names of the agents on the signs that mark each row. The established ones are predictably enough very busy but he can see more than a few with nothing to do, gazing out into space, either eating something (at Frankfurt everyone is eating or drinking all the time) or falling back on that old staple, reading a book. He wonders how many of the smaller agents will be back next year – the hotels are scandalously over-priced and if you add up the cost of the flights, rentals, and the like, along with dwindling advances, the Cassandras are probably right: the best days of Frankfurt, London, the BEA in New York, and every other rights fair, big and small, may well be over. He remembers a time when on the eve of

Frankfurt every agent would flood publishers with their best submissions of the year, hoping enough would bite so that a heated auction could take place, with the winner more often than not paying seven or eight times what the book was worth. Those days are over, but he wouldn't write Frankfurt off just yet. This year the digital revolution is the focus of the fair and its leading proponents have gathered here, a sign that the fair, which is as old as Gutenberg and has insouciantly negotiated every convulsion in the publishing business, will probably figure out a way to ride the digital wave successfully as well.

He sees the Dutch publishers with Julia rising from their seats, kissing her cheeks one-two-three times, and leaving. She glances around, waves him over. She looks impossibly fresh in a dress that is both light and formal, and he thinks the same thing he thinks every time he sees her after an absence – there is nothing he wouldn't do to win her back.

———

He has already taken the first major step in that direction at some cost to himself. After his return from Toronto he had finally managed to summon up the resolve to break up with Mandy. Over pizzas at an Italian restaurant, he had said his piece without equivocating as he had in the past, and he was grateful she had absorbed the news without throwing a tantrum. They had parted civilly enough and he had felt a great sense of relief not unmixed with guilt as she walked towards her Tube station. Within a week she revealed an unexpected side to her personality; he discovered that she had managed to hack into his computer and send a message full of squalid fabrications about him to everyone on his Contacts list. She had followed that up with phone calls to anyone who was willing to listen to her stories about his unconscionable behaviour. He had never given the relationship a chance, but this was contemptible. He had been surprised by the calm manner in which she had received his announcement that it was over, and although he had been preparing himself for the possibility that she might lash out at him, he was blindsided by the dishonesty and malevolence of her reaction. Although Julia was upset on his behalf, she had counselled restraint, as had most of his close friends. A few had suggested he retaliate in kind, but after giving the matter sufficient thought he had decided it would be beneath him to do so; the best course was to put as much distance as he could between himself and the drama that was being enacted.

As the weeks passed Julia's attitude towards him began to soften perceptibly. She still refused to move in with him, but when he had proposed that at some point in the future, Christmas maybe, she might consider doing so, she had said she would think about it seriously.

———

"God, I love the Dutch," Julia says happily as he takes his seat at her table. "After all these years I still don't know how they do it. Such a tiny country, and yet I'm sure they buy more foreign fiction than any other country in the world per capita, and make it work. And they continue to pay decent advances."

"So I guess your UEA chap is going well."

"Better than well, Zach. I've just sold him to the wonderful people at Haarlem after an auction between three publishers drove the advance to more than twice the floor I'd set."

"That's fantastic."

"Yep, and there's interest in three more territories, which if I manage to close will take the total up to seven. The new McEwan they are calling him."

"Now all you need is for him to get on to the shortlist of the Booker and you're all set—"

"Hey, don't go saying that, you'll attract the evil eye," she says grinning, the English irregularity of her teeth giving her a waifish charm. He is so happy for her, he so wants to be with her, he so wants her to be happy with him, he feels his head could burst with the emotion of it all.

"Have dinner with me tonight," he blurts.

She frowns. "You know I can't do that, Zach. Why, what's the matter? Why can't this wait until we get back to London – you know I have a packed schedule. I still don't get how one is expected to sell a book in something like thirty seconds to a prospective publisher."

He laughs. "You know, I was talking to this Israeli publisher who said he could tell in ten seconds whether a book was going to work in his market or not."

"Good thing people seem to like my guy. But non-stop pitching takes a lot out of you!"

"I know, I just thought you might want to take some time off."

She looks at him as if he were mad. "You can't be serious, this is Frankfurt. Don't you have any appointments this evening?"

He does, a dinner that he must go to with the German publisher of *Storm of Angels*. But he had hoped in an impulsive moment that he and Julia could just have a quiet, intimate dinner together.

"I do," he says grumpily.

"Oh, come on, Zach, don't be a bore." Seeing that he still looks unhappy, she makes a face, pulls out her BlackBerry, checks her schedule, and says, "OK, maybe I could do an after-dinner drink. Just one, all right?"

His mood lightens immediately. "Woo-hoo," he says, "you're on."

"Hey, I saw the Archangel Gabriel wandering about here earlier today. He looks sensational, but how did he get through security?"

"Come on – he's an archangel."

She laughs. "You're the toast of the fair, Zach. This morning I opened the daily newsletter and who should I see but Seppi on the front page."

"Yes, it's been great. Seven Star Studios just bought the option, and they're going to fast-track the movie for a Christmas release next year."

"When do you launch the book?"

"We're hoping to drop it in for Christmas this year, we'll do the movie tie-in next Christmas, mass market the year after, and on the day the world officially comes to an end we're proposing to launch the trade paperback – a hundred lucky winners get a ticket to heaven with the archangels as escorts."

"You're joking!"

"I just made that up," he confesses, "but why not? By the time December 2012 rolls around the crazies will have amped up doomsday scenarios to such an extent that a free pass to Heaven might not seem too implausible. Perhaps we could get Virgin to provide the spacecraft to get there."

"You're nuts, you know that, don't you?"

"Only about you," he says.

"OK, you're going to have to go now, I can see the worthies of Gallimard approaching. See you this evening."

———

In all the years he has been visiting Frankfurt he has never been to an authentic German eatery, preferring like most foreign visitors to limit his choice to more familiar cuisines – Italian (good), Japanese (just once and it was awful, for some reason most of the food had a sweetish taste) and Thai (not bad). Upon hearing of this gaping hole in his gastronomic experience of the city, Dieter, Seppi's German publisher, has suggested they meet at a restaurant that has been serving authentic Hessian food for over two hundred years.

After he has showered and changed for dinner, he joins one of the unending queues for taxis outside the hotel. A thin evil rain is falling. He has barely been in line for a few minutes before a Canadian publisher whom he had just missed during his visit to Toronto hauls him out of it. He insists that Zach have a drink with him. Zach demurs briefly before they go back into the lobby, where they join a genial group of Canucks, some of whom he knows. His friend introduces him to the people he doesn't know, orders two whiskies, and joins the conversation, which seems to be about an agent prone to erratic behavior. From there the discussion drifts to an order fulfillment problem that all are facing back home. Zach finds it heavy going, and after ten minutes or so when there is no sign of the subject being abandoned, he is about to excuse himself and leave when the whisky he has forgotten has been ordered for him arrives.

He pours in some soda from a beaker on the table, takes a swig, and almost gags at the hideously sweet taste. Fucking German whisky, he thinks, but he does not want to appear rude, so he continues to sip from his glass and listen in on the conversation, which continues to bore the hell out of him. Finally, he can take it no longer. He sets his glass down and whispers to his friend that he is leaving.

"What whisky is this?" he asks as he gets up to go.

"Oh, I don't know some single malt, Macallan, I think."

"Does it taste odd to you?"

"No, why?"

"Mine did it was kind of sweet."

He points to his glass. His friend's eyes fall on the beaker next to it that he has been using to dilute the liquor.

"Christ, Zach, you must have a serious case of Frankfurt fatigue. No wonder your whisky tasted sweet, you've been mixing it with lime cordial." He leaves with their laughter ringing in his ears.

———

He takes a taxi to Sachsenhausen, bypassing the queue outside the Marriott by walking to the train station close by and quickly finding a cab there. He finds Dieter waiting for him outside the Wagner restaurant. It's chilly so they decide not to dine on the patio but to look for a place inside.

"Mein gott," Dieter mutters as they make their way into the astonishingly loud, crowded room, "I haven't been here for a year, I've forgotten how busy it can get."

Nobody pays the slightest attention to them; the burly waiters carrying huge platters of food seem exceptionally harassed.

"Come on," Dieter says, and wades into the room, heading for one of the long wooden tables at the back that already has four loud-voiced patrons occupying it. At one end, there is space for two more.

"This place doesn't take reservations after six so I hope you don't mind sharing a table," Dieter yells.

"Hey, no problem. After visiting the fair for ten years, I figure it's about time I had an authentic Frankfurt dining experience."

"Oh, you'll get that my friend, don't you worry. I hope you like meat, lots of it."

Dieter flings his coat on a hook on the wall, indicates to Zach that he should do the same, and takes his seat at the table. Zach follows suit. The big, red-faced fellow next to him gives him a friendly nod, then turns back to his companions, all of whom are talking at the same time.

"You'll let me order, ja? No dietary restrictions?"

Zach shakes his head.

"Apfelwein?"

"Never drunk it."

"Well, give it a try. Only don't drink too much, you'll get – how do you say it? – the runs."

"I'll give it a go, I've drunk whisky mixed with lime cordial this evening, I don't see why I shouldn't try apfelwein."

"Wunderbar!"

Dieter grabs hold of a passing waiter, orders their drinks and food, and settles back, giving Zach a huge grin. "I hope you've brought along a big appetite, you're going to need it," he says.

The apfelwein arrives within minutes in a large ceramic pitcher. The waiter puts down two glasses with a diamond-pane pattern next to the wine, and is gone without any ceremony.

"Not exactly the Hessischer Hof," Dieter shouts, "but you won't get anything more authentic anywhere in Germany. They boast that they have been making their wine and food the same way for more than a hundred years."

Zach takes a deep swig from his glass. The wine tastes like a combination of filtered lager and apple juice with a sour aftertaste. Dieter has been watching and asks whether he likes it. "Tastes just fine," he yells.

While they wait for the food to arrive they carry on a shouted conversation. Dieter tells him that while the German book industry is in somewhat better shape than a few years earlier, the current recessionary trends, along with the changing nature of the marketplace, means that every major publisher has to fight to stay afloat, never mind increasing profit.

"I must thank you, my friend," he says, raising his glass in a toast. "Without *Storm of Angels* I don't think I would have been able to make my sales number this year." He explains that he has collapsed his translation and production schedule in order to have the book out by Christmas. Zach tells him about the movie deal that has just gone through, and Dieter beams with happiness. He leans across the table and says, "You know my deepest regret until *Storm of Angels* came along was that I didn't bid enough for Hilary Mantel when I had the chance a few years ago. Have you read *Wolf Hall?*

Zach shakes his head.

"It's a great book, the best novel I've read this year. I think it will win the Booker."

The food arrives quickly; they have scarcely been here fifteen minutes. On an enormous white platter are piled mounds of meat – pork sausages, grilled pig's knuckles, pork belly, and other bits and pieces he can't identify – with heaping sides of sauerkraut and fried onions. Nary a green vegetable in sight. Dieter looks amused as he sees Zach eyeing the mountain of animal protein.

"When in Germany . . ." Dieter says, and tucks his napkin into his collar.

Zach remembers a night in Singapore, somewhere on the water, where after donning a huge white bib he had waded into some of the biggest crabs he had ever seen in his life.

This will require a similar effort, he thinks. He takes a long swig at the apfelwein, mimics Dieter and dives in. Forty-five minutes later, there is still enough food on the serving dish to fill a decent-sized stroller or feed a starving refugee family (pick your nationality) of four.

"I'm done, Dieter," he says.

His host cups a hand to his ear.

"I'm done. *Basta!*" he roars. Dieter smiles, and asks if he would like dessert or coffee. "Just coffee, my friend, just coffee," he says weakly.

Later, as he waits on the pavement outside the restaurant for the taxi Dieter has summoned, he reckons he has never in his life eaten so much meat at one sitting. His stomach is distended and he feels as ungainly as a hippo.

"What's this I hear about Litmus being sold?" Dieter asks, lighting a cigarette.

Fuck, Zach thinks, Frankfurt, a place where nothing is sacred, no secret safe.

"Absolutely untrue," he says, looking Dieter steadily in the eye. "We're in excellent health, and I know that Gabrijela values our independence. And now with *Storm of Angels*, it looks like we'll have our best year ever."

"Everyone knows that Globish has had its eye on you for some time now. And someone told me that they saw you, your boss, and the big guy at Globish having breakfast this morning at the Marriott."

"True enough, my boss and Mortimer are old friends."

"Mortimer has no friends," Dieter growls. "You had better watch out; you know his reputation in the industry."

"I'm just the publisher, my friend," he says, "all I do is publish books, I leave corporate wheeling and dealing to my superiors. But I can say with confidence that Gabrijela will not easily give up control of the company she has fought so hard to build."

"How much of it does she own?"

"Enough," he says, "I don't know, but enough to keep her from surrendering so easily."

His taxi arrives; he bids Dieter goodbye and asks to be driven to the Marriott.

———

At eleven at night, the lobby of the Marriott is still full. To survive a Frankfurt Book Fair you need the stamina of a marathon runner and the iron frame of a mixed martial arts fighter, he thinks. None of these people will go to bed before two, a third will probably pair off for further highjinks, and maybe one per cent will go at it all night, or morning rather, before they drag their weary carcasses off to a breakfast meeting. Oh, to be twenty-nine again, the year of his first Frankfurt! He feels disgustingly bloated; he must be giving off the smell of meat. He heads for the loo off the lobby , where he runs into a publisher he is acquainted with. A long-haired hellraiser in a corduroy jacket and jeans, the man has just finished doing a line of coke; he cleans up the evidence next to the wash basin, raises a languid hand to Zach, drawls, "How's it hanging, mate?" and wanders back into the fray outside.

Julia is perched on a sofa in the far corner, her coat still on. She is utterly exhausted. She spots Zach before he sees her, and a tired smile animates her face. She is glad they are beginning to repair their relationship; she knows that she is making him work hard, but he ought to — he's given her enough trouble, hasn't he? But perhaps the time has come for her to ease up a bit. She doesn't doubt his love for her, and while she doesn't know if things will work smoothly if they get back together, she is more confident than she once was that they will be able to make a go of it.

———

Just then Zach catches sight of her, waves. She smiles at him as he comes up to her.

"Hey, falling asleep?" he says.

"This is crazy, I don't think I can move another step, think another thought, pitch another book."

"That makes two of us, now I know what it means, literally, to eat an ox — or rather a pig!"

"That's gross," she says. "Where have you been?"

"The Wagner."

"Oh, really," she says, "that's a Frankfurt institution."

"Not for you, honey," he says gently. "It's only for certified — no, certifiable — carnivores. You're not allowed entry unless you can prove that you can eat a hippo. Medium-rare."

"Ugh!" She wrinkles her nose, and the well-remembered gesture drenches him with a huge longing.

"Julia," he says huskily, having difficulty getting the words out, "move back in with me now, please. I love you so much."

"That's sweet," she says, "but you're drunk, better hide the flowerpots."

He is sober enough to look abashed. In the early days of their relationship, they had gone to a party in Knightsbridge, not a neighbourhood they frequented much, but they had been at a loose end and had tagged along with a friend to the palatial apartment of a stockbroker who was throwing a large bash to celebrate his fortieth birthday. Zach had quickly become bored with the people there, hotshots who worked in the financial industry and their vacuous girlfriends, so had begun to drink his host's whisky a bit more quickly than was wise. He had got separated from Julia after a while, but was quite sloshed by then so he hadn't really noticed she was no longer around. Finding the living room (where he had stationed himself for the past three or four drinks) claustrophobic, he had wandered out onto a balcony with a rather splendid array of potted plants. Two or three people were standing around, smoking and drinking. He knew none of them but they all seemed to be very friendly, and he was beginning to have a good time. The apartment was seven or eight floors up, and at some point in the conversation one of his new friends, a tall brunette, had wondered whether they would be able to hear the sound of something that fell from this height and smashed against the pavement, over the noise of the traffic and the background hum of the city. It was but the work of a moment for him to hoist a largish pot with a flowering shrub in it (the blooms were purplish, he recalls) over the wall and send it sailing into space. For a moment everyone froze but then they began clapping and cheering him on. Another flowerpot hit the pavement. They all thought they could hear the sound of the impact faintly, but just to be sure they weren't imagining it he was getting ready to tip another pot over when Julia was by his side, restraining him, leading him away over his protestations, getting him out of the apartment. Her tiny frame was almost bent over with the effort of supporting his body, which refused to stay upright, into the lift and into a cab. To this day he does not know how or if she squared things with the host, but when she brings up flowerpots it is his cue to go easy on the booze.

She gets up, wearily slings her bag onto her shoulder, and says, "Come on, let's get that drink, probably mineral water for you, and then I must go. We will have time enough to discuss our relationship back in London."

———

He rarely stays for all five days of the fair but he has to this year because of details surrounding the upcoming publication of *Storm of Angels*. The plan is to have a single lay-down date of 21 December 2009 for all the English-language editions, the Italian edition, possibly the German edition if Dieter is able to swing it and any other translated editions that might be ready by then. It's almost three in the afternoon before he finishes with his last appointment. Everywhere in the giant fairground, only a skeletal staff remain, watching as the public, who are let in on the final day, denude the stalls of sample copies of books, posters, leftover goody bags, whatever they can lay their hands on.

Gabrijela comes up to the Litmus stall. Like everyone at Frankfurt by now, she has pouches under her eyes, her lips are cracked, and she's moving as though she were underwater.

"How are you?" she asks.

"Bone tired but it was a great fair. May the spirit of Seppi rejoice among the angelic hosts, it was all because of him," he says, casting his eyes upward to the less than inspirational steel beams and roof of Halle 8.

Gabrijela smiles, then walks across to a locker and pulls out a bottle of champagne and a couple of plastic glasses. "Cristal," she says, pops the cork, and fills the glasses, hands one to him, and is about to take a sip when she pauses, puts her glass down, gets up, and fills a couple more glasses and takes them across to the two young women who have been manning reception. She fills another one for their international sales manager, who will be supervising the shipping of their remaining books and other fair-related paraphernalia back to London. She spends a few moments with him, returns, and raises her glass in a toast.

"To Litmus," she says.

"To Litmus."

"When do you get back?"

"Early tomorrow."

They sit in silence for a while, the sounds of the dying fair rustling around them. A few people are still walking around, the proprietors of the stall across the aisle are packing up, but for the most part tired exhibitors are putting up their feet and relaxing as the 2009 edition of the Frankfurt Book Fair winds down.

"When did you last read a book, Zach?" Gabrijela asks, breaking the silence.

"Don't know, two days ago, finished the proof copy of *The Arc*, Julian's book for the spring, great new talent –"

She interrupts him. "Did you enjoy it?"

He turns the question around in his head. "I suppose I did. I think we could have done a little bit more work on it, the ending is a bit flat, but schedules being what they are . . ."

"You know, I was thinking there are over a hundred thousand of us here, all of us focused on nothing but books, all of us living, breathing, exhaling books, but what I find sad is that so very little of it has to do with what brought us to books in the first place."

She is not looking at him but down at her drink, at the bubbles rising and exploding against the plastic sides of the glass. "How old were you when you first read a book all by yourself?"

"Oh, I don't know, six or seven?"

"What was it?"

"Probably an Enid Blyton or something like that."

"Umm . . . I guess we all have favourite kid's books but, you know, the first book that made a real impression on me, a book that I can recite passages from to this day, was something my father gave me to read when I was fifteen maybe, an extraordinary collection of stories entitled *The Encyclopedia of the Dead* by a writer called Danilo Kiš, known as the Serbian Kafka. There was one passage that stuck in my mind, it described a train pulling into Belgrade, and I related to it so fervently I suppose that I blame it for my addiction to this business – the words were so simple, so mesmerizing: 'The train wheels clatter as they pass over the metal trestles, the Sava flows mud-green, the locomotive blows its whistle and loses speed.' It was exactly as I remembered it from train journeys I took as a little girl. What about you?"

Her reminiscing illuminates a long forgotten corner of his memory. "I was in college, and I'd just finished wading through a monumental tome by Lawrence Durrell, *The Alexandria Quartet*. I tried to reread it recently but gave up. I found it too ponderous and dated, but if there is one fragment of prose I'll remember all my life, it was something I read in that novel, in which he describes a scene in Alexandria: 'A basket of quail burst open in the bazaar. They did not try to escape but spread out slowly like spilt honey.'"

He wonders where this conversation is going, he doesn't have a good feeling about it; the last time he and Gabrijela had had a conversation like this in the coffee bar in London he'd thought it was the end. Fortunately things had turned out otherwise.

"I'm sad that every one of us reads books without actually *reading* them, savouring them as we once used to," she says. "We read books for work, we read books to fix them, we read the books of our competitors; if we are good at what we do we take the time to read the books of the day, the books of tomorrow, the books of yesterday. Books, books, and more books – but when was the last time we really immersed ourselves in them?"

"On vacation?" he ventures.

"Yes, of course, now and again by accident we might slip out of our professional personae and actually sink into a book. But what of it? There's so much we lose."

"We're better off," he says, "than all those others who have even less to be thankful for."

"Fair enough," she concedes. She sits up straighter in her chair. "I'm getting out, Zach."

"*What?*" The import of what she has just said kicks in; he tries to keep it at bay, but Gabrijela is carrying on inexorably.

"I wanted you to know well in advance. I am not going to disappear tomorrow," she assures him, "but I'm going. As you know we've been talking for a while about getting Litmus to firm ground and our dear departed friend Seppi has ensured that will take place, God rest his soul.

"But I hadn't realized how determined Morty was to get his hands on Litmus, he needs a presence in the UK desperately if he is to be a player of any consequence. His own small company here has not made a go of it, so acquisition is the only route open to him. I thought *Storm of Angels* would frighten him off, make us too expensive to acquire, but he has simply raised his price, and it was way too much for William to turn down. He phoned me last night to say he was going to accept Globish's offer, and that three of the other directors were also inclined to accept. That leaves just Andrew and me and it's just a matter of time before he folds as well. There's no way I can fend off Morty."

"But surely you can stay on, you'll still hold a large chunk of the company."

"I could stay on for a while, but I couldn't work for Morty," she says ruefully. She takes a sip of her drink. After a while she asks, "Do you know what CEOs really do?"

"Run companies?"

"I suppose we do that, but unless we retain control of some operational areas of our firms, in terms of actual, hands-on work we do very little. Oh, we manage teams, we keep track of earnings and costs, prepare reports, chair meetings, fly here and there, make speeches, formulate strategy, fire-fight. . . all very necessary, no doubt, but what we are paid the big bucks to do is take decisions, hundreds of them, thousands of them, all the time. As you know, taking a real decision is one of the toughest things to do in business – or in your personal life for that matter. When a junior assistant or manager wonders why the CEO pulls down his or her six- or seven-figure salary, it's because at every other level of the company you are paid a fair wage for your craft, the things you were trained to do, while at the very top you're often a long way from what you were trained to do, but you're being paid for your ability to make decisions when often there is not enough information on which to base such decisions. You're being paid for your strategic instincts, your people management skills, your intuition. Business schools and work experience can prepare you for the role, but they can't teach you how to perform it."

"Do you want me to take over from you?" he asks in some alarm. "I'm not interested, Gabrijela, all I would like is for you to stay."

She laughs for the first time since they began talking. "No, Zach, I'm not suggesting you become CEO. I think you are a very good publisher with the potential to become a great publisher, and that's what you should focus on. The reason I'm talking about the CEO's role is so you will have an understanding of what life will be like as part of the Globish organization. At Litmus I was CEO but I was an integral part of a small, tightly knit group, and was therefore able to devote a lot of time to what you and the others did, but when you become part of Globish it is likely that you will find your lack of access to the man at the top frustrating. In a company the size of Globish the CEO is spread really thin, not surprising when you realize that he is managing something the size of a small country. Not that you should worry about that too much – it is probably a good thing you won't be working directly with Morty. In fact, come to think of it, you will in all likelihood report in due course to Hayley, the UK CEO. Now that's a whole different story."

She takes a sip from her glass, grimaces. "Champagne tastes foul when drunk out of a plastic glass," she says. "Let's go to your hotel bar and have a proper drink."

They collect their bags, bid goodbye to the people remaining at the stall, and leave, with Gabrijela talking as they go.

"I'm fifty-four years old, Zach, and I have been head of this company for a couple of decades now. It was fun at first, but after a while I found I wasn't enjoying life so much, especially once Litmus had grown to something approaching its present size. This is probably because I have always been a bit of a worker bee, and while I liked directing the course of the company, and have never shied away from taking tough decisions, I felt I wasn't as fulfilled as I once was. I wasn't being hands-on enough. To be honest, even though I would find it difficult to work for Morty, the real reason I'm going is because I would like to taste and feel books and work with authors again. I'm going to take a long break after I leave Litmus and then I'll probably start a small company that will publish the sort of books I once published. It'll lose money, I'm sure, but I'll be able to afford it."

She bends down and, to his astonishment, takes off her shoes, stuffing them into her bag and laughing at his expression. For just an instant he glimpses the vivacious young woman she once must have been.

"What they never warn you about at Frankfurt is how much punishment your feet have to take. I've always wanted to do this, and as I suspect this will be my last Frankfurt for a while, I don't care if my stockings are shredded to bits."

"You sure you don't want to take the shuttle bus?" he asks.

"Absolutely," she says firmly, "I'm making a statement here."

He shrugs and they walk on.

"As I was saying, a couple of years into my role, I came to the realization that being the CEO of a largeish company was fine for the time being. I was competent enough but I wasn't as excited by the job as I was when I was publisher; that in turn meant that I would never be great at the role, which was the other problem with being CEO. If I wasn't going to excel, that simply wasn't good enough for me. Like any industry, publishing has all kinds of CEOs. There are some disastrous ones and many who are competent, who form the majority; they keep their companies sailing steadily onward but don't have a clue about how to take the big intuitive leaps or formulate innovative strategy. The good

CEOs increase the value of their companies, meet their annual targets, keep shareholders happy, strategize effectively. Morty is one of these; he's a very clever guy, make no mistake, he wouldn't have got to where he has otherwise.

"Then there are the beloved CEOs, the ones everyone in the company would kill for, and everyone in the industry would die to work for. They are rare; and even rarer are the game-changers, the extraordinarily talented individuals who are often tunnel-visioned or crazy, who make the sort of intuitive leaps that they themselves can't explain to you, who see the field of play and take decisions with blinding clarity, rather like how Roger Federer in his prime could figure out exactly where to whack a tennis ball three strokes in advance of winning the point. They will be remembered long after they are gone, the founders of great companies, the fixers of broken companies . . .

"Morty's problem is that he would like to be thought of as one of the great ones when he knows he doesn't have it in him to be one. Not that that is going to hold him back, and in his desire to be recognized as one he will stop at nothing, I fear. He is a few years older than me, and figures he has another ten or twelve years to get to where he wants to be, which is not a whole lot of years in the world of business, especially when he works in an industry that is past its prime, so he's a guy in a hurry and the acquisition of Litmus is just one of many steps to get him to where he wants to be. It simply won't do for his ego to retire as the head of the seventh-largest English-language publishing company in the world."

They leave the fairgrounds behind, and are passing the Maritim Hotel when Gabrijela says she cannot walk one step further without a drink to revive her. They walk into the lobby, head for the bar, which is relatively noiseless and uncrowded today. She orders a large gin and tonic and he settles for a mineral water.

"I know you probably have lots of questions for me," she says, "but there is no rush, we have plenty of time to work through them. I just wanted to give you enough information so you're able to ask the right questions."

"The only question I have right now," he says, "is whether I should be looking for another job?"

"Not at all," she says. "In fact, you are probably Litmus's most valuable asset after Seppi, so Morty will take very good care of you, he will not ignore you the next time you meet, believe me. But you should also know the kind of person you're dealing with. I've already told you why the fact that he will never be what he wants to be makes him rather difficult and unpredictable, but the real reason you will need to be cautious around him is more complicated. You may know that he and I went out together briefly many years ago. Well, just before we got together Morty was let down badly by a friend and he has never trusted anyone completely since – nor has he been trustworthy. Over the years many of his employees have learned that about him when they were shown the door after they had outlived their usefulness, or became a threat to him, or made a mistake that he thought would reflect badly on him. At Litmus we were truly a family, I would like to think we looked out for each other, but at Globish you will have to learn to watch your back. Remember that and you'll do just fine."

6.

NEW YORK

If publishing has an evolutionary scale, after hundreds of years of natural selection what has risen to the top is a formidable creature – the Manhattan-based publisher of a large publishing company. Capable of stopping a Bengal tiger in mid-spring or charming a swallow out of its nest, this paragon is usually a woman of indeterminate age, with the ability to bend a room full of New Yorkers (unanimously regarded as the toughest and most cynical people in publishing anywhere) to her will, or to make a steely agent see reason, or to have one of the planet's biggest authors eating out of her hand. Each of these ladies, and there are less than a half-dozen of them present on the scene at any one time, has put more bestsellers on the *New York Times* list than God, and for as long as they are around publishing will not perish. At least that's the way it seems to Zach as he watches the publisher of Globish Inc.'s US company in action in the seventeenth-floor board-room of the company's midtown headquarters.

Casey Travers has published more bestsellers than all but three other legendary women in the pantheon of great US publishers and as she is far from done yet the odds are that she will stand alone at the summit when she finally bows out. Her appearance belies the enormous power she wields within the company and in the marketplace. She is a diminutive, brown-haired woman, dressed in a grey pantsuit and possessing an unexpectedly deep voice. As Zach watches her in action, a character in a western novel he read when he was a schoolboy crosses his mind. Dusty Fog was a short, insignificant-looking gunfighter, but his prowess with the twin ivory-handled Colts he wore in crossdraw holsters was so deadly that when he entered a crowded saloon his presence intimidated every person there. There must be about fifty sales reps, marketing staff, editors, and sundry other company people sitting at the enormous oval boardroom table, but there is no question about who counts the most. At the moment proceedings have ground to a halt because Casey is tearing a strip off a rep who has made a suggestion that she thinks is risible. He is astonished by how these grown men and women can take a public dressing-down without protesting, and is beginning to get a sense of the culture of a large corporation like Globish – or perhaps it's the way they do things here in America; back home publishing is much more collegial. Here it seems – he searches for the right word – gladiatorial. You are expected to get in the ring and fight to the death for your books. Or perhaps it is just the sheer force of Casey's personality that determines how these meetings are run.

The door to the conference room opens and Mortimer Weaver walks in and takes a seat at the back. His arrival hasn't escaped Casey's attention and she snaps, "You're late, *Maarty*," with just a glimmer of a smile to acknowledge the fact that he is her boss.

"Sorry, was delayed by a phone call," he mumbles sheepishly. Casey resumes her berating of the hapless rep, and the morning session of Globish's December sales conference carries on. Usually, this conference would have taken place in a venue out of town, but the company is cutting costs this year. This delights Zach; New York is a city he is always happy to visit. Although the conference is devoted to the coming year's summer list, the earlier lists having already been sold into the stores, he has been invited to present *Storm of Angels*, which everyone is hoping will be dropped as planned into December, although the production deadline is extraordinarily tight.

Events have moved swiftly after Frankfurt. Gabrijela has worked out a deal with Globish wherein the formal acquisition of Litmus will be completed and announced to the media as close as possible to the release of *Storm of Angels* on 21 December, 2009. This is expected to work well for both parties. The share price of Globish's parent company will rise, and she has been able to include a clause that will give Litmus's shareholders a bonus on top of Mortimer's already generous offer if the share price gets to a certain level. It has been agreed that Gabrijela will stay on as Litmus's CEO until April 2010, by which time all staff will have moved into Globish's London offices in a featureless low-rise in Camden Town. This development has been met with a great deal of unhappiness, but only four people have quit. In these troubled times it is madness to chuck up a good job, although given Globish's reputation there is no doubt that cuts will come soon. But Gabrijela has managed to include a provision in the takeover agreement that no Litmus employee can be fired for a year from the date of the sale being finalized except for justifiable cause. It's the best they could have hoped for in the circumstances.

———

He has a lunch appointment at Balthazar and decides to walk to the restaurant; to his mind nothing quite matches the experience of wandering through the streets of Manhattan. The streets of Hong Kong are busier, the streets of Bombay are rattier, the streets of Paris are filled with more elegant people, the streets of Singapore are cleaner, the streets of Rome have more architectural delights, but none comes close to matching the sheer variety and energy and excitement of New York's streets. He relishes the chaotic traffic barely contained by the sidewalks, the thunder of people surging in every direction, and everywhere the blaring noise of construction, car horns, hot dog vendors, shouted conversations, arguments – everybody and everything in a constant state of flux. This is, after all, a city whose every inhabitant is convinced they know how to catch that goddamn falling star, make that next million, star in the third act of their lives. Never mind that they may be delusional; to be a New Yorker is to want to do it all, win at all costs, fill every minute of every day with whatever will sway the world, and this translates into an extraordinary force field of energy that all are plunged into the moment they set foot in the city – energy so powerful it could resurrect the dead and make the living levitate. By the time he gets to Balthazar he feels drained and energized at one and the same time.

He is looking forward to his meeting with Alfred Rothstein, a man who has been part of the New York publishing scene for over fifty years. And although he has handed off the day-to-day management of his literary agency to his successors, he keeps close tabs on everything about the publishing business, much like Ramesh in Delhi, and Zach has come away from every meeting with Mr. Rothstein (he will always be Mr. Rothstein to him) with a deeper appreciation and understanding of his profession. In the dim aqueous light of the bistro, he finds it hard to spot his host. Matters are not helped by the fact that the maître d' seems run off his feet as he attempts to maintain some order in the clamorous room. As he waits he thinks Balthazar, with its zinc bar, red leather banquettes, and glasses sparkling like mermaid's conches, is the perfect setting for a meeting with a renowned New York publishing personality. He can imagine Kerouac or Fitzgerald or Hemingway deep in conversation with Maxwell Perkins over in one corner, while Alfred Knopf or Nelson Doubleday inks a contract with another New York literary lion at the bar.

When he is led to his table he finds Mr. Rothstein already there, looking through a copy of that day's *Times*, a partially crumbled roll on the tablecloth in front of him. He is impeccably turned out – polka-dot bowtie, dark suit, blinding white

shirt, his few remaining strands of hair neatly combed over
the large domed head speckled with liver spots. Although
he is nearly ninety, the quick birdlike movements and the
sharp inquisitive mind would be the envy of a much younger
man. Zach goes with Mr. Rothstein's recommendation and
orders the calf's liver. His guest has a Kindle lying next to his
paper and Zach asks him whether he is at all worried about
the effect ereaders and other manifestations of the digital age
might have on the publishing industry. After admitting that he
loves his Kindle and can't wait to get his hands on an iPad
when it is launched next year, Mr. Rothstein says that he is
not concerned at all about the ability of the publishing business to negotiate any challenge that might be thrown down.
He says he has watched it morph from a business of small
independent houses, where the proprietor's knowledge of
stock turnover was limited to running his hands over the piles
of books in the warehouse to gauge how quickly they were
moving from the amount of dust that had collected on them,
to one of giant conglomerates with sophisticated sales and
marketing and warehouse management systems. He has seen
the coming of the paperback and the mass market edition;
vertical integration; the virtual disappearance of the independent bookstore and the rise of mall stores, superstores, and
online bookstores. With every new development enough
people were ready to write off the publishing industry, he says,
but it has weathered every crisis. When Zach asks whether he
thinks that the forces that have sorely tested the newspaper
and the music business might prove too difficult to handle,
Mr. Rothstein leans across and levels a finger at him.

"You must remember," he says, "relatively speaking, you work for a tiny, quirky industry, and that alone gives you a lot of protection from the forces of change, as some astute observers have pointed out. Publishing has never been and will never be as mainstream as the newspaper business or the music industry. Two centuries ago, literacy levels limited its size, and today its size is limited by the plethora of entertainment and information options available to the consumer. Why, the world's seven largest consumer publishing companies, including your own, Globish (it feels strange to be addressed as an employee of Globish, Zach thinks), put together aren't even a third the size of Amazon, let alone Apple or Google. So that gives you a certain amount of protection, the giant corporations don't think of your turf as something that is big enough or profitable enough to invade."

"But some have already started aggressively edging onto our turf."

Mr. Rothstein waves the objection away. "Publishing is way too small for them to bother with so they will just reach an accommodation with you guys. What is important to bear in mind is that your core customers are extremely loyal, better educated than the average guy, more affluent, and more mindful of the need to keep you all alive. What I think might happen over time is that publishing companies might not be able to afford to be as large as Globish and some others are today, too much cost, not enough revenue, and so you might see a return to the days of smaller independents who fulfil a specific editorial and marketing role. One way or the other publishing will go on, the industry is full of smart people like you who will incorporate what you need to take on board to keep you viable and you'll go on."

Zach has been ignoring his BlackBerry, but it has started to buzz insistently and he excuses himself to take a look at his messages. The most urgent one is from Rachel in London and it does not bear good news. No matter how hard they push, she says, there is no way they are going to make a December pub date for *Storm of Angels*. She says that Gabrijela has already e-mailed Mortimer, and followed up the message with a phone call, but has suggested that Zach meet with him as well. The message casts a pall over the rest of his lunch, and he refuses coffee and dessert. His host, who has seen it all before, tells him to get going, and Zach races out of the restaurant, flags down a cab, and makes his way back to the office and a meeting with Mortimer that he is not looking forward to.

————

Mortimer has called a strategy meeting after lunch, in the small boardroom on the fifteenth floor. He has lunched alone in his office – a BLT and mineral water that his longtime secretary, Edna, has organized – and has spent the past half-hour brooding about what he would like to do to Casey Travers if only he could. He dislikes her arrogance, her American forthrightness and aggression, but most of all he hates her disdain for him; she barely masks the fact that all she does is tolerate him. He knows he needs her more than she needs him (she would be long gone if that weren't the case), but she could at least hide her contempt better. This sort of nonsense would never happen in London, no matter what a subordinate thought of him it would be suitably camouflaged.

He is swept by a wave of homesickness. He would like to be back in the UK, the acquisition of Litmus should make it possible for him to spend more time in London. Although he has spent nearly a decade in the States, two of them even married to an American woman – the two most distressing years of his life, filled with endless talk about every shade of their emotions and how they were doing as a couple, and sex, and love, and pretty much everything in between; God, these people liked to talk every single thing to death and beyond – stolid, repressed London would be a nice change. The moment passes. He puts Casey from his mind. It is something he does well, this ruthless closing down of one window of his mind and the opening of another. It is the only way to survive as a chief executive; with a million things that need to be addressed simultaneously, nothing can be dwelt on for too long, especially if he doesn't have a solution to the problem. Suck it up and move on, there will come a time when Casey is no longer needed.

A message lands in his inbox and a few moments later Edna buzzes him to say that Gabrijela is on the phone. *Storm of Angels* cannot be released this month, she tells him; they cannot even get him an advance copy for his presentation tomorrow, he will have to make do with a jacketed dummy. *Fuck, that's not good*, but there's not a whole lot he can do about it. It would have been great to have the Seppi revenues this year, but to have them next year shouldn't be too bad, and his announcement of the Litmus acquisition and the impending arrival of a new Seppi should do the share price of Globish's parent company no harm. He looks at his expensive watch, a present from his new love interest, the widow of a wealthy Philadelphia banker, whom he fortunately has to see only about once every eight weeks or so, and gets up from his desk to go to his meeting. He pauses for a moment by the window, looks down at the traffic crawling down Park Avenue, the cabs so alarmingly yellow, so New York, and then heads to the elevator.

When he gets to the conference room he finds the rest of his management team already there. He feels a slight twinge of irritation; he always likes to be the first to arrive for a meeting, it gives him a slight edge to be present in advance of the others. He finds it useful to watch each of his subordinates come in, so he can figure out how best to tackle them that day, the cocky ones, the submissive ones, the ones who don't say anything, the mediocrities who have got to where they are by virtue of being long serving, or servile, or because they are useful to him. He thinks CEOs who like to stride in late, make a grand entrance, are losing out on a valuable advantage.

He takes his seat at the table, greets them, calls the meeting to order, then lets a moment of silence develop; it is another stratagem he uses to control a meeting – before he spells out the direction the meeting will take, agendas notwithstanding, the others at the table will be unsettled for just a moment and that will be to his advantage. To Mortimer, running a business is like waging a war, but before you join battle with your competitors and enemies it is necessary to be completely in control of your own troops, so he regards all his internal meetings as skirmishes, where he pits himself against his key lieutenants, those who would take his crown from him given the chance. He is not the sort of leader who is a conciliator, who welds his team into an effective fighting unit by playing up their strengths. No, for him management is all about pitting man against man or woman, keeping them guessing at all times, making sure that no one person gets too powerful. A history buff, he is particularly taken with the tactic used by the great strategists of empire – *Divide et impera*, Divide and conquer. It was how a handful of Englishmen got to rule the world and it's how he survives and thrives. The three men and the sole woman at the table wait in silence for their boss to speak. There's Frank Mayhew, the unexciting and dependable CEO of his American company, who can be relied upon to do exactly as he is told. A tall, rangy man, with thinning hair and a weak chin that he hides with a trim goatee, he looks like a complacent greengrocer (the standing joke about Frank is that he is a great listener – because he has nothing of any consequence to say). Hayley Caldwell, the head of his UK company, is a bit mercurial and bossy, but careful never to let him feel threatened; she is going to be tested by Gabrijela, he thinks with grim satisfaction. C.K. Lee is the youngest person present and the head of Globish's fledgling Australian company - Mortimer is hoping that Lee will in due course be able to reach out to China and points beyond. The fourth person is his CFO, Bob Nougat, the only person in the group he trusts to the extent he trusts anyone;

he has known Bob for twenty-five years and brought him into the company when he took over.

He breaks the silence, reviews the year to date with the group. They had no hope of making their annual targets at the end of the third quarter, he reminds them, and they had nothing in the bag that would have helped them do so, until he pulled out the Litmus acquisition. Their applause rolls over him, and he smiles and accepts it graciously while privately thinking how they must hate him for constantly reminding them that the only reason they hold down their jobs, earn their bonuses, is because of his brilliance. He has no doubt that they slag him off behind his back, but he doesn't care – he is not here to win a popularity contest, he is here to win, to look good for his boss. He has survived as president for four years, which is three years longer than his five predecessors and he intends to continue in the position for as long as he can.

As the praise dies down he drops his bombshell: *Storm of Angels* is going to be delayed to April next year. As their faces fall he tells them he has activated Plan B, which should salvage the year through the release of certain provisions; he adds that the delayed launch of the Seppi novel is probably a blessing in disguise because it will make their twenty-fifth anniversary celebration in April 2010 even more special. He wants the company to put together a promotional campaign for the anniversary that is both spectacular and useful; he is not inter-ested in mere pomp, he wants to use the milestone to lodge the Globish brand firmly in the minds of the public. The way things are trending, if they do not have a recognizable brand with which to attract authors and consumers, they might not be celebrating their fiftieth anniversary. And the first place to start, he says, is by reviewing and restating the company's values. As he says this, he smiles inwardly at the memory of his initial reaction to the obsession of large American companies with values that went beyond their core competencies, usually empty-sounding words and infantile slogans that were a smokescreen for skullduggery. However, he very quickly figured out how to use company slogans to his advantage and now, at least on the surface, he is an ardent believer in them. He asks each member of the group for a single word that they think best describes Globish and what it stands for.

"Perfection," says Hayley, always the first off the mark.

"Solid," says Frank, dull as ever.

"Paranoid," says C.K. Lee puzzlingly, and possibly insultingly. Thank God, Mortimer thinks, that the Australian company represents less than half a per cent of their turnover, it would be worrying otherwise to have someone who thinks like Lee in charge.

"Innovative," says Bob, loyally repeating the trait he has planted.

He pretends to be thinking about their suggestions for a minute or two, then says, "I like Bob's suggestion, it is imperative that we are seen as 'innovative' so let's take that on board. And maybe 'successful' is more positive than 'solid.'"

Frank says, "Fine."

"How about 'honest?'" he asks. The group agrees, as he knows they will.

"Let's have one more," he says. When no suggestions are forthcoming he suggests "thoughtful," adding, "We are a publishing company; it would be a good idea to plant the idea in the mind of the consumer that we are thoughtful about what we do."

"We could have the acronym printed on T-shirts that could be handed out to employees, authors and customers on our anniversary," Hayley says enthusiastically.

"Successful. Honest. Innovative. Thoughtful. *S.H.I.T.* Would people really want to wear that on their chests?" Bob asks drily.

The group laughs nervously – they know Bob holds a privileged position, but this is dangerously close to being offensive, and that simply won't do with Mortimer. Everyone knows how much he resents Casey's effrontery. But Mortimer is not offended. He is sure Bob didn't mean to displease or make fun of him, and he was smart to catch the obvious danger with the slogan.

"Let's take 'honest' out, that should solve the problem, it's a self-evident trait anyway, everyone knows that we are renowned for our honesty. And perhaps 'thoughtful' as well."

No one contradicts him, the discussion about values has gone on long enough. They will only be taken seriously in this country; the subsidiaries will adopt them grudgingly and jettison them at the first opportunity.

"Moving on," he says, "I would like every CEO to examine the Globish ecosystem closely, see where we can effect improvements at minimal cost." Lately, he has found himself using whatever management buzzwords are current – "ecosystem," "DNA," and the other claptrap that disguises imprecise, lazy thinking – it's either another step in his development as a CEO or it is the beginning of the long slide down. As quickly as the thought arises he suppresses it, the meeting needs to go on, he will have time later to examine his use of the English language.

"Do we need to meddle with our logo, freshen it up?" he asks. "In some of the new media the face of the cougar looks too bloated, sluggish." There is no response and he thinks, *And I'm going to handle this decade of change with this lot, with not one original idea among them!* They are a handpicked bunch, he reminds himself, noted for their personal loyalty, and for their lack of enterprise and brilliance. Those qualities are fine lower down the pecking order, but not at this level, where they can be too threatening. For every advantage, a disadvantage! He picks up the clicker next to him, switches on the laptop, projects some images of the redesigned logo on the screen – the body of the cougar is trimmer, the visible eye is larger and a bit more benign. There are no objections, he didn't expect any, and he moves on to the last item on the agenda that deals with the logistics of the anniversary celebration. There will be press conferences and parties in New York and London, each with a keynote speaker, and he checks that all arrangements have been made; he is very particular and detail oriented about these things, and they spend half an hour discussing menus, floral arrangements, and seating for honoured guests. He has made arrangements for his image to be projected on a giant screen behind him when he makes his chairman's speech, in the manner of Steve Jobs and Bill Gates – he was careful to run this particular idea by Greg, his boss, who given the extremely competitive nature of the software industry, was very supportive of it. Naturally, everyone in this group thinks it is a great idea. He intends tomorrow's year-end presentation to be a dry run of what they are planning to do next year.

Bob takes over and gives a PowerPoint presentation on the company's P&L and balance sheet. Mortimer's attention drifts, he knows the figures to the last cent, so he is thinking instead about the new midnight-blue Kiton suit he has ordered for tomorrow's presentation – he will cut a dashing figure, of that he is sure.

As the discussion on the financials and three-year plan comes to a close, Lee, who appears to have been asleep for much of the conversation, pipes up and asks how they are going to achieve their growth targets in 2011 and 2012 with nothing that comes close to matching the Seppi revenues.

"Casey is confident half a dozen of her repeaters will get bigger," he says looking across to Frank for confirmation, which he gets. "In addition, we will have various paperback formats of *Storm of Angels*, and I am confident that we can get Litmus's publisher to dream up new projects with the Seppi estate." The Seppi franchise is one of the reasons he has been able to value Litmus handsomely, and while he hasn't talked to Zach about it yet, he is sure that they will be able to publish some sort of new Seppi book annually for at least the next three years.

"What if sales dwindle when it is clear that the books are written by someone else?" Hayley asks. "I haven't checked figures but I think with the Ludlum and Bond franchises, unless there were movies attached, sales of posthumously ghost-written books were nowhere near as high as the original books. Fans of books with freakishly high sales are fanatical, they want the original article."

"I'm aware of that," he says calmly. "The guy who runs Seven Star Studios is a friend of mine and they are as keen on the Seppi franchise as we are and they will keep it going for as long as possible. I'm not worried, I think we'll be able to wring a lot of sales out of Seppi."

———

Mortimer operates by the rule that, until proven otherwise, all New Yorkers are crazy – either good crazy or crazy crazy. It doesn't matter if they got here last week or are sixth-generation locals, they all possess that crazy streak. Others might characterize them as unique or cynical or just plain cussed; each to his own, he prefers crazy. This craziness makes them difficult to impress, and as New Yorkers constitute approximately seventy per cent of his employees he has had to come up with a twenty-fifth anniversary presentation (or, to be more accurate, a trial run) that is daring and different.

At six P.M. on the day of the year-end party, which is traditionally held on the last day of the sales conference, the four-hundred-seat hotel ballroom is filled to capacity with Globish employees. Frank climbs the steps to the raised platform at the front of the room, welcomes the gathering, and introduces Mortimer. The lights dim. Mortimer rises to his feet, makes his way to the podium. He wishes his classmates who had kicked him around in school could see him now, all those hapless morons spinning their days out in their stately homes or in empty pomp. His repaired heart pounds strongly in his chest as he looks out over the assembled gathering. "Friends," he begins, "the coming year will mark an important milestone in the history of our great company. We stand on the threshold of an extraordinary future – what we do today will determine how we get to our long-awaited destiny of becoming the most celebrated, the most innovative publishing company in the world."

To everyone's astonishment, Mortimer then shrugs off his expensive Kiton suit jacket, twirls it thrice around his head, and flings it into the audience, where it lands on the surprised Hayley. He then pulls off his tie and unbuttons his shirt to reveal the black T-shirt underneath, on which is printed the new-look Globish logo over the letters *SI*: *Successful. Innovative.* "Today, we remind ourselves of what Globish stands for," he thunders. "Each one of you is our future; let these words lodge in your hearts and minds, as you look to the coming year." The music swells, it's Dvorák, and on the giant screen behind him a movie begins to roll. It opens with a shot of the Panjshir mountain range in Afghanistan and then cuts to the terrifying sight of silos in a thinly populated region north of Islamabad opening as they prepare to launch nuclear missiles. The warheads take flight at the same time as a host of deadly missiles roar forth from army bases in India. World War III has begun. THE END OF DAYS appears in flaring letters on the screen. DECEMBER 21, 2012. And then four great beings fill the sky – Michael, Gabriel, Raphael, Uriel – and over, above, and everywhere around them, the incandescent face of God. The missiles explode harmlessly against the glowing presence of the Celestials, and the music swells to a crescendo, as *Storm of Angels* and "Massimo Seppi" appear in gold type on a black background. The music dies away, and a giant image of Mortimer appears on the screen, towering over his presence at the microphone. *Suck that up, Steve. On your bike, Bill. This is Mortimer Weaver, prophet of the future.* He launches into his speech – perhaps the best one he has made this year, the silly gimmick with the jacket notwithstanding. Ten minutes later he is finished, and as the applause rolls over him he thinks with satisfaction, *Nothing can stop me now.*

———

Zach is seated at the back of the room and he thinks that the presentation was terrific; judging by the mood in the room a lot of the others feel that way too. Then he hears a young assistant in the row ahead of him ask her neighbour, "What was that about, then? Must have cost a fortune, do you think we'll get a raise this year?"

"Fuck knows," her neighbour says. "All I know is that if I don't make more money I can kiss my apartment goodbye."

———

At the lavish dinner that follows, where his employees choose between salmon and New York strip loin for the main course (the seventeen vegetarians get eggplant parmesan), Mortimer is mobbed by the more unctuous and ambitious elements within the company; the expense has been worth it, he thinks, the anxiety caused by the recent layoffs Globish has had to make has been neutralized. Between dessert and coffee he introduces the speaker for the evening to the sated and largely disinterested audience. Timothy Hellman has worked with some of the most impressive Silicon Valley start-ups and now runs an innovative blog on developments in the digital world.

As Hellman begins his speech the image of an enormous statue appears on the screen behind him. The figure has four arms and is ringed by a wreath of fire. His right leg is planted on a grotesque dwarf, his left leg is raised. A cobra uncoils from his right forearm; his upper right hand holds a drum, and flames shoot from his upper left hand; his other right hand forms a mudra; a crescent moon and skull are twisted into his long hair, which is caught up in a topknot. A great serpent encircles his waist.

The speaker points to the figure on the screen, which for all its size and complexity is exquisitely sculpted and perfectly balanced. "Can anyone tell me what that is?" he asks.

The ten people in the audience who are paying attention, Zach among them, look to where he is pointing. Nobody answers, and Zach feels the tension building within the pit of his stomach, the same sensation that he had felt all those many years ago when he was preparing to answer the question another keynote speaker had put to a class of publishing wannabes.

"Nobody?" Hellman asks.

"Nataraja," Zach says.

"Exactly right," Hellman says, "Now who was that?"

Zach raises his hand.

"Could you stand up, please?"

He does so. Reluctantly. He sees Mortimer looking at him and gives him a weak smile.

"And what do you know about Nataraja, my friend?"

"He is an avatar of Shiva, the Hindu god of destruction."

"And creation," Hellman says, motioning for Zach to take his seat. "In the great Hindu trinity, Shiva is the god of both destruction and creation. This image was created about a dozen centuries ago, and it is the perfect metaphor for all of you who are involved in the creative industries. In it, Lasya (creation) and Tandava (destruction) are held in perfect balance. As Shiva dances, old worlds collapse under his thundering feet, to be replaced instantaneously by new worlds. The mantra that a lot of companies are muttering to themselves today as they try to reinvent themselves to cope with a rapidly changing world is 'Creative Disruption.' That is what the Dance of Shiva symbolizes, that is what creative disruption means: break everything you know and reassemble it in new and unheard-of ways. That is the future of the book, my friends, and it is incredibly exciting."

Hellman takes them on a swift journey through all the relevant developments taking place in the digital world, then predicts that in five or ten years these developments will be seen as the first stuttering steps taken in a transformation that will be more wide-ranging than anyone today can foresee. But he says this should not worry them because the future is there to be grasped by those who have the vision and the courage to do so. "For two hundred years, the reading of books, the telling of stories has been a largely passive experience, but as the wheel turns it is being returned to what it once was, a lively, enriched, layered experience in which the soul of a culture resides. The future is not something you should be afraid of. Just as Shiva destroys the old and brings forth the new, so will the world of books and publishing rise, and rise again in fresh and exciting ways." He bows to the assembled crowd, holds his interlocked hands up, and says by way of parting, "Range far and wide, mash it all up, the future has never been as exciting."

As Hellman returns to his seat, Zach glances across at Mortimer. The president's face is alive with excitement. Zach thinks about his rousing speech, his obvious determination to make Globish a leading player in the digital age and feels that being part of Mortimer's company might not be such a bad thing at all, Gabrijela's reservations notwithstanding.

7

SYDNEY

The old men stagger wearily out of the coffee-coloured ocean and head for their burrows, shaking the moisture from their bedraggled waistcoats. They are about a foot tall and look grumpy. No wonder, Zach thinks, he has never been as cold and miserable in his life and he is just visiting. He and a bunch of other tourists have waited for over an hour in driving rain to watch the parade of fairy penguins on Phillip Island. Their guide explains their mating and nesting habits, and then as quickly as it has begun the show closes and they take the van back to their hotel in Melbourne.

On the long drive back, as the chill gradually leaves his bones in the heated interior, his mind lazily drifts over the events of the last six months. The highlight, without a doubt, was the day Julia invited him to her parents' home in Surrey for Christmas lunch. He had taken the train on a clear, crisp morning and had been met at the station by her father. He had always got on well with his parents-in-law, and with

Julia's younger sister, Natalie, and the family had seemed to view the first slow steps towards a rapprochement positively. After lunch, where he had eaten and drunk too much, Julia and he had taken the family's Labradors, the black one named Troilus and the golden one named Cressida, for a walk. He has always liked the English countryside – its domesticated palette of colours, the orderly hedgerows, the disciplined tweeting of birds – and on this afternoon it was at its glorious best. Julia was chattering about the abrupt exit of a well-known publisher. "His farewell party was like something out of *The Tudors*," she had said, while struggling to control Cressida. She had finally let the Lab off the leash, and it had bounded ahead, farther into the woodland where they were walking. *This is what makes me happy,* he had thought - the woman I love beside me, talking of everyday things! Before he had left to catch his train, he had asked her when exactly she was intending to move back in with him, and to his great relief she had replied that she was all packed and ready and would return to their Kensington flat before the year was out.

She would have loved the fairy penguins, he thinks. It is unfortunate she couldn't make the trip, but she had to spend time with her mother, who was in hospital. He is in Australia for the Sydney Writers' Festival; before he gets to Sydney he has taken a couple of days off in Melbourne to visit friends and, naturally, along with koalas, cockatoos, and kangaroos, he has been told to take in the little penguins.

He laughs as he thinks about his initial impression of the city; after he had passed through the sprays and sniffer dogs with which the island nation tried to keep out unwelcome imports, he had spent a few hours worrying about unexpectedly encountering some of the world's deadliest snakes, most of which (somehow this was what bothered him the most) had astonishingly innocuous names – brown snake, fierce snake, tiger snake and so on – it was almost as though the Aussies were so tough that they couldn't be bothered to give their venomous cohabitants scary names. His nervousness had gradually dissipated – after all he was born in the land of the king cobra and the krait. Once he discovered that Gorgon's knots of writhing reptiles that could kill you in the blink of an eye weren't suspended from every street lamp, he had given himself over to enjoying the city and its friendly people.

A couple of days later he is in Sydney where he has been invited to participate in a panel discussion on the editor's changing role in publishing, and to give a talk on the life of Massimo Seppi and the five great Angels books.

A week before he arrived in Australia, *Storm of Angels* had been published and predictably shot to the top of the bestseller lists on the day it was launched. The inconvenience of a volcanic eruption in Iceland had delayed the launch slightly from April to the second of May, but nothing could dim the euphoria over the publication of Litmus's biggest book of the year, although the general feeling of well-being was soon tempered by everybody's sadness over Gabrijela's departure a day after the launch and their move to Globish's London headquarters. As the senior surviving member of staff, Zach had done his best to lift people's spirits. The main thing was that they were all still together, he'd said, and the four people who had quit notwithstanding, that was indeed the case.

Mortimer had agreed to dedicate Litmus's existing sales and marketing staff to Litmus's books, and although three people in accounting and admin were absorbed into the Globish back office, by the end of the first week of the merger people had begun to relax and take an interest in their work again.

He saw very little of Mortimer after the launch, as he visited London only once a quarter, and he found working with Hayley, his new boss, uncomplicated.

———

We never know what it is about the world's most iconic objects that make them real to us, helps us make them our own. He remembers that when he first saw the Taj Mahal it wasn't its slender minarets outlined against the sky, or its perfect symmetry, that grabbed hold of him; its beauty made a real impact only when the guide who was taking them around shone a torch on the marble, and revealed the translucence of the stone and the delicacy of the gems embedded in it. From within the stone, the gorgeous workmanship spoke to him, and the Taj Mahal was no longer a clichéd abstraction, a commonplace image, but something that he would carry within him forever. In similar fashion, the soaring petals of the Sydney Opera House, resplendent under clear blue skies on a crisp winter's day, would have remained just another picture-postcard image if it wasn't for the opening ceremony of the festival that took place in the enormous main hall of the building.

In an inspired move, the festival's organizers had invited an Aborigine elder to give them permission to hold the festival on his people's ancestral ground, and bless the activity that was about to take place. The man had cut a rather unimpressive figure as he approached the microphone, but as he launched into the welcome ceremony his whole aspect had changed. His ancestors had sung this land into existence and on this evening their whispering spirits filled the building for just a moment, hallowing it.

The next day, at the editors' session, the room is filled with aspiring writers who are hoping the panel will impart to them the magic formula that will make them famous published writers. They have no formula, magic or otherwise, to give the aspirants but they do their best, relaying whatever wisdom they have – about the craft of writing maybe, but not the art. He reminds one persistent woman about Saul Bellow's observation that he didn't probe too much into where his art sprang from, that he left it well alone. He tells her she should read, read, and then read some more, strategically and intelligently; there was no writer, alive or dead, who hadn't benefited from a careful reading of the greatest writers in whichever genre they were working in. But it is in the nature of this particular aspirant to question and question, to seek concrete suggestions on how it is done. He has nothing to give her beyond standard tips on pacing, characterization, plotting, POV, and the like, stuff that can be got for nothing online or for a few dollars in any of the dozens of books and writing programs that claim to be able to teach writing, and she sits down frustrated and angry. The panellist next to him, who works for one of the big Australian independents, leans across and whispers in his ear, "We get her every year; she has been coming here for at least five years, with nothing to show for it. She seems to hold it against us that she hasn't been able to publish anything."

The Q and A that ends the discussion is uneventful except towards the very end, when he finds himself defending the global publishing corporations because he is the only one on the panel who works for one. This is a novel experience for him but the defence is easy to mount. He points out that the Big Seven corporations between them publish more first novelists than most of the other houses put together, they keep the careers of thousands of midlist writers alive, and if it weren't for them the book trade would be severely diminished. He accepts that the big players might not be as responsive to the needs of every writer as some of the indies but as demerits go that was a small one.

He has a couple of hours to himself after the sessions end and decides to go for a walk, he would like to track down some opal earrings for Julia. It is her birthday next month and he has always liked giving her jewellery. Up a steep sloping street he finds a cluster of opal emporia, and selecting the one that looks the most promising he goes in. He often thinks he might easily qualify for the title of world's worst shopper, but he has found that because his incompetence is so manifest sales people tend to take pity on him and help him out. A friendly middle-aged saleswoman, noticing the utterly helpless look on his face as he regards display case upon display case stacked with opals, takes him in hand, tells him how to choose opals, ascertains his budget, finds out who the gift is for, and then starts pulling out stones to show him. He finds one stone in particular completely spectacular, a gem-quality Lightning Ridge black opal with a harlequin pattern – reds, violets, purples, greens, and blues pocking a deep midnight-blue background – a stone that might have surfaced from the imagination of some demented disciple of Seurat who had decided to shoot bullets of colour into the night sky. It would look perfect on Julia, he thinks. But the stone is several thousand dollars over his budget so he settles for a pair of earrings that has green lightning flashes and bands against blue. After buying the opals he walks around downtown for a while, then goes back to the festival hotel for a quick nap before the evening program begins.

He wakes up refreshed, and after a quick shower joins one of his fellow panellists in the bar downstairs. He finds the stories his drinking companion has to tell about his nation's publishing environment fascinating. For a small country Australia has several world-class publishers, ranging from independents like Text Publishing and Allen & Unwin to the outposts of the Big Seven, but here, like everywhere else, things are getting tougher and the publishing community is nervous about what the future might hold.

After a couple of the local beers, a clean-tasting golden yellow lager, they go across to a party hosted by a festival sponsor at one of the piers. He gets a drink, is introduced to a festival volunteer, and is entirely sincere when he tells her he is enjoying himself. They talk about the day's sessions and his event tomorrow. Once that's done he will be free to take in some of the other events, and he is looking forward to catching Christopher Hitchens and Peter Carey later in the week.

As the evening progresses, he takes off his name tag – he has always had a problem with identifying himself publicly – gets himself a refill, and wanders off to look at a book display in a corner of the enclosure. A gang of publishing people or festival volunteers, he has no idea who they are, are chatting animatedly next to the display; one of the women, skeletally thin, bears a startling resemblance to the figure in Munch's *The Scream*. He is beginning to move away to somewhere less noisy when a striking woman, almost as tall as he is, introduces herself as Betsy Molloy. He is nonplussed – how does she know who he is, he doesn't have his name tag on – and he would have noticed if she had been at the morning's session. The mystery is explained when she says she was working as a scout in London for an Australian publisher when the first *Angels* book was published and recommended it for publication. It's the only book she has recommended that has enjoyed such a level of success, she says; he says that is true of him as well. There is a lot he likes about her; she is easy to talk to, very attractive to look at, honey-blonde hair, blue-grey eyes, and a voice that suggests more than a nodding acquaintance with whisky and cigarettes. At any other time he would have hoped their encounter would lead to something else, but he can let nothing interfere with the delicate rebuilding of his relationship with Julia. At the point at which the conversation looks as though it might take a turn towards something more intimate he excuses himself, pleading work waiting for him back in his hotel room, now that the UK has woken up.

He walks back along the waterfront; the piers, alive with readings, parties, and music, push long, illuminated fingers into the dark waters. It's a glimpse of the future, he thinks; everywhere cultural festivals are proliferating, and there will come a time when the integration of music, drama, food, festivity, and literature will become commonplace, just as it was for hundreds of years – the wheel turns and turns and turns, and comes to where it once was and turns again. He is feeling good about himself, he will not deny it; the encounter with Betsy has heightened his sense of well-being, all he needs now is Julia's voice whispering in his ear. He will sleep well; it is his third day in Australia and with his brief nap in the afternoon the jet lag is beginning to lose its potency.

———

Later he will think about how some of the biggest events in his life have crept up on him unawares. This one begins in Hamilton, an unremarkable industrial town not far from Toronto. When he turns on his BlackBerry in his hotel room in Sydney he finds an e-mail from Rachel saying that while there is nothing to be concerned about, he should know that the Google Alert they have switched on for *Storm of Angels* has turned up an interesting observation about the book, posted by a Hamilton blogger called Night Owl. The blog, to which Rachel has provided a link, says that Night Owl has found a few similarities between the text of *Storm of Angels* and a 1930s fantasy series about angels by an Irish writer called Eileen Keane. "Watch this space," the blogger writes, "I might be on to something big." Zach isn't too worried about the post, virtually every one of the world's biggest writers, including J.K. Rowling and Stephenie Meyer, has been accused by less successful writers of plagiarism and the charges have usually been thrown out of court. This will probably fizzle out in the same way.

It does not. A day later Night Owl blogs that she has run *Storm of Angels*, and the books that she alleges it has been plagiarized from, *God's Messengers* and two others by Eileen Keane, through a comparison software program, and claims that approximately a third of Seppi's book is identical to the earlier works.

———

On the morning of the same day, in Toronto, Simon Prescott walks into his office at *Bibliomania* after a week's vacation at a friend's cottage. As he switches on his laptop he is feeling a little resentful that he has had to work hard during his holiday, cleaning and cooking and running errands, but he supposes that is the reality at the lower end of cottage life, when you don't have a staff and a cottage of your own. It could have been worse, he thinks. I could have been stuck in Toronto all summer long with all those other poor saps who haven't yet discovered or, worse, disdain the pleasure of driving for three hours, one way, in bumper-to-bumper traffic for the dubious rewards of being eaten alive by black flies and mosquitoes and eating indifferent home cooking. Nothing much seems to have taken place during his absence, a few new deals to be reported, and a couple of personnel changes at a West Coast publisher. As he scrolls down the mail in his in-box his Google Alerts page points him to the blog about Seppi.

Bibliomania's coverage of the publication of *Storm of Angels*, the biggest event in Canadian publishing in 2010, has been non-stop, and Simon is determined to wring as much juice from the story as possible. He had even tried to elicit Megumi's comments on the Seppi phenomenon by presenting her with a copy of *Storm of Angels*: she had declined the book, saying restaurant policy prevented her from accepting gifts from customers. He was crushed but not for long; he had decided that this was pretty much his last attempt to get her interested, and that if this gambit did not work he would stay away from her. He had thrown himself back into the magazine's coverage of *Storm of Angels*. He had done phone interviews with Caryn and Giuseppe, done an e-mail interview with Zach, and provided daily updates in the online edition of *Bibliomania*. Gradually, though, there was not a whole lot left to say. Until now.

He sends Night Owl an e-mail saying he would like to cover her story. She replies immediately and by that afternoon he is on a GO train to Hamilton. From the station he takes a bus to the address that Night Owl has given him. It turns out to be a housing development of identical two-storey, red-brick row houses with minuscule, unkempt front yards. Night Owl turns out to be a woman in her thirties with long, dishevelled black hair. She is dressed in a flowing purple caftan. She is vague about what she does for a living but he gathers she is some sort of freelance computer programmer. The air in her living room smells musty and he can see why: it appears as if the windows have not been opened for a long time.

He clears a pile of books off the only sofa and sits down as she takes a seat at her desk, pops open her laptop, and begins a monologue in a high-pitched voice about the outrage being perpetrated on the fans of Eileen Keane and Massimo Seppi. She tells Simon that she has been visited by angels since she was three, glowing naked men with tremendously developed pectorals. Her face is flushed and she sprays him with spit as she talks about her obsession (*sexual?* he types into his laptop). At the age of thirteen she discovered a long out-of-print book by Eileen Keane at a neighbourhood garage sale and was overjoyed at having found a soul sister. Her greatest regret was that Miss Keane had been dead twenty-two years so there was no chance of meeting her. But she tracked down every one of the nine books (three on non-angelic themes) Keane had written, devoured every word, and communed with the object of her adoration through dreams.

She takes him through the angels' hierarchies, and he wishes he had brought a recording device along with him. He isn't sure he is getting all these names down properly, who would have thought angels lived in such a complicated world! He makes a joke, and Night Owl, whose real name is Jennifer (she forbids him to use it, either while speaking to her or in his article) glares at him and says with the rage of the true jihadi that he must *never ever* make light of angels, that they are capable of wreaking the most horrific vengeance. He assumes a contrite expression and the interview goes on. She has read every book written about angels, fiction and non-fiction, and he records this fact dutifully in his laptop, although part of his mind wonders if that is even possible, given her description of the wide world of angels – a world that stretches across religions, races, time. Surely she couldn't have read everything there is about angels in Arabic or Urdu.

He snaps his wandering mind to heel. Night Owl is talking now about Seppi. When *Angels Rising* appeared she was overjoyed; here was the new master, the guru who would take her by the hand and help her negotiate the labyrinth of angels. Seppi's reclusiveness was a problem; she had travelled to Toronto every time she learned of an author event, a reading, a bookstore signing, or a fantasy convocation that featured him, but the closest she had ever got was a brief hello when he signed her books after a reading. And then, as his fame grew, *Angels* events simply stopped featuring him, to her frustration. But as long as the books kept coming, at least that was some consolation. She was devastated when he died. But incredibly, there was talk of a new book, and finally she had experienced the thrill of holding *Storm of Angels* in her hands. One hundred and seventy pages into the novel, disillusionment began to set in. By page two hundred she was sure. After that it was simply a matter of feeding all the words of Seppi's new novel and the novels of Keane into a comparison software program and her suspicions were confirmed. Of the 278,000 words of *Storm of Angels* 97,742 were identical to various passages in Eileen Keane's angel books.

As he read and compared the work of the two writers, Simon could see there was no mistake: entire paragraphs, in one case a chapter, had been lifted from the one and transposed into the work of the other with only the names and locales changed. His mind was beginning to seize up with excitement.

For a moment he wondered if he should approach the *Globe and Mail* or *Maclean's* with the story, perhaps even the *New York Times,* but out of loyalty to his own publication he decided to write the story for *Bibliomania.* He knew what people said about his paper – that it was read by all of six people including its staff of four, that its value if anyone ever wanted to buy it would barely max out the credit card of a grad student, that it got its facts wrong constantly. He would show them all what was what when he broke the literary story of the century. He would have to move fast, for all he knew the other papers were already on to the story; at least he had got to Night Owl first. He would phone Caryn Bianchi when he got back to the office, and also see if he could get a reaction from the publisher of Litmus.

"You've done an astonishing thing, Night Owl," he says sincerely. "I'm putting you on the front page of my magazine." He does not tell her that *Bibliomania* does not exist anymore in print form but he does not think that would matter to a blogger.

"Cool," she says, "Eileen would be pleased."

"Do you know if she has any family?" he asks, wondering if he should fly to Dublin, interview surviving family members. Not enough time, he thinks, even if he could scrape together the money for the airfare. He gets Night Owl to e-mail the text comparisons to him and takes a taxi to the train station with his last remaining dollars. During the long ride back he prepares a rough draft of the story.

It's past seven when he gets into the office, and it's in darkness. He gets settled at his desk, phones Caryn, and gets voice mail. Now what? he thinks, as he puts the phone down without leaving a message. She could be out of town on holiday or merely be away from home for a few hours, what should he do? He decides to write the article, leaving openings for quotes from Caryn if he is able to get hold of her before the midnight deadline he has imposed upon himself. As he writes the story he thinks that Caryn's quotes aren't necessary for it to hold up, unless she is prepared to be absolutely honest about the deception.

He finishes the piece, picks up a coffee at his neighbourhood Timothy's and takes the subway to Caryn's place. The house is in darkness and there is no car in the driveway. He wanders around the neighbourhood for half an hour or so, but when he returns there is still no sign of activity at the house. An hour later he calls it quits, and posts the story online.

———

In Sydney, several hours ahead of Toronto, Zach reads the story and is knocked sideways by it. The irony, he thinks, the crowning achievement of his life undone by a nincompoop with an unfulfilled fixation on the hostess of a sushi bar. He phones Rachel on her mobile, and without apologizing for waking her up asks her to quickly find copies of the Eileen Keane books Prescott is referring to and compare them to

Storm of Angels to make sure the claims are inalienable. He tries calling Caryn in Toronto and gets her voice mail; he keeps trying but after leaving her five messages he gives up.

A few hours later he is talking to his boss in London. Hayley Caldwell hears him out, and says the allegations will have to be brought to Mortimer's attention; the crisis is too big for the London office to handle. He spends a couple of tense and anxious hours, and then phones Caryn again. Still no reply, she is probably on holiday. He has no idea what he is going to say to Mortimer. He supposes he could say, plausibly enough, that no one could have read every book on angels there is; that the author, or in this case the translator, warranted to them that the book was an original work and that they had had no option but to take her at her word. Publishing lacks the resources to undertake independent fact-checking, it's a business that has historically been based on trust, and if there are a few rotten apples who breach that trust from time to time, that's just plain bad luck — there is little anyone can do to prevent or anticipate such deception. He recalls his slight concern about the difference in style between this manuscript and the preceding books in the series and wonders if he should share that bit of information with Mortimer. Would Globish's president pin the blame on him? Zach dismisses the concern; they are all in it together, and no matter what people have said to him about Mortimer's reputation for letting his people down, and his initial misgivings at their meeting at Frankfurt, the Globish boss has been nothing but supportive in the past few months. He will share his suspicions with him about

Caryn. What made her do it? Vengeance for being cheated out of what was rightfully hers? A fanatical desire to carry on the Seppi legacy at any cost? An attempt to show that she was a creative artist in her own right? Although he is extremely upset with her, the more he thinks about it, the more his anger is mixed with sorrow. He remembers the charm and the wry sense of humour that emerged from behind the iron veneer she presented to the world. How lonely she must be feeling right now, how besieged, he must not be too harsh on her!

But no matter how humane his and the company's treatment of her, she will have to be held to account; reparations will have to be made. Caryn and Giuseppe did sign contracts vouching for the authenticity of the work, but if Litmus sued, how much money would they be able to recover? And if any members of Eileen Keane's family sued for copyright infringement, who would pay? And what of all the publishers Litmus has sold rights to? It can return the advances, and not all forty-eight have published yet, but still ... And that doesn't even start taking into account the Seppi fans who have bought the book, close to two million of them already. Will any of them sue? What of Litmus's reputation? His head aches from the sheer immensity of the problem, the myriad ramifications that he is sure haven't occurred to him yet. While waiting for New York to wake up, he calls the airline and books a flight back to London that evening.

———

His phone call to Mortimer is uneventful. Mortimer tells him, his voice neutral, that he too will fly to London as quickly as possible so they can plan a strategy to deal with the fallout of the plagiarism.

Mortimer seems calm when they meet in the office he uses when he is in London. Hayley is present but Morty does all the talking. He asks Zach to take him through the entire situation, from the time he met Caryn in Toronto, all the way to the first intimation that something was very wrong. When Zach comes to the end of his account, he says quietly, "We'll have to find Caryn as soon as possible; I'll talk to our office in Toronto. We will also have to get in touch with all the publishers we have licensed rights to, say that we will repay every cent of every advance paid to us. If necessary we will make a public apology to all Seppi fans, hopefully that will mollify them. We will say we feel as aggrieved as any of them but we must stress that we acted in good faith. For now, I would like you to hand in your resignation to Hayley. I'm sorry, we have given this a lot of thought, but for an error of this magnitude we have no choice but to let you go."

Mortimer's decision slams into him, terrorizes him briefly; his job is one of the two most important stanchions that support his life. But there is nothing to be said; the firing has taken him completely by surprise, and he could not have mounted a defence even if he were thinking lucidly. It is clear the meeting is over. He gets up, as does Mortimer, who walks him to the door. They do not speak. As the door closes behind him, he thinks Gabrijela wouldn't have hung him out to dry; she would have stood by him, fought through the

crisis with him. But Gabrijela is no longer here; he will need
to deal with the situation as best he can. To his surprise, even
though the worst thing he could think of has taken place,
after the initial moments of panic he is calm; although he
isn't thinking clearly yet, he believes he can handle the situation. And he certainly isn't going to get down on himself
because of someone like Morty. *Fuck him*, he thinks, and
walks down the corridor to the bank of lifts.

After Zach and Hayley have left, Mortimer sits at his desk
for what seems to him a long time but is only about five
minutes, looking out the window, not particularly focusing
on activity in the street outside. Firing Zach hasn't left much
of an impression on him, to be honest he hardly knew the
guy; Zach was a means towards an end, he screwed up therefore he had to go. Mortimer didn't even have to practise his
sad face before the mirror, something he usually does before
firing someone. He makes a few notes on his laptop about
practical matters that will have to be acted upon immediately:
he will draft the press release announcing Zach's resignation;
Hayley should be the point person for the media and the
publishers they have licensed rights to; he will get Frank to
take charge of the hunt for Caryn. He closes the computer
and thinks about what else will need to be done to contain
the situation. This is a blow that he will not find it easy to
recover from, he had taken a big gamble when he overpaid
for Litmus. Now it will be difficult for Globish to make its
numbers over the next two quarters and, more worryingly,
the media storm will have an effect on the parent company's

share price. He has done what he can to protect himself – the firing of Zach, the attempts to head off lawsuits – but these actions will not be enough when he is called to account by his boss, because in the world of business, as he knows only too well, any prolonged downslide of performance, especially in times like these, will not be tolerated. Unless he has a killer Plan B up his sleeve, which he does not have, he might survive for a little while but he will have to start looking for his twelfth job soon, unless by some miracle Globish turns in a stellar performance this year or at least the next. Except Mortimer does not believe in miracles. He picks up the phone to call Monterey.

———

When Zach gets home, Julia meets him at the door. He isn't expecting to see her, he thought she would still be at work where he had phoned her with his news, but he is enormously glad she is here, for the strength she gives him by just being around. Nothing is ever lost, he thinks, when you have someone you love and trust to fight your corner.

———

The news of the Seppi fraud makes the front pages of every US and UK paper the day of Zach's meeting with Mortimer. Unusually, the story makes the front pages the next day as well, because of a tragic update: the body of a forty-four-year-old woman identified as Caryn Bianchi, a Montreal native, has been found in an upscale Bermuda hotel room. Preliminary investigations rule her death to be suicide from an overdose of sleeping pills. There is no suicide note.

———

Within forty-eight hours of the story breaking worldwide *Storm of Angels* begins to slide off the bestseller lists, and within a week it has fallen off the Amazon Top 100 and keeps heading downwards. Globish's reps countrywide in the US, and other major markets are besieged with phone calls from all their accounts seeking to return stock earlier than usual for full credit. All requests are acceded to. The media refuses to let go of the story, despite the best efforts of the in-house marketing and publicity department and of the high-powered spin doctors Mortimer has hired. The share price of Globish's parent company, Amadeus, starts to slip almost immediately, losing a dollar and a half, before rebounding slightly to settle at a full eight points lower than its level before the scandal broke. Mortimer flies to Monterey for an unpleasant meeting with Greg Holmes; he is not fired as he was expecting but he is put on notice that unless the company posts increases in both revenues and profits throughout 2011, he should not expect his contract, which comes to an end that year, to be renewed. It is better than he had hoped for, certainly better than the treatment he has meted out to Zach. He has time to come up with something and he is sure he will.

PART THREE

Ithaca gave you the beautiful journey;
Without her you wouldn't have set out on the road . . .

And if you find her poor, Ithaca didn't deceive you.
As wise as you will have become, with so much experience,
You will understand, by then, these Ithacas; what they mean.

– from "Ithaca" by C.P. Cavafy

8.

ITHACA

A month later, on an idle afternoon, Zach watches a documentary about a Slovenian man called Martin Strel whom he has never heard of before. A difficult childhood had led to a life lived on the margins until one day Strel decided to start swimming the greatest rivers in the world. He began with the Danube. A few years later he swam the entire length of the Mississippi. Next, he tackled the Yangtze, one of the most polluted rivers in the world, and nearly died. Finally, in his fifties, fat and washed up, he decided he would swim possibly the most dangerous big river in the world, the Amazon, a feat no one had ever attempted before. He was no Michael Phelps, he had high blood pressure, his resources were meagre, his training poor, and he fuelled himself with wine and beer while he swam. His son, who narrates the story of the quixotic feat, says the reason his father made up his mind to swim the Amazon was because he wanted to stop the destruction of the rain forest, but nobody quite knew how he intended to do that. If Strel knew, he wasn't explaining it very well to his people. Everyone thought he would die, his doctor made him sign a waiver saying she would not be responsible for the consequences if he went ahead. Strel signed, and by the time he got to the end of his journey he was almost out of his mind.

He returned to Slovenia and the destruction of the Amazon rain forest went on. We are not told if this disheartens Strel, the only thing we are told is that he is done, his days as the Big River Man are over. There is no real point to this story, except that you probably shouldn't swim the Amazon on cheap Slovenian wine. All it illustrates is that as we make our journey through life, deep down we have no real idea of why we do what we do and even less control over what the outcome will be. All we can do is make the journey.

9

ENDS AND BEGINNINGS

I n the old house in Yercaud, midway up the hill, with its timbered rafters, tiled roof, uneven floors, and its immense character, well remembered from the years he spent growing up there, Zachariah Thomas sits at an octagonal teak table in the glassed-in front verandah, drinking tea and looking out at the mist sculpting a fantastical bestiary out of the trees and shrubs in the garden. There is work to be done on the house and the garden, and he will also need to settle his parents' affairs, which he has been guilty of neglecting. All this will take at least three months if not longer.

It's been almost six months since he was fired from Globish. At first he did very little, simply mooned around their London flat, reading, listening to music, or watching incredibly violent Hong Kong cop movies in Mandarin (a language he does not know) without subtitles, which he found oddly soothing. Lately though, Julia and he have begun trying to figure out the future. For the moment their finances are holding up, but it is clear he will need to find a job fairly quickly. The big decision is where that job will be – in London where the publishing industry is tanking, or here in India where the prospects are much better? But if he were to move to India, would Julia give up her job or would they have a long-distance relationship? They haven't really talked about it, it is not a question that lends itself to easy resolution, especially so soon after their rapprochement.

He has been up since dawn, when he drove out to the cemetery to tend to the graves of his parents. And although the place could be better maintained, their final resting place is well chosen, with its long view of the hills and the mist rolling in over the trees. He has found the cemetery conducive to silent reflection, and has visited it often since coming to the Shevaroys a fortnight ago. In this quiet place, he has found that the anger and dismay that have corroded his life for much of the past six months are slowly seeping away. This morning, as he was sweeping fallen jacaranda flowers off his parents' graves with an improvised broom of twigs, he had wondered, as he has done often since returning, about the trajectory of his life, the odd symmetry of it. Would it end here, where it had begun?

Manjula, the housekeeper, comes into the room and announces that he has a visitor, Nagesh, the postman. Nagesh has been retired for decades now, but he's continued to keep in touch with the family, with his parents when they were alive, and now Zach whenever he visits. The invisible network of watchers that records all the comings and goings in this small town had alerted Nagesh as soon as Zach had returned, but he had been busy with workmen the last time the old postman visited. This time he offers him tea, gives him his full attention.

Nagesh was an integral part of his adolescence when his parents first came to live in this corner of the Shevaroys. At the corner of the driveway, where it takes a sharp turn to go down-hill, stands an old cypress with a branch that sticks out just low enough for a teenage boy to rest his forearms. From this vantage point he would look out across the valley to the winding road that led to town. At some point in the morning, depending on the number of stops he had had to make that day, the tiny figure of the postman would come into view, sliding jerkily down the road like a dun-coloured beetle, the bearer of good news, bad news, and all the neighbourhood gossip.

It is hard to tell how old Nagesh is, the broad flat planes of his face are only lightly dusted by wrinkles, but one eye is clouded with cataracts, and he tells Zach that his once power-ful legs, which used to carry him effortlessly over the hill roads, have given way; he is practically crippled by arthritis in the winter, and he finds it painful to walk even on the good days. He has had to make the journey from Yercaud town, where he lives, by bus, where once he would have walked.

Nagesh reminisces about Zach's parents, and then tells him about his own family, his children, and his grandchildren. The visit stretches on, but Zach is in no hurry – he realizes with some surprise that this is probably the longest he has ever spent in the company of Nagesh. It is no imposition, he has the time, but more than that he finds himself genuinely fasci-nated by the stories the postman has to tell, real stories of triumph and tragedy, of lived lives, not stories strained through the filter of fiction, which has been his preferred way of seeing the world for far too long.

In the old way of the hills, Nagesh lets it be known that he has heard of Zach's misfortune only towards the end of his visit. He leans forward, earnestly takes Zach's hand in his own, and quotes a Tamil proverb: "The letters of fate are written on your head, you cannot escape your fate even if you shave your head."

Ah yes, Zach thinks, fate or karma or kismet, or whatever you choose to call it, that old standby to explain why things do not work out as expected or when your life is dramatically altered. At one time he would have cast such reasoning aside, but who is he to scoff at the wisdom of the ancients, especially when it is relayed to him by a man who has had a deep and intimate view of the lives of others?

Nagesh gets up to leave, puts his hands together in a namaskaram. Zach returns the greeting and they walk down the driveway together. When they reach the old cypress on the corner he tells the postman about how he would watch out for him every day. "I know you did," Nagesh says with a smile. "My eyes were very good back then." Before he goes, he has one more thing to share. "I know these hills better than anyone else," he says with pride, "from walking up and down them every day of the week. Sometimes though, because of a sudden storm or landslide or accident, I would find the road blocked, and I would have to patiently find another route to complete my rounds.

"You cannot escape your fate," he continues, "but your

journey hasn't ended. All that has happened is that you have been pointed in a different direction – keep on, keep on." One more namaskaram and a refusal of Zach's offer of a ride home, then the old man makes his way slowly down the hill.

Zach walks back to the house. The insights of the postman are not new, it's just that somehow they have a weight to them because of the place they have been drawn from, that is why they are so compelling. And so that is what he will do. Piece by piece he will begin to reassemble his life, point it in a new direction, taking his time about it, and one day the angels will take wing again.

ACKNOWLEDGEMENTS

I would like to thank the following people (family, friends, and publishing colleagues) for helping in a myriad ways during the writing, editing, designing, and publishing of this book – K.D. and Nini Singh, Ruth and Rajendra Swamy, Dilsher and Pia Sen, Arjun and Mallika Nath, Mooma, Erik, and Shakuntala Carlquist, Doug Pepper and Susan Burns, David Robertson and Simone Lehmann, David Godwin, Pragati Sahni, Bipin Nayak, V.K. Karthika, Thomas Abraham, Michael Levine, Eva Frank, and Michael Zachs, Nilanjana Roy and Devangshu Datta, G. Mihajlovic, Khushwant Singh, Andrew Franklin, C.S. Richardson, Kendra Ward, and Anne Holloway.

I would also like to thank the following copyright holders for giving me permission to use material within copyright in the book:

"Ithaca" translated by Daniel Mendelsohn, from COLLECTED POEMS by C.P. Cavafy, translated by Daniel Mendelsohn,

A NOTE ABOUT THE TYPE

The text of *Ithaca* has been set in a digitized form of Bembo, a typeface based on an old-style Roman face that was used for Cardinal Bembo's *De Aetna* in 1495. Bembo was first cut by Francisco Griffo in the early sixteenth century.

BOOK DESIGN BY CS RICHARDSON